THE EDGE OF NOWHERE

MARGOT QUINN

First published in 2025
Concept created by Black Swan Digital. Developed by Annie Kenyon.

PROLOGUE

The truck-stop parking lot was nearly empty, the asphalt glistening under the flicker of a failing neon sign. Somewhere in the distance, a dog barked, its sound echoing through the stillness of the night.

Lara tightened her grip on the steering wheel, her knuckles pale under the faint glow of the dashboard lights. Beside her, Mia sat frozen, her breath coming in shallow gasps, her hand trembling in her lap. The faint scent of diesel and winter air drifted through the cracked window, mingling with the metallic tang clinging to their clothes. No words. No explanation. Just the harsh, bitter truth of what they had done.

"Say something." Mia's voice was barely a whisper, cracking like it had been dragged over gravel.

Lara swallowed hard. Her gaze locked on the dimly lit highway ahead. She couldn't look at Mia, not now, not with the image of his lifeless body burned into her mind. The blood. The way his head had hit the ground with a sickening thud.

Her chest tightened, a vice grip of guilt and panic threatening to crush her. She clenched the steering wheel tighter, her nails digging into her palms. What could she say?

That they'd made the worst mistake of their lives? That Mia's reckless charm had once again dragged them both into chaos? Or that maybe, just maybe, Lara was just as much to blame because she hadn't stopped it?

She shook her head, her grip tightening further. "What do you want me to say?"

Mia shifted, curling inward like she was trying to disappear into the seat. Her fair waves, damp with sweat, clung to her neck.

"I didn't mean..."

"Don't." Lara's voice was sharper than she intended, slicing through the fragile space between them like a blade. She winced as the word hung in the air, laden with everything they couldn't say.

Mia flinched but said nothing more, her face turned toward the window. The headlights of an approaching jeep washed over her features, illuminating the streaks of mascara smudged beneath her eyes and the raw, jagged fear carved into her expression. Then, just as quickly, the glare vanished, leaving them in darkness again, except for the glow of the dashboard lights.

The silence stretched again, brittle and suffocating. Outside, the vast emptiness of the night sprawled in every direction, a dark canvas of endless cornfields and abandoned rest stops. The highway stretched like a vein, pulsing faintly with the occasional trucker barreling through the night. Nowhere to run. Nowhere to hide.

Lara shifted into drive, her foot hovering over the accelerator. Her brain screamed at her to stop, to think, to breathe. But her instincts roared louder. *Keep going. Don't look back.*

"We need to move, fast," she said finally, her voice cold and steady, like she wasn't about to drive them into the unknown.

Mia's head snapped toward her. "What?"

"We can't stay here. It's only a matter of time before someone finds..." Lara stopped herself, her throat tightening. She couldn't say his name. Couldn't let it become real.

The words hovered between them, sharp and undeniable. Somewhere, far behind them in the dark, lay a truth they could never escape.

"You mean run?" Mia's voice was small, fragile, but her eyes searched Lara's face, desperate for some kind of reassurance.

Lara turned to her, her chest tightening at the sight of her best friend, no, her anchor—looking so completely shattered. "It's not running, Mia. It's surviving."

The words felt like ash on her tongue, but they ignited something in Mia. She nodded slowly, her lips trembling yet pressed together, like she was bracing for a storm. And Lara knew this was it. They'd crossed an invisible line tonight; one they could never return from.

With a deep breath, Lara pressed her foot to the gas. The truck stop faded in the rearview mirror, swallowed by the dark highway stretching endlessly ahead. Outside, the cold night dissolved into a sea of shadows. The headlights carved a narrow path onwards, but the world beyond them remained unknowable, unrelenting. Somewhere up north, past the invisible border that separated their old lives from whatever came next, lay a chance. Maybe even freedom.

But for now, all they had was the road. And each other.

1

The monitor flat-lined.

The shrill, unrelenting whine filled the small, South Bronx apartment, ramping up the already unbearable tension. Lara's arms burned as she continued compressions, each pump to the young man's chest echoing like a scream inside her head. Sweat trickled down her neck, her paramedic uniform clinging like a second skin.

"Come on, kid," she muttered under her breath, willing him back to life. The med bag lay splayed open beside her, syringes and ampoules scattered across the stained carpet. Her partner, Sam, crouched at the boy's head, his voice calm and practiced as he counted her compressions. Somewhere outside, the blaring siren of their ambulance faded into the city noise.

But nothing worked. No pulse. No movement. Just the pale, waxy skin of a teenager who'd barely lived long enough to call himself a man.

"Lara," Sam said, his voice softer now, edged with the kind of resignation she hated. "It's been over fifteen minutes."

"Don't," she snapped, her voice sharper than intended. Her arms screamed for her to stop, but she couldn't. She wouldn't.

Not when the boy's mother slumped in the corner, her sobs barely audible over the flatline. Not when his sister—maybe twelve, clung to the doorframe, her wide, terrified eyes locked on her brother's body.

The apartment reeked of despair, stale cigarette smoke, greasy takeout, and the sharp chemical tang of the drugs they'd tried to flush before Lara and Sam arrived. The wallpaper peeled in places, its floral pattern faded and torn, and the furniture looked like it had been there longer than the boy had been alive. Everything in the room felt like it was caving in, suffocating her.

She couldn't stop. She didn't know how.

"Lara," Sam said again, more insistent this time. His hand landed on her shoulder, firm but steady. "We have to call it."

Her hands stilled mid-compression, hovering above the boy's chest. His ribs were too fragile under her palms, his body too small, too light, too young. Her chest tightened as the stigma of failure settled in, heavier than the air in the room. She dropped back onto her heels, her arms falling limply at her sides.

Sam reached for his radio, murmuring something into it, words Lara couldn't process. Her gaze stayed fixed on the boy, on his hollow cheeks, the faint track marks along his arm, the unnatural shade of blue on his lips.

Overdose. Her stomach churned. It wasn't the first, and it wouldn't be the last.

The boy's mother let out a wail, the kind that reached deep into Lara's chest and twisted, making it hard to breathe. Sam knelt beside her, his voice low and soothing, though his words were lost beneath her grief.

"I did everything I could," Lara said, though the words felt hollow even as they left her mouth.

The boy's sister didn't respond. She just stared at her

brother, silent tears streaking down her cheeks. Lara wanted to say more, to offer some kind of comfort, but nothing felt right. Nothing ever did.

By the time they stepped outside onto the streets of New York, the sun had begun to rise, painting the crumbling brick of the apartment complex in muted shades of orange and gold. The early morning light felt like a cruel contrast to the deep despair lingering in the air. Lara took a deep breath, trying to shake the feeling that she'd left part of herself behind in that room.

"You need coffee," Sam said, breaking the silence as they loaded the stretcher back into the ambulance. He slammed the doors shut with practiced efficiency, giving her a sidelong glance. "And sleep."

"I'm fine." The lie slipped out automatically, though they both knew better.

"Lara." Sam's tone softened; his weathered face lined with concern. "You've been running yourself into the ground."

She didn't respond, pulling her jacket tighter against the morning winter chill. Running herself into the ground was better than standing still. Better than having time to think.

The hospital was just coming alive when they arrived, the lobby already buzzing with its unique blend of chaos. Nurses in scrubs wheeled patients past the triage desk, while the unmistakable aroma of antiseptic and bad coffee filled the air. Lara barely registered the commotion as they unloaded their gear and headed to the supply room to restock. She kept her head down, avoiding the familiar faces of colleagues who might ask questions she wasn't ready to answer.

"Hey, Lawson," a nurse called from across the hallway, her tone light but tinged with sympathy. "Rough morning?"

"Just another day," Lara replied, forcing a tight smile that didn't reach her eyes. She busied herself re-organizing the med bag, her hands moving mechanically. Sam stood beside her; his silence comforting in its own way. The other paramedics chatted quietly in the background, their laughter and small talk like static in her ears.

She pulled out her phone and scrolled mindlessly through her notifications, trying to ignore the ache in her chest. A text from Emily sat unopened at the top of her screen: *We should talk.*

Lara's stomach clenched. She stared at the message, her thumb hovering over the screen before locking the phone and shoving it back into her pocket. She wasn't ready to talk. Not now. Maybe not ever.

Instead, she stood, her body weary with fatigue but her mind still racing. She grabbed her bag and left the station without a word, stepping back into the chaos of the city. The streets were alive with noise and motion, the world moving forward as it always did—indifferent to the lives left behind in its wake.

Outside the station, the city was waking up, the rhythmic rumble of passing cars blending with the faint chatter of people heading to work. Lara adjusted the strap of her bag on her shoulder, her eyes scanning the sidewalk for a distraction, anything to quiet the thoughts clawing at the edges of her mind. She didn't make it far before Sam fell into step beside her, his broad frame and steady presence grounding her in a way she couldn't quite articulate.

"You know, there's this little diner a couple of blocks down," Sam said, his voice casual but purposeful. "Best coffee in the city or so they claim. Couldn't hurt to test their theory."

Lara shook her head, the ghost of a smile tugging at her lips. "I appreciate the offer, but I think I'll pass."

"You've been passing on everything lately," Sam replied, his tone light but not unkind. "Coffee, a decent night's sleep, maybe even a social life. You keep this up, and I'm gonna start taking it personally."

Lara stopped, turning to face him. The morning sun highlighted the lines etched deep into his weathered face, his gray-streaked hair peeking out from under his cap. He looked at her with the kind of concern she didn't know how to handle, gentle but insistent, like he wouldn't let her slip away as easily as she wanted to.

"I'm fine," she said again, though the words felt thinner this time, less convincing.

Sam snorted, crossing his arms over his chest. "Sure you are. And I'm twenty-five with a full head of hair."

She huffed a quiet laugh despite herself, the sound feeling foreign after the morning they'd had. "You really know how to sell it, Sam."

"Just calling it like I see it." He paused, his expression softening. "Look, kid, I know today wasn't easy. Hell, none of them are. But you've gotta let yourself breathe once in a while. You're no good to anyone, not to your patients, not to yourself, if you're running on fumes."

The word *running* struck something deep in her chest, a jarring reminder of Emily's voice, sharp and raw as it rang out across their cramped apartment during their last fight.

"You never stay," Emily had said, arms crossed tightly over her chest like she was holding herself together. "Whenever things get too real, you just... run. You shut down. You put up a wall, and I can't, I won't keep banging my head against it."

"That's not fair," Lara had argued, though the words had felt empty even then. Emily wasn't wrong. Not entirely.

"What's not fair is that I've been here, Lara. I've been fighting for us, for you. But you won't even let me in." Emily's voice cracked, frustration giving way to something more fragile. "I can't do it anymore. I'm tired."

The memory stung like an open wound. Lara forced herself back to the present, shaking her head as if she could dislodge the thought.

"Lara?" Sam's voice pulled her back. His brow furrowed as he studied her, and she realized she hadn't answered him, her silence lingering too long.

"Sorry," she muttered, adjusting the strap of her bag again. "Just... thinking."

Sam didn't press, though concern lingered in his eyes. "Look, I'm not trying to pry. But if you ever feel like talking or even just grabbing that terrible coffee, I'm here. No pressure."

She nodded, grateful for the offer even if she wasn't ready to take it. "Thanks, Sam. I'll think about it."

"Good. That's all I ask." He clapped her lightly on the shoulder before turning back toward the station, leaving her alone with the city and the noise in her head.

As she watched him go, Lara exhaled a breath she hadn't realized she was holding. The band of tension in her chest remained, but for the first time in a long while, it didn't feel quite so debilitating.

The sun climbed higher, its warmth brushing against her face as she started walking again. Her phone buzzed in her pocket, but she ignored it, already knowing it was from Emily. She wasn't ready. Not to face her, not to face herself.

For now, all she could do was keep moving, one step at a time, even if she had no idea where she was headed.

2

The engine rumbled beneath her as Lara navigated the ambulance through the dense downtown traffic, the rhythm of the city both familiar and relentless. New York moved like a machine—constant, unyielding, grinding up anyone who dared to pause for even a second. Lara was no exception.

She leaned forward slightly, one hand on the steering wheel, the other gripping her coffee—already lukewarm and far too bitter to be worth the two dollars she'd paid for it.

Beside her, Sam thumbed through their dispatch tablet, his graying eyebrows knitting together in concentration. He muttered something under his breath about insurance paperwork, but Lara wasn't really listening. The chaos of the morning still clung to her like a second skin, and no amount of coffee—bitter or not—could wash it away.

"You're still too quiet," Sam finally said, his voice cutting through the noise of the engine.

"Just tired," she replied automatically, keeping her eyes on the road.

Sam snorted, the faintest smirk tugging at his lips. "You're always tired, Lawson. Doesn't mean you shut down like this. Something's eating at you."

Lara tightened her grip on the wheel, her knuckles whitening. "I'm fine."

"Sure, you are." Sam leaned back in his seat, resting a hand on his thigh as he studied her. "You've been 'fine' for months, but you look like you're carrying the weight of the whole damn city on your shoulders."

His tone was light, almost teasing, but the words landed harder than they should have. Lara bit the inside of her cheek, keeping her eyes locked on the road.

"I don't need a therapy session, Sam."

"And yet, here we are." He chuckled, shaking his head. "Look, I'm not trying to pry. But you can't keep bottling everything up. It'll eat you alive, kid."

His words hovered, filling the small space of the cab. Sam had a way of seeing through her, his steady, unshakable presence like a mirror she didn't want to look into.

She could still hear Emily's voice, sharp and cutting, from their last fight.

"Do you even know how to let someone in?" Emily had asked, arms crossed tightly over her chest as she stood in the middle of their too-small apartment. "Or are you just going to keep building walls and shutting people out until there's no one left?"

The memory twisted in Lara's stomach, sharp and fresh. She exhaled through her nose, forcing herself to shove it aside.

"Are we gonna talk about it?" Sam asked, his tone softer now, more careful.

"Talk about what?"

"Whatever's been eating at you since we left that scene this morning. Or maybe what's been eating at you for the last six months," he said, his eyes narrowing slightly.

Lara's jaw tightened. She didn't want to talk about it—the boy she couldn't save, the fight she couldn't forget, or the gnawing sense that everything in her life was teetering on the edge of collapse.

Instead, she steered the conversation away. "What's our next call?"

Sam sighed, shaking his head like he knew exactly what she was doing but chose not to push. "We've got some breathing room for now. Dispatch says we're on hold until something comes in."

Lara nodded, relieved by the temporary reprieve. She guided the ambulance into the station's parking lot and cut the engine, the sudden silence almost jarring.

As she stepped out, the early afternoon air nipped at her skin. The sun hung higher now, casting long shadows across the pavement. She pulled her jacket tighter, her boots crunching against the gravel as she made her way toward the station's doors.

Inside, the atmosphere was a strange blend of chaos and calm. The scent of antiseptic and burned coffee lingered in the air, mingling with the low vibration of conversation and the occasional crackle of the dispatch radio. Paramedics and EMTs moved through the halls, their voices measured, their faces set with the quiet determination that came with the job.

Lara paused by the bulletin board near the breakroom, scanning the notices tacked haphazardly across the cork. Training schedules, charity fundraisers, and a poorly drawn cartoon of a paramedic sprawled across a stretcher with the caption: "Don't mind me, just saving lives."

"Lawson," a voice called from behind her.

She turned to see Tara, one of the triage nurses, striding toward her with a clipboard in hand. Tall and no-nonsense, Tara had sharp eyes and a quick wit that made her a favorite among the station's staff.

"Got a minute?" Tara asked, her voice clipped but not unkind.

"Sure," Lara said, straightening. "What's up?"

"I just wanted to check in about this morning," Tara said, her tone softening. "Sam mentioned it was a rough call."

Lara's stomach tightened. The events of the morning still raw. "It was fine. Just another day."

Tara raised an eyebrow, skeptical. "You keep saying that like you're trying to convince yourself."

Lara's lips twitched, but it wasn't quite a smile. "What do you want me to say?"

"I want you to take care of yourself," Tara said, her voice firm but laced with concern. "You're one of the best paramedics we've got, Lawson. But even you can't carry all of this on your own."

Lara looked away, her throat tightening. She hated this—the concern, the well-meaning advice, the way everyone seemed to think they knew what was best for her.

"I'll be fine," she said finally, her voice quieter now.

Tara studied her for a moment, then nodded. "Just... don't forget you've got people here who care. Okay?"

"Okay," Lara said, though she wasn't sure she believed it.

As Tara walked away, Lara exhaled slowly, her shoulders sagging. She glanced at her phone, her thumb hovering over Emily's unopened message.

We should talk.

The words stared back at her, sharp and unrelenting. She locked the screen again and shoved the phone into her pocket.

Not today.

. . .

By the time Lara reached her apartment, exhaustion had seeped into her bones. Her boots felt heavier with each step up the narrow staircase, the threadbare carpet barely muffling her footsteps. She fumbled with her keys, fingers sluggish, and nudged the door open with her hip.

The smell hit her first—something sour and vaguely burnt. Lara wrinkled her nose as she stepped inside, scanning the dimly lit space. The kitchen, which bled into the cramped living room, looked like a tornado had ripped through. A precarious stack of plates teetered in the sink; their edges crusted with what looked like dried tomato sauce. An empty pizza box sat on the counter, its lid gaping open to reveal a few rogue crusts. A half-full coffee mug balanced dangerously close to the edge; its contents congealed into a thick sludge.

"Of course," Lara muttered, kicking the door shut behind her with more force than necessary.

She dropped her bag onto the tiny dining table, Jess's unofficial dumping ground for bills, flyers, and whatever else she couldn't be bothered to deal with. The table wobbled under the weight, one of its legs slightly shorter than the others. Lara exhaled a long sigh.

"Jess!" she called, her voice sharper than she intended. She didn't care. She was too tired to care.

There was no answer, only the faint strains of music filtering from Jess's bedroom. Lara's jaw tightened as she made her way to the sink, her boots scuffing against the faded linoleum. She turned on the tap and grabbed a sponge, her movements stiff and jerky as she scrubbed at the plates.

The apartment wasn't much to look at. Just a two-bedroom shoebox with peeling paint and windows that rattled in their frames whenever the wind picked up. The radiator worked when it felt like it, and the showerhead had a habit of spraying water in every direction except down. But it was all Lara could afford, and after the breakup with Emily, she hadn't had the energy to look for something better.

She'd found Jess through a Craigslist ad, describing her as a bubbly twenty-something who worked nights at a bar and spent most of her free time either sleeping or hosting impromptu get-togethers that inevitably ended with someone puking in the bathroom. Lara didn't like her, but she tolerated her. Barely.

"Seriously, Jess!" Lara called again, louder this time, as she rinsed a plate and set it on the drying rack. The music from Jess's room cut off abruptly, followed by the sound of footsteps.

The door creaked open, and Jess appeared, her blonde hair piled into a messy bun, a pair of oversized headphones draped around her neck. She wore an old hoodie that might have once been white, paired with leopard-print leggings that clashed violently with her neon pink socks.

"What?" Jess asked, blinking at Lara like she'd just woken up. "Why are you yelling?"

Lara gestured at the kitchen with the sponge still in her hand, water dripping onto the floor. "This. Again. I've had a long day, Jess. The least you could do is clean up after yourself."

Jess rolled her eyes and leaned against the doorframe. "I was going to get to it."

"Really? When? Next week?" Lara snapped, exhaustion sharpening her words. "I'm not your maid."

Jess huffed, crossing her arms. "Okay, chill. I didn't realize you were in such a twenty-four-seven clean freak."

Lara clenched her teeth, counting to five in her head. She didn't have the energy for this fight. Not tonight. "Just... don't let it happen again."

Jess shrugged, unapologetic. "Fine. Whatever." She turned and disappeared back into her room, the music starting up again a moment later.

Lara sighed, tossing the sponge into the sink before leaning against the counter. Her reflection in the dark window above caught her eye, and for a moment, she barely recognized the woman staring back. Strands of hair had slipped from her ponytail, clinging to her damp forehead. The circles beneath her eyes looked darker than usual, her skin pale and drawn. She looked as exhausted as she felt.

Pushing off the counter, she grabbed a glass from the cabinet, filled it with water, and downed it in one go. The apartment was quiet now, save for the faint bass thumping from Jess's room. The silence felt too big so she left the kitchen and made her way to her bedroom, stepping over a pile of Jess's shoes in the hallway.

Her room was the only space in the apartment that truly felt like hers. The walls were mostly bare, except for a single framed photo from a trip to Colorado two years ago—her and Emily, smiling against a backdrop of snow-dusted mountains. Lara's stomach twisted as her gaze lingered on it, the memory both distant and painfully fresh.

She sank onto the edge of her bed, shoulders slumping forward as she kicked off her boots. Her phone buzzed in her pocket. Pulling it out, she hesitated, her thumb hovering over the screen.

We should talk.

Emily's message stared back at her, unyielding.

Lara's throat tightened. She could still hear Emily's voice, soft but firm, as she packed up her things.

"You never let me in, Lara. I tried. God, I tried. But you don't know how to stay."

The memory hit like a punch to the chest. Lara exhaled a shaky breath, locking her phone before tossing it onto the nightstand. She didn't want to think about Emily, or the boy she couldn't save this morning, or the pile of dishes still waiting in the sink. All she wanted was sleep.

She lay back, staring up at the dusty lightshade as memories of the day settled over her. Outside her window, the city pulsed with its usual chaos—sirens wailing in the distance, car horns blaring, voices drifting up from the street. It all blurred together into a dull roar, a reminder that the world kept moving, no matter how stuck she felt.

For once, she wished it would all just stop.

3

The atmosphere in the small townhouse was electric, as if the walls had absorbed every argument, every unspoken resentment, every broken promise, bouncing static back into the rooms. The blinds in the living room were drawn tight, shutting out the winter sun that showed up every flaw, like the dents in the cupboards, the scuffs on the linoleum floor and the gloom clung to everything, including her.

At the sink, Mia plunged her hands into soapy water, the clean scent of lemon dish soap tickling her nose. Above her, the cheap fluorescent light buzzed faintly, the bulb a tired, fragile thing—just like everything else in this house.

She scrubbed harder at the pan, the metal sponge grating against the burned-on grease. The repetitive motion kept her hands busy, her thoughts at bay, her mind from wandering too far down the dark paths it always seemed to take.

Behind her, the voice on the TV filled the space, some sports commentary Dane always left on, even when he wasn't watching. A half-empty beer can sat on the coffee table, surrounded by crumpled snack wrappers and an overflowing ashtray, the staleness of old smoke settling into the furniture.

“Are you just going to stand there all night, or are you actually going to get dinner ready?”

The words sliced through the kitchen like a blade, sharp and biting. Mia’s shoulders stiffened, but she didn’t turn around. She didn’t have to. Dane stood in the doorway, his broad frame filling the space, leaning against the doorframe like he was the center of the universe because, in every way that mattered, he was.

“It’s coming,” she said quietly, keeping her voice as steady as she could. She rinsed the pan and set it on the drying rack, reaching for the next dish.

“Not fast enough,” Dane snapped. His tone was cold, clipped. The kind that made her stomach clench. He stepped into the kitchen now, his shadow stretching long across the tiled floor.

“You’re home all day, Mia. All day. And you can’t even have dinner ready when I walk in the door?”

Mia’s grip on the plate tightened, her knuckles whitening as she stared down at the sink. She wanted to say something, to defend herself, but the words died in her throat. They always did.

“I’ve been working my ass off,” Dane said, his voice rising, rough with frustration. The veins in his neck bulged slightly, a warning sign Mia knew all too well. “And what have you been doing? Sitting on *your* ass, watching TV, ignoring everything you’re supposed to be doing around here?”

“That’s not fair,” Mia said softly, turning off the faucet. She wiped her hands on a dish towel, but it did nothing to stop their shaking. She hated it, hated that he could always make her feel so small.

“Not fair?” Dane let out a sharp, humorless laugh. His dark eyes locked onto her, daring her to push back. “What’s not fair is me coming home to a disaster every damn day. This place is a mess, Mia. You're a mess. You can't even keep up with the bare minimum."

Mia's stomach twisted as she glanced around the kitchen. It wasn't spotless, but it wasn't the disaster Dane made it out to be. A stack of unopened mail cluttered the counter, because *he* insisted on opening everything that came through the letterbox, a few dishes sat in the sink that *he* wouldn't dream of washing, but she'd spent the day scrubbing the bathroom tiles as per *his* instructions, folding *his* laundry. It was never enough for him. Nothing ever was.

"I'm doing my best," she murmured, her voice barely above a whisper.

"Well, your best isn't good enough," he snapped, stepping closer. His broad shoulders loomed over her, the heat of his presence prickling against her skin. "And you wonder why Noah doesn't respect you."

The words hit like a slap. Mia's breath caught, her grip tightening on the counter to steady herself. "Don't bring Noah into this."

Dane's smirk sharpened; his eyes gleaming with something cold, cruel. "Why not? He sees it. He sees how useless you are. You think he doesn't notice? You think he doesn't see how you let everyone walk all over you?"

"Hey!"

The voice cut through the room, sharp and unyielding.

Both Mia and Dane turned.

Noah stood in the doorway, his frame filling the space. At seventeen, he was tall and lean, his dark hair slightly disheveled, his blue eyes blazing. He had Dane's sharp jawline but none of his father's venom, and for a moment, Mia felt both pride and heartbreak swell in her chest.

"Don't talk to her like that." His voice was firm, louder than Mia had ever heard it.

Dane turned fully, his body tensing. "Stay out of this, Noah. This doesn't concern you."

"It does when you're yelling at her for no reason." Noah stepped further into the room, his shoulders squared, fists clenched.

Dane's sneer deepened, his eyes narrowing. "You think you can walk in here and tell me how to run my house?"

Noah didn't flinch. "I think someone has to."

Mia's heart pounded as she looked between them, panic clawing at her throat. Noah was so much like his father in some ways, stubborn, headstrong, but he had her heart, her softness. She couldn't let this escalate.

"That's enough!" Her voice finally broke through the tension as she stepped between them, pressing a hand against Noah's chest. His heartbeat thrummed beneath her palm, fast and unrelenting. "Noah, go to your room."

"Mom..."

"Please," she whispered, her voice splintering. "Just go."

Noah hesitated, his jaw tensing as his gaze flicked between her and Dane. A long beat passed before he exhaled sharply and stormed out. His bedroom door slammed down the hall, the sound ricocheting through the house. Mia flinched.

She turned back to Dane, her breath coming fast and uneven. His eyes remained narrowed, his jaw locked, but he didn't speak. Instead, he shook his head and walked out of the kitchen, muttering under his breath. A moment later, the front door slammed as he marched into the blackness of a November night, leaving Mia alone in the middle of the kitchen, her hands trembling.

The silence that followed wasn't comforting. It gave her too much time to think, to despise herself for allowing Dane to control every aspect of her life. She hated being cooped up in the apartment all day and longed to go to work, take a job anywhere, even part-time just so she could escape for a few hours. Dane forbade it and she didn't dare go against him because it never ended well. Defiance wasn't something her husband could deal with. And she couldn't cope with the bruises.

She glanced toward the hallway, toward Noah's room, her heart plummeting as she thought of him on the other side of the door. She wanted to go to him, to tell him she was sorry—that she wished she were stronger, that she could give him the life he deserved. But the words wouldn't come.

Instead, she leaned against the counter, her head bowed and let the tears she'd been holding back finally fall. Once they were shed, she wiped her face quickly with the back of her hand, sniffling as she tried to compose herself. There was no time to wallow, no space in her life for falling apart. Turning off the kitchen light she walked down the narrow hallway toward her bedroom.

Noah's door was shut tight, but she could hear faint music playing on the other side, a playlist he always turned to when he needed to calm down. Her heart ached as she passed by, her hand hovering over the doorknob for a moment before she forced herself to move on.

Her room was small and sparsely decorated, just like the rest of the house. The bed was unmade, its pale blue sheets twisted from another restless night. Against one wall stood a dresser with peeling laminate, its top cluttered with a mismatched collection of jewelry, an old perfume bottle, and a photo frame turned face-down.

Mia shut the door quietly behind her and leaned against it, eyes slipping shut as she exhaled a long, unsteady breath. Exhaustion dragged at her, her limbs leaden and aching, but her mind refused to stop spinning.

The fear was always there, a constant undercurrent

humming in her veins. It wasn't just the yelling or the cruel words. It was the unpredictability—the way Dane's anger could shift in an instant, turning from cold and cutting to explosive and physical. She had learned to tiptoe around him, to anticipate the changes in his mood, but it never stopped her from feeling like she was walking a tightrope with no safety net.

Her gaze drifted to the corner of the room, where a small shoebox sat tucked beneath her nightstand. She crossed the room and knelt, fingers brushing against the worn cardboard as she pulled it out.

Inside were the pieces of a plan. Small, scattered fragments of hope she clung to like a lifeline.

A handful of crumpled bills, painstakingly saved from grocery money and the occasional odd job she'd done for neighbors. A burner phone, bought with cash and hidden beneath the bills. A folded map of the city, its surface marked with circles around bus stations and shelters, places she had looked up late at night when Dane was asleep.

Mia sat cross-legged on the floor, the shoebox in front of her, as she unfolded the map and smoothed it out on the carpet. Her laptop rested on the nightstand, its screen casting a faint glow in the dim room. She had bookmarked a dozen websites, domestic violence resources, legal aid offices, job postings, but just seeing them made her heart pound.

Every time she opened one of those pages, a wave of a thousand doubts washed over her. What if Dane found out? What if he caught her before she could leave? What if she failed?

Her fingers hovered over the touchpad as she navigated to one of the shelters she had researched. The page loaded slowly; the Wi-Fi as temperamental as everything else in the house. She scanned the information, her eyes flicking over the bullet points: *Emergency housing. Counseling services. Safety planning.*

Her throat tensed as she read the words which were a sharp reminder of just how bad things had gotten. She hated the burn of shame in her chest, hated that she had let herself sink so far into this mess.

But it wasn't just about her anymore. It hadn't been for a long time.

Her gaze drifted to the shoebox, to the thin stack of bills, the sum total of every spare dollar she had managed to hide. It wasn't much, just under two hundred dollars, but it was something. It was a start.

Mia closed the laptop, her hands trembling as she shoved the map and phone back into the shoebox. She slid it under the nightstand again, her movements quick and furtive, as if Dane could walk through the door at any moment and rip it all away.

She stood and crossed to the window, pushing the curtain aside just enough to peer down at the street. Dane's car was nowhere in sight, but the empty driveway did little to loosen the knot in her stomach. Her eyes swept the street, her mind playing tricks on her, conjuring his figure emerging from the darkness, his expression cold, unyielding.

Mia let the curtain fall back into place and leaned her forehead against the cool glass. The thought of leaving terrified her almost as much as the thought of staying. She didn't know what life looked like beyond this house, beyond Dane's control. And the idea of taking Noah with her, uprooting his life, his friends, his school made her sad.

But what kind of example was she setting by staying? What kind of mother was she if she let Noah watch her shrink into herself, let him believe this was what love looked like?

She pressed her palms against the window frame, her breaths coming faster, shallow and uneven.

"You have to do this," she whispered, her voice trembling. "You have to."

Her reflection stared back at her in the dim glass, eyes hollow and tired. She didn't look like the person she used to be, the girl who loved baking, who dreamed of owning a little café, who laughed so hard she cried. That girl felt like a stranger now, buried beneath years of fear and disappointment.

Mia straightened, brushing her hair back from her face as she forced herself to stand taller. She couldn't let Dane take any more from her. She couldn't let him steal what little hope she had left.

Her phone buzzed on the nightstand, the sudden sound making her jump. She snatched it up, her stomach twisting as Dane's name flashed across the screen. Her thumb hovered over the answer button, her heartbeat thudding against her ribs.

She let it ring.

4

The phone rested in Lara's hand as she paced the length of her tiny living room, her thumb hovering over Mia's contact name. The small lamp on the side table cast a warm, uneven glow across the space, barely illuminating the faded couch and the stack of old magazines she kept meaning to deal with. The apartment was quiet now, save for the distant sound of traffic outside the window. Too quiet.

She glanced down at the screen again. Mia's name stared back at her, the small photo beside it captured the two of them laughing at a college party years ago. They had been so young then, carefree in a way neither of them could even imagine anymore. She swiped a thumb across her jaw and sighed.

It had been weeks since they'd last spoken. A few quick texts here and there, nothing of substance. But that was how it always went. They didn't need constant communication to stay connected. Mia was one of the few people in Lara's life who still felt like home, even if home itself had become a distant memory.

Before she could talk herself out of it, Lara tapped the screen and pressed the phone to her ear. It rang twice before Mia's voice came through, soft and familiar.

"Lara?"

"Hey," Lara said, leaning against the wall and sliding down until she was sitting on the floor, her knees pulled to her chest. "Hope I'm not catching you at a bad time."

"No, no, it's fine." Mia's voice was slightly breathless, and Lara heard the faint clatter of dishes in the background. "Just finishing up in the kitchen. You know how it is."

Lara smiled faintly, though it didn't quite reach her eyes. "Still pulling off those Pinterest-perfect meals?"

Mia let out a small laugh, but it sounded strained. "Not exactly. Tonight's masterpiece was boxed mac and cheese. I even burned the pot a little."

"Sounds gourmet to me," Lara teased, her voice lighter than she felt. She picked at a loose thread on her pajama pants, the fabric soft and worn from too many washes.

"What about you?" Mia asked, the clatter fading as her voice softened. "How's work?"

Lara hesitated, the question hanging in the air. She wanted to tell Mia everything, that she felt like she was drowning, that she couldn't stop thinking about the boy she'd lost that morning, that Emily's voice still echoed in her head, accusing her of running away. But the words stuck in her throat, too raw and tangled to come out.

"Same old, same old," Lara said finally, forcing a lightness she didn't feel. "You know, saving lives, being a hero. No big deal."

Mia laughed again, but this time, warmth softened the sound. "I swear, you're the only person who can make a job like that sound easy."

"It's not," Lara admitted quietly, her fingers tightening around the phone. "But you just... keep going, I guess."

A pause stretched between them, long enough that Lara wondered if Mia was about to press her for more. She wasn't sure if she wanted her to.

"Yeah," Mia said at last, her voice softer now. "I get that."

For a moment, the gap made by things unsaid stretched between them, a fragile thread connecting two women who wanted to speak but didn't know how.

"How's Noah?" Lara asked, steering the conversation away from herself. It was easier that way. Safer.

Mia exhaled, the sound laced with both affection and exhaustion. "He's good. Teenagers, you know? Stubborn and moody, but... he's a good kid. Too good, sometimes. I just wish..."

Her voice trailed off, and Lara waited, her chest tightening at the hesitation in her friend's words.

"Wish what?" she prompted gently.

"Nothing," Mia said quickly, the forced brightness in her tone making it clear it wasn't nothing at all. "Just wish I had more time to spend with him, that's all."

Lara frowned, leaning her head back against the wall. "You okay, Mia? You sound... I don't know, tired."

Mia's laugh came through the line, thin and brittle. "Who isn't tired these days?"

It was a deflection, and Lara knew it, but she didn't push. Instead, she settled into the familiar rhythm of their conversations, the safe topics that never dug too deep.

"Remember that time in college when we skipped class and drove to the beach?" Lara asked, a smile tugging at her lips.

Mia groaned, though there was warmth in the sound. "How could I forget? You insisted on taking your old Jeep, even though it overheated halfway there."

"And we waited three hours for a tow truck," Lara added,

laughing. "I think we ate an entire bag of gummy bears while sitting on the side of the road."

"That was the worst sunburn of my life," Mia said, her voice lighter now, the exhaustion slipping away for just a moment.

Lara's laughter faded as the memory settled between them, bittersweet in its simplicity. She could almost feel the sun on her skin, the sticky heat of the car's vinyl seats—the freedom of being twenty, reckless, and believing the world was still full of endless possibilities.

"You ever think about those days?" Lara asked softly.

"Yeah," Mia said after a pause. "All the time."

Lara wanted to say more, to ask Mia what was really going on, to tell her about Emily and how much she hated the person she'd become. But instead, she fell back into the familiar rhythm of their friendship, the way they danced around the truth without ever quite stepping into it.

They talked about little things, the weather, the latest Netflix series Mia had started but never finished, the overpriced coffee shop down the street from Lara's apartment. Safe topics that wouldn't unravel them.

But even as they talked, Lara couldn't shake the feeling that Mia's voice carried something heavier, something unspoken. And she wondered if Mia could sense the same in her.

As their conversation drifted on, Lara leaned her head back and closed her eyes, letting the sound of her friend's voice fill the empty space around her.

For now, it was enough.

Mia's laughter trailed off, leaving only the faint crackle of static on the line. Lara leaned her head against the wall, the soft thud grounding her for a moment. She didn't mind the silence —it was the kind that came with old friendships, where every pause didn't need filling.

And yet, something about this stillness felt different. Tense. Charged.

"I've been thinking," Mia said suddenly, her voice bright—too bright.

"About?" Lara asked, dragging out the word, suspicion creeping into her tone.

"We should go on a trip," Mia blurted out, the words rushing forward like she'd been holding them back too long.

Lara blinked, caught off guard. "A trip?"

"Yeah," Mia said, her voice quickening with excitement. "Just the two of us. Like we used to. Get out of the city for a while, take a break from… everything."

Lara pulled the phone away from her ear, staring at it like it had just started speaking a foreign language. She could picture Mia now—probably pacing her small kitchen, one hand tugging at her hair, energy bubbling over the way it always did when an idea took hold.

"Okay," Lara said slowly, pressing the phone back to her ear. "And where exactly are we going on this imaginary trip of yours?"

Mia hesitated. Lara could almost hear her chewing on the inside of her cheek, a nervous habit she'd had since college.

"Canada."

"Canada?" Lara repeated, eyebrows shooting up.

"Yeah, why not?" Mia said quickly, her words tumbling over each other. "It's not that far. Less than seven hours. We could drive up to the Falls, rent a cabin or something. I mean, doesn't that sound nice? Fresh air, no traffic, no responsibilities for a few days…"

Lara let out a short laugh, shaking her head. "Mia, are you serious?"

"Yes, I'm serious," Mia said, her voice rising with a mix of desperation and determination. “Look, I know it’s random, but I need this, Lara. I need to get out of here. Just for a little while.”

Something in Mia’s voice made Lara pause. A crack, subtle but unmistakable, threaded through her words, raw and vulnerable, no matter how hard Mia tried to hide it.

“You okay?” Lara asked softly.

“I’m fine,” Mia said, too quickly. “I just... I’ve been stuck in the same routine for so long, you know? And Noah’s old enough to handle a couple of days on his own. I just need a break, Lara. I need to feel like myself again.”

Lara leaned her head back against the wall, eyes slipping shut. She wanted to press Mia, to ask what was really going on, but the toll of her own day pressed down on her, too ingrained to shake off.

Emily’s voice rang in her head, sharp and accusing. *You don’t know how to stay. You always run when things get hard.*

Lara opened her eyes, staring at the ceiling. Maybe Emily was right. Maybe she did run. But right now, running felt like exactly what she needed.

“You’re really serious about this?” she asked, her skepticism still there but softened now.

“Completely,” Mia said, a fragile but insistent spark of hope in her voice. “It’ll be fun, Lara. Just like old times. We’ll hit the road, suffer through terrible playlists, and eat enough junk food to make us sick. Come on, you know you want to.”

Lara hesitated. She thought about the fight with Emily, how the words had cut deeper than they should have. She thought about the boy she couldn’t save, about how her apartment felt more like a cage when she was alone.

“Okay,” she said finally, the word slipping out before she could second-guess herself.

“Wait, really?” Mia asked, her voice bright with disbelief.

"Yeah, really," Lara said, a small smile tugging at her lips despite herself. "But don't make me regret this, okay?"

"You won't," Mia said, her excitement bubbling over. "I promise. You're going to love it. I'll start looking up cabins tonight, and we can leave in a couple of days. Oh my God, Lara, this is going to be amazing."

Lara couldn't help but laugh, Mia's energy infectious even through the phone. "Calm down, I haven't even packed yet."

"I'll text you the details," Mia said quickly, her words tumbling over each other in her rush. "Seriously, thank you for saying yes. I owe you big time."

"You owe me more than you know," Lara said lightly, but a strange sense of relief curled in her chest, softening the edges of her exhaustion.

They stayed on the phone a little longer, talking through logistics and laughing about what snacks they'd bring, to take warm clothes and to remember their passports, until Mia's excitement gave way to something softer, quieter.

"Thanks, Lara," Mia said as they prepared to hang up. Her voice was lower now, threaded with something earnest, something that reached through the line and settled deep in Lara's chest.

"Anytime," Lara said, and meant it.

As she hung up, Lara stared at her phone for a long moment, her faint reflection staring back from the dark screen. A road trip. Canada. It was impulsive, completely unlike her.

But maybe that wasn't such a bad thing.

5

The parking lot was almost empty when Lara stepped out of the car and stretched. The sun warm on her face despite the cool wind. The car, a glossy red 1968 Chevrolet Impala she'd rented for the trip gleamed under the sunlight, its chrome trim catching every glimmer. Running a hand over the hood, she grinned to herself. It had been an impulsive splurge, but if they were going to do this, they were going to do it in style.

She spotted Mia before she heard her, emerging from behind a silver sedan parked a few spaces away. Her dark hair tumbled over her shoulders in loose waves, and she wore a faded denim jacket over a long, knitted dress that swayed lightly in the breeze.

"Mia!" Lara called, waving as she leaned casually against the Impala's door.

Mia's face lit up the moment she saw Lara, her entire posture relaxing as a wide grin spread across her face.

"Lara!"

She crossed the lot quickly, her sandals crunching against the gravel, and wrapped her arms around Lara in a hug that was both fierce and warm.

"Oh my God, it's so good to see you," Mia said, squeezing tightly.

"You too," Lara said, laughing as she hugged her back. "Though I gotta say, you look way too put together for a road trip."

Mia pulled back, her hands still resting on Lara's shoulders, eyes sparkling with amusement. "Hey, just because we're hitting the road doesn't mean I can't look cute." She paused, her gaze shifting to the car behind Lara. "Wait. Is that...?"

Lara smirked and stepped aside to give Mia a better view. "Yep. 1968 Impala. Full tank of gas, no GPS, and probably a questionable suspension system. What do you think?"

Mia's jaw dropped, eyes widening as she circled the car, running her fingers lightly over the polished surface. "Lara, this is... amazing. How did you even...?"

"Found a rental place online," Lara said, shrugging like it was no big deal, though she couldn't quite hide her grin. "Figured if we're going to do this, we might as well do it right."

Mia laughed, shaking her head in disbelief. "You're unbelievable. This is the kind of car they'd drive in an old movie. It's perfect."

"Damn right it is," Lara said, opening the driver's side door and nodding toward the passenger seat. "Now, come on. Let's hit the road before you change your mind."

Mia climbed in, the leather seats creaking faintly as she settled in. She ran her hands over the dashboard, her smile widening as she took in the retro dials and chrome accents. "This is so cool."

Lara slid into the driver's seat, adjusting the rearview mirror before turning the key. The Impala roared to life, its deep, throaty rumble sending a thrill through her chest.

"Buckle up," she said, shooting Mia a playful look.

"Yes, ma'am," Mia said, clicking her seatbelt into place.

The car rolled out of the lot, tires crunching over gravel as they pulled onto the road.

The I-87 North stretched ahead; the kind of empty, open highway that made you feel like you could drive forever. For a while, they rode in companionable silence, the rumble of the engine and the rustle of wind through the open windows filling the space between them. Then Mia turned, eyes bright with excitement.

"Okay, so what's the plan?" she asked. "Where are we going first?"

Lara glanced at her, one eyebrow lifting. "The plan? You mean the incredibly detailed itinerary I definitely didn't make?"

Mia laughed, tossing her head back. "You didn't plan anything?"

"Not a thing," Lara admitted, grinning. "I figured we'd just... go. See where the road takes us."

Mia shook her head, still laughing. "You're full of surprises today, you know that?"

"Gotta keep you on your toes," Lara said, turning the wheel as the road curved gently along the water's edge.

Mia leaned back in her seat, her fingers playing idly with the sleeve of her dress. "This feels... surreal," she said softly, her voice almost lost to the wind. "I haven't done anything like this in years. Just... let go, you know?"

Lara glanced at her, her smile fading slightly. "Maybe it's time we both let go a little."

Mia met her gaze, something unspoken passing between them in the quiet. Then she smiled, small but genuine—and nodded.

"Yeah," she said. "Maybe it is."

They drove on, the scenery of the Hudson River Valley shifting as the sun dipped lower in the sky, casting everything in shades of gold and amber. The road ahead felt endless, full of possibilities they hadn't dared to dream of in far too long.

"Okay," Mia said suddenly, sitting up straighter. "First rule of the road trip: music. What's your playlist situation?"

Lara laughed, reaching for her phone and handing it over. "You're in charge of DJing. Just don't embarrass me."

Mia grinned, scrolling through Lara's music library. "No promises," she said, selecting a song and cranking up the volume. The opening chords of an old pop anthem filled the car, and Mia started singing along, loud and unabashed. Lara shook her head, laughing as she joined in, their voices blending with the thrum of the engine and the rush of wind through the windows.

The road stretched ahead, winding through dense forests that occasionally gave way to rolling farmland. Fields of golden corn swayed in the breeze, dotted with weathered barns that leaned slightly with age. Here and there, a windmill stood silhouetted against the sky, its blades creaking lazily. The late afternoon sun dipped lower, washing the landscape in hues of amber and soft pink, like a watercolor painting come to life.

Inside the car, the warm, worn leather seats carried the faint scent of polish and nostalgia. The dashboard gleamed, its chrome accents catching the light as Mia traced her fingers over the dials. A small hula dancer figurine bobbed gently on the dash, her grass skirt swaying with every bump in the road.

"This car is ridiculous," Mia said, laughing as she adjusted the radio dial. "I mean, look at this—an actual cassette player. When was the last time you even saw one of these?"

"Right?" Lara grinned, tapping the oversized steering wheel. "It's like stepping back in time. No Bluetooth, no GPS. Just vibes and a questionable sense of direction."

"Good thing we have a map," Mia teased, pulling a folded

paper map from the glove compartment. "You know, just in case we end up stranded in the middle of nowhere."

"We're not getting lost," Lara said, though her tone was playful. "And if we do, it's all part of the adventure."

They passed a wooden sign welcoming them to a small town with a name neither of them could pronounce. Mia squinted at it, trying to make sense of the jumble of letters.

"Think the whole town fits into one diner?" she mused.

Lara chuckled, glancing over at her. "Probably. Bet they have the best pie, though."

"Now you're speaking my language," Mia said, tucking the map back into the glove box.

The car rattled as they hit a stretch of uneven road, and Lara tightened her grip on the wheel, though she didn't seem concerned. The Impala felt solid beneath them, its deep engine purring like a contented cat.

"You ever think about the old days?" Mia asked suddenly, her voice quieter now, the laughter slipping from her tone.

"All the time," Lara admitted. "Why? Something on your mind?"

Mia hesitated, "I don't know. I guess... sometimes I wonder how we ended up here, you know? Like this—" she gestured vaguely at the car, the road, herself. "This isn't exactly what I pictured when I thought about my future."

Lara glanced at her, curiosity flickering across her face. "What did you picture?"

Mia smiled, though it was tinged with something bittersweet. "I used to want to open a bakery."

Lara raised an eyebrow. "A bakery? You never told me that."

"I didn't think it mattered," Mia said with a small shrug. "It was just a silly dream. But yeah, I used to picture this little place on the corner of some quiet street—a big window with my name painted on it, shelves full of pastries, the smell of fresh bread in the air. I'd wear one of those cute aprons, and everyone would call me by my first name. It was simple, but it felt like mine, you know?"

Lara didn't respond right away, her eyes steady on the road. When she spoke, her voice was soft. "It doesn't sound silly. It sounds... beautiful."

Mia's smile was faint, her gaze drifting out the window to the blur of trees passing by. "Yeah, well. Life had other plans."

Lara let the silence settle before speaking again. "I used to want to be an astronomer."

Mia turned to her, eyebrows raised. "Really? You?"

Lara nodded, a small smile playing at her lips. "When I was a kid, my dad got me this cheap telescope for Christmas. It wasn't much, but I used to sit on the roof for hours, staring at the stars. I was obsessed with constellations—I'd draw them in my notebooks, make up stories about them. I thought maybe one day I'd work for NASA or something."

Mia laughed softly. "I can totally see that. Little Lara, mapping out the stars and solving the mysteries of the universe."

"Yeah, well," Lara said with a shrug. "Turns out I'm better at fixing people than at calculating orbital mechanics."

Mia tilted her head, studying her. "Do you miss it?"

Lara didn't answer right away. Her grip tightened slightly on the wheel. "Sometimes," she admitted. "But it feels so far away now, like it belonged to someone else. Someone who doesn't exist anymore."

Mia nodded, her smile fading as she looked down at her hands. "Yeah. I get that."

The companionship between them was enhanced by the comforting, steady rumble of the car. The road curved ahead, winding through a small valley where the sun dipped low, streaking the horizon with orange and pink. A herd of deer grazed at the meadow's edge, their heads lifting as the car passed.

"This is beautiful," Mia said softly, almost reverent.

Lara glanced at her, a small smile tugging at the corner of her mouth. "Yeah. It is."

Mia shifted in her seat, turning toward her. "You know, we're allowed to want more than this."

Lara's smile faltered, her brow creasing. "More than what?"

"Than the lives we ended up with," Mia said, firm but gentle. "The bakery, the stars... all of it. We're allowed to want those things, even if they feel impossible."

Lara didn't answer right away. Her gaze stayed fixed on the road, her fingers tight on the wheel. After a long moment, she exhaled slowly, her grip loosening.

"Maybe," she said finally, her voice quiet.

Mia smiled and reached over, resting a hand on Lara's arm for a moment before pulling back. "Well, for now, we've got this. And I don't know about you, but I'm starving."

Lara laughed, the tension easing from her shoulders. "Fine. Let's find that diner with the world's best pie."

The car sped on, the road stretching endlessly ahead carrying them toward something neither could name but both desperately needed.

6

The sun hung low on the horizon, a burning orange disc sinking slowly into a bed of pink and violet clouds. Trees lined the road, their dark silhouettes swaying in the chilled evening breeze. The Impala cruised steadily along the winding highway; its deep, steady engine noise punctuated by the occasional crackle of gravel beneath its tires.

Inside the car, the air was warm and easy, filled with laughter and the faint strains of an old pop song Mia had queued up on Lara's playlist. Mia had her feet propped on the dashboard, her sandals discarded on the floor, her head tilted back against the seat.

"Okay, okay," Mia said, laughing as she swiped at the screen of Lara's phone. "Here's one. If you could live anywhere in the world, no limits, no strings, where would it be?"

Lara glanced at her, one hand resting casually on the wheel. "That's easy. Colorado. Somewhere up in the mountains, where the air's thin and the stars feel like they're right on top of you."

Mia raised an eyebrow. "You'd pick Colorado? Out of the whole world?"

"Why not?" Lara shrugged. "It's quiet. Peaceful. No traffic, no noise, just... space. Plus, I've always been a sucker for a good mountain view."

Mia hummed thoughtfully, tapping a finger against her chin. "I can see that. You'd have a little cabin, maybe a dog, spend your nights stargazing like you used to."

Lara smiled faintly, her eyes flicking back to the road. "Yeah, something like that."

"What about you?" she asked, shifting the conversation. "If you could live anywhere, where would it be?"

"Paris," Mia said without hesitation.

Lara snorted. "Paris? Seriously?"

"What's wrong with Paris?" Mia laughed, feigning offense.

"Nothing, except I didn't peg you for the croissants-and-Eiffel-Tower vibe," Lara teased.

Mia rolled her eyes, though her smile didn't fade. "I've always wanted to go there—walk along the Seine, eat pastries for breakfast, shop in those little markets. It just seems so... magical, you know?"

Lara shook her head, a soft laugh escaping her lips. "You're impossible."

"And you're predictable," Mia shot back, smirking.

Their laughter faded into a comfortable silence—the kind that didn't need filling. Outside, the last light of day stretched across the horizon, the sky deepening into shades of indigo and gold. As they drove deeper into the forest, the trees grew taller, their branches intertwining overhead to form a dense canopy that swallowed what remained of the sunlight.

"Hey, are we actually heading anywhere?" Mia asked, breaking the quiet.

"Sort of," Lara said, her tone playful. "There's a little town up ahead. I figured we could stop there for the night, grab some food, maybe find a place to crash."

"And by 'find a place to crash,' you mean one of those

charming motels with questionable sheets and a vending machine in the lobby?"

"Exactly," Lara said, grinning. "You're catching on."

Mia groaned dramatically, but there was a spark of excitement in her eyes. "You're lucky I'm in a good mood."

The road curved sharply, the trees lined up on either side, their shadows stretching longer, darker, as the last traces of daylight bled from the sky. Lara's gaze alternating between the road and the dense forest beyond.

"You know," Mia said, her voice softer now, "this is the most fun I've had in... God, I don't even know how long."

Lara glanced at her, the tension in her shoulders easing just slightly. "Me too."

Mia smiled and turned to the window, watching the world blur past. "It's nice. Being out here with you. Feels like... I don't know, like we've left everything behind."

Lara exhaled, her eyes settling back on the road. "Yeah," she murmured. "It does."

The words had barely left her lips when something shot out from the shadows—a blur of movement appearing out of nowhere.

"Lara!" Mia's voice cut through the quiet, sharp and panicked.

Lara slammed the brakes. The Impala's tires screamed against the pavement, the car lurching violently forward. Her heart pounded against her ribs as they skidded to a halt—just feet from the massive buck frozen in the middle of the road.

The deer's wide, dark eyes stared back at them, its antlers stark against the glow of the headlights. For a moment, everything was silent—the road, the car, even the forest seemed to hold its breath.

"Jesus," Lara muttered, gripping the wheel so tightly her knuckles turned white.

Mia sat motionless in the passenger seat, her chest rising and falling in shallow, rapid breaths. "Is it... is it okay?"

The deer blinked once, ears twitching, then, with a sudden burst of movement, bounded off into the trees.

Lara exhaled shakily, easing her grip on the wheel. "It's fine. We're fine."

Mia let out a breathless laugh, pressing a hand to her chest. "That was... oh my God, my heart is still racing."

"Yeah," Lara said, her voice tight. "Mine too."

They sat there for a moment, the Impala idling quietly in the middle of the road. Adrenaline still thrummed through Lara's veins, her pulse pounding in her ears.

"Guess that's what we get for driving through deer country," Mia said, her voice laced with forced humor.

Lara glanced at her, a faint smile tugging at her lips despite the tension still coiled in her chest. "You okay?"

Mia nodded, though her hands trembled slightly as she brushed her hair back from her face. "Yeah. Just... didn't see that coming."

"Me neither," Lara admitted, shifting the car into drive.

The Impala rolled forward slowly, its tires crunching over the pavement as they continued down the road. The laughter and lighthearted chatter from earlier had vanished, replaced by a quiet tension neither woman acknowledged but both felt.

As the forest thinned and the first lights of the small town came into view, Mia broke the silence.

"Well, that's one way to start a road trip," she said, her voice still a little shaky but carrying a trace of her usual humor.

Lara let out a soft laugh, glancing at her. "Here's hoping the rest of it isn't quite so exciting."

Mia smiled, leaning back in her seat as the town grew closer, its warm glow cutting through the darkness. For the first time since they'd started this journey, the excitement in her chest was tempered by something else—something heavier, more uncertain.

But she didn't say it. And neither did Lara.

The Impala rumbled into the gravel parking lot, its headlights slicing through the inky darkness. The neon sign for Pine Hollow Bar & Rooms flickered faintly, casting an uneven glow over the weathered wooden building. A string of mismatched Christmas lights hung haphazardly along the roofline; their colors muted against the night. The only other cars in the lot were a couple of dusty pickups and an old Harley parked near the entrance.

Lara killed the engine, the sudden quiet inside the car almost deafening. She leaned back in her seat, exhaling slowly as her grip on the steering wheel relaxed.

"This is... something," Mia said, peering through the windshield.

"Yeah, well," Lara said, cracking a wry smile. "Beggars can't be choosers."

They stepped out of the car, the cool night air biting at their skin as they stretched their legs. Gravel crunched beneath their boots as they made their way to the entrance, where the faint sound of music and muffled voices spilled out each time the door swung open.

The scent hit them the moment they stepped inside, a mix of spilled beer, fried food, and stale cigarette smoke that clung to the air like an old memory. The bar was dimly lit, its walls lined with hunting trophies and faded photographs of fishermen posing with their prized catches. In the corner, a jukebox played a scratchy rendition of an old country song, its melancholic twang barely audible over the low murmur of conversation.

Lara glanced around, taking in the scene. A group of locals clustered around a pool table in the back, their laughter punctuated by the sharp clink of billiard balls. The bar itself was long and wooden, its scarred and sticky surface lined with mismatched stools. Above it, a row of neon beer signs flickered dimly, casting a bluish glow over the bottles arranged against the mirror.

"Quaint," Mia murmured, her lips twitching into a faint smile.

"Quaint is one way to put it," Lara said, leading them toward a small table near the wall. It wobbled slightly as they sat, the chair legs scraping against the worn floor.

"Be right back," Lara said, pushing up from her seat and heading toward the bar.

The bartender, a burly man with a thick beard, wore a baseball cap pulled low over his forehead. As Lara approached, he gave her a brief nod, wiping his hands on a rag that had seen better days.

"What'll it be?" he asked, his voice gravelly but not unkind.

"Bourbon. Large. And a Budweiser," Lara said, her tone steady.

The bartender raised an eyebrow but didn't comment, pouring bourbon into a short glass and cracking open the beer. Lara carried the drinks back to the table, setting the Budweiser in front of Mia before dropping into her seat with a sigh.

Mia eyed the bourbon, her brows lifting. "Rough night?"

"You could say that," Lara said, picking up the glass and tossing it back in one smooth motion. The bourbon burned on the way down, sharp and warm. She exhaled slowly, savoring the heat as it settled in her chest.

Mia hesitated before wrapping her fingers around the beer bottle. "I'm not much of a drinker, you know."

"I remember," Lara said, a small smile tugging at her lips. "But if there was ever a night to start, this might be it."

Mia let out a nervous laugh, lifting the bottle to her lips and taking a tentative sip. Her nose wrinkled slightly at the taste, but she kept going—drinking faster than she probably should have.

"Whoa, slow down," Lara said, chuckling. "It's not a race."

Mia set the bottle down, her cheeks flushing. "Well, you made it look so easy."

"That's because I'm a professional," Lara said, leaning back in her chair as she gestured for the bartender to bring another bourbon.

Mia laughed again, softer this time, almost hesitant. The tension from earlier still lingered beneath the surface, but for the first time in hours, it felt like they could breathe again.

The jukebox switched to a slow, bluesy tune, its mournful notes drifting through the bar as the bartender slid another bourbon onto the table. Lara picked it up, swirling the amber liquid in her glass as she glanced around the room.

"Here's to surviving," she said, raising her glass slightly.

Mia hesitated, then lifted her bottle with a small, determined smile. "To surviving."

Their glasses clinked softly; the sound nearly lost in the hubbub of the bar. Outside, the wind whispered through the pines, rustling their branches as the neon sign flickered—on, off, then on again, casting faint, uneven shadows across the gravel lot.

For a moment, it was just the two of them. Sitting in a dive bar in the middle of nowhere, their lives suspended in this strange, fleeting bubble of quiet.

And for now, that was enough.

7

The bar had filled out as the night deepened, the buzz of conversation swelling, punctuated by bursts of rowdy laughter and the occasional crash of a glass hitting the floor. The jukebox in the corner cycled through country and rock songs, its speakers crackling slightly with each new track. A haze of cigarette smoke clung to the air, mingling with the aroma of cheap beer and fried food. It was the kind of place that felt frozen in time. Worn, gritty, and unapologetically rough around the edges.

Lara nursed her third bourbon, the glass cool in her hand as she leaned back in her chair, her gaze sweeping the room. The locals were exactly what she'd expected: rugged men in trucker hats and flannel shirts, women in denim cutoffs and tank tops that clung to their sun-kissed skin. It wasn't exactly hostile, but there was an edge to the atmosphere, a charged energy that made Lara's instincts fizz with caution.

Mia, on the other hand, was clearly having the time of her life. She sat a little too upright, her cheeks flushed from drinking her beer far too quickly. Her laugh rang out above the noise, bright, unguarded as she leaned across the table, engrossed in conversation with the man who had joined them a few minutes earlier.

His name was Trent. Late thirties, dark hair slicked back, his smile just a little too sharp. He wore a leather jacket that looked like it had seen as many fights as he probably had, and his jeans were frayed at the knees. Confidence clung to him, toeing the line between charm and arrogance, the kind that felt more practiced than genuine. Lara had pegged him as trouble the moment he sauntered over, but Mia, caught up in her excitement, hadn't noticed.

"So, you ladies just passing through?" Trent asked, his voice smooth as he leaned closer to Mia, ignoring Lara entirely.

"Something like that," Mia said, twirling a strand of dark hair around her finger. She giggled. Her words slightly slurred. "We're on a road trip."

"Road trip, huh?" Trent's gaze flicked to Lara, though his smirk didn't waver. "Bet you've got some stories."

"Not yet," Lara said coolly, lifting her glass to her lips. "We just got started."

Mia elbowed her playfully. "Don't listen to her. We've already had some excitement. Almost hit a deer on the way here. It scared the crap out of us."

Trent chuckled, though the sound didn't quite reach his eyes. "Yeah, those things are all over the place up here. You gotta watch the roads at night."

His gaze drifted to Lara, smirk widening. "What are you driving, anyway?"

"'68 Impala," Lara said, her tone clipped. She didn't like the way his eyes lingered, like he was sizing her up.

"Classic," Trent said, nodding appreciatively. "Bet she purrs."

"She does," Lara replied evenly, turning her attention back to her drink, hoping he'd take the hint and move on.

But Trent wasn't here for her. His chair scraped closer to

Mia's as he leaned in, voice low and intimate. "You ever been up here before?"

Mia shook her head, her smile wide and uninhibited. "Nope. First time."

"Well, welcome to the Northwoods," Trent said, tipping an imaginary hat. "We don't get many tourists this time of year. Guess that makes you special."

Mia laughed. Too loud, too open. "I don't know about special."

"Oh, I'd say you're special," Trent said, his gaze dipping briefly to her bare shoulders before flicking back to her face. "A woman like you? Hard to miss."

Lara's grip tightened around her glass, her jaw clenching. "Mia," she said, her tone sharper than she intended. "Maybe we should—"

"Relax, Lara," Mia said, waving her off. "We're just talking."

"Yeah, we're just talking," Trent echoed, but his smirk had taken on an edge that made Lara's stomach twist.

The bartender appeared at their table, a woman in her fifties with graying hair pulled into a tight ponytail. She cast a glance at Trent, her expression unreadable. "Need another round?"

"I'm good," Lara said quickly, shaking her head. "Mia?"

Mia hesitated, then shook her head as well. "No, thanks."

The bartender lingered, her gaze flicking between Trent and the two women. Then, with a small nod, she turned to leave but not before shooting Lara a look. Something wary. Almost a warning.

Trent didn't seem to notice. He leaned in closer to Mia, his voice dipping lower. "You know, there's a great spot down by the lake. Quiet. Beautiful. I could take you there sometime."

Mia laughed again, but this time, it sounded thinner, her buzz wearing off under the scrutiny of his attention. "That's nice of you, but—"

"Three's a crowd," Lara cut in, her voice sharper now. "And we don't have time for sightseeing."

Trent's eyes flicked to her, his smirk faltering for the first time. "And what's that supposed to mean?"

"It means we're just passing through," Lara said evenly, her gaze locked onto his. "And we're not looking for company."

Mia shifted uncomfortably in her seat, her smile fading. "Lara..."

"Don't worry," Trent said, his voice cooler now. "Just being friendly."

"Yeah, well, we're all set on friendly," Lara said, standing and grabbing her jacket. "Come on, Mia. Let's call it a night."

Mia hesitated, her cheeks flushing as she glanced between Trent and Lara. "I... okay."

Trent leaned back in his chair, his smirk returning as he watched them gather their things. "You ladies take care now," he said, his tone dripping with sarcasm.

Lara didn't respond. Her grip on Mia's arm was firm as she guided her toward the door. The cool night air hit them the moment they stepped outside, crisp and biting, a stark contrast to the stifling heat of the bar. Lara exhaled slowly. Her breath visible in the dim glow of the parking lot lights.

"Lara," Mia started, her voice softer now.

"Not here," Lara said, shaking her head. "Let's just get to the car."

The night air hit them like a splash of cold water, cutting through the alcohol haze that had settled over the last few hours. Gravel crunched beneath their shoes as Lara strode toward the Impala, her jaw tight, irritation and concern warring in her chest. Behind her, Mia trailed slightly, the flush in her cheeks still visible even under the flickering glow of the Pine Hollow Bar & Rooms sign.

"Mia," Lara said sharply, spinning to face her once they reached the car. "What the hell was that?"

"What was what?" Mia shot back, folding her arms across her chest, her tone instantly defensive.

Lara exhaled, struggling for patience. "You were flirting with a guy who's practically dripping with bad news," she said, her voice edged with worry. "He's not just some harmless local, Mia. I don't like the way he was looking at you."

Mia huffed, brushing a strand of hair out of her face. "Lara, I'm fine. It's not like I was about to run off into the woods with him."

"No, but you don't know him," Lara pressed, her voice dropping but losing none of its firmness. "And you've been drinking. You're not thinking clearly."

Mia rolled her eyes, a humorless laugh slipping past her lips. "God, Lara, would you just stop? I'm not a child. I can handle myself."

Lara exhaled slowly, her hands curling into fists at her sides. "I'm not saying you're a child. I'm saying this isn't you. Since when do you..." She gestured back toward the bar. "... do this?"

Mia hesitated, her arms wrapping around herself as if to ward off the accusation. "Maybe I'm tired of being predictable," she murmured, her voice barely audible over the distant chatter of crickets. "Maybe I just... need this."

Lara stared at her, the words sinking in. She wanted to argue, to push harder, but something in Mia's expression, a fragile mix of defiance and desperation made her stop. Before she could respond, the crunch of footsteps on gravel made them both turn. Trent emerged from the bar, his leather jacket slung over one shoulder, his smirk firmly in place.

"Everything okay out here?" he asked, his voice smooth as his gaze flicked between them.

Mia's posture straightened, her demeanor shifting as she turned toward him. "Yeah. Everything's fine."

Lara's stomach twisted. She saw the way Mia's face lit up, the way she unconsciously leaned toward Trent.

"You coming back in?" Trent asked, his gaze locked on Mia.

Mia hesitated, glancing at Lara for a brief moment before nodding. "Actually, I think I'm going to go back inside."

Lara's jaw tightened. "Mia, are you serious?"

"It's fine," Mia said quickly, her voice firm, though her smile was too bright, too forced. "I'll see you later, okay? Just... go get us a room and rest up."

"Mia," Lara started, her voice low, edged with warning, but Mia was already stepping closer to Trent, her fingers grazing his arm as she smiled up at him.

"Night, Lara," she called over her shoulder, her tone light but unmistakably final.

Lara stood frozen, her heart pounding as she watched them disappear back into the bar. She wanted to go after Mia; to grab her by the arm and drag her out of there but something held her back. Maybe it was the exhaustion creeping in, the alcohol dulling her edges, or that small, stubborn voice in her head whispering, *She's an adult. Let her make her own choices.*

Even as she turned toward the Impala, unease coiled in Lara's stomach. Inside, the bar pulsed with noise and laughter, clinking glasses, raucous male conversation. Through the window, Lara caught the bartender watching Mia, her expression one of concern. Lara's fingers tightened around the car door handle. She hesitated. Then, with a sigh, she turned and walked towards the motel.

The twin room Lara rented was small and plain, the kind of place that looked clean enough on the surface but had probably seen its fair share of questionable moments. The bed was stiff, the sheets scratchy, and the single window overlooked the parking lot, where the Impala gleamed faintly under the moonlight.

After she'd texted Mia the room number, Lara kicked off her boots and sat on the edge of the bed, hands resting on her knees. Her mind raced. Each scenario worse than the last. She didn't trust Trent. His smirk, his slick confidence, the way he had looked at Mia like she was something to be conquered.

But Mia had made her choice. And Lara had to respect that. Didn't she?

She leaned back against the headboard, closed her eyes and tried to doze. Time dragged until eventually, the sound of footsteps echoing in the hallway, the door next door closing put Lara on alert. A muffled laugh, Mia's, filtered through the thin walls, and Lara's jaw tightened. Had Trent already checked into the motel and by coincidence, he was the room next door? Or was it intentional?

She told herself it was fine. Mia was just letting her hair down, cutting loose in a way she hadn't in years. Maybe she needed this. Maybe Lara needed to stop overthinking everything. But even as she closed her eyes, wishing herself to sleep, unease gnawed at her, a quiet whisper in the back of her mind.

Something wasn't right.

In the next room, the laughter faded, replaced by the slow creak of bedsprings and hushed voices. Outside, the neon sign for *Pine Hollow Bar & Rooms* flickered once, twice, then went dark.

8

Lara lay flat on her back. Her body was tired, exhausted really, but her mind refused to shut off. She kept replaying the moment Mia had walked away with Trent, her arm brushing against his, that giddy, careless look on her face.

"Let it go," Lara muttered to herself, turning onto her side. The lumpy mattress groaned under her weight, and the musty smell of the room, like damp carpet and stale smoke only made her more irritable.

But she couldn't let it go. Not really. Through the thin wall separating their rooms, she could hear muffled voices. Mia's giggle drifted through, followed by Trent's deeper, smooth tone. She couldn't make out the words, but the sound of it set her teeth on edge.

Another burst of laughter came, louder this time, and Lara groaned, pulling the scratchy pillow over her head. *She's an adult. She's fine. She's just having fun.*

But fun wasn't the word that came to mind when she thought about Trent. His arrogance, the predatory way he'd leaned into Mia like he already owned her, the way he'd dismissed Lara like she was invisible. It all felt wrong.

Another giggle, then a soft thump against the wall.

"For fuck's sake," Lara muttered, tossing the pillow aside. She sat up, rubbing her hands over her face.

She didn't want to hover. She didn't want to play the overprotective friend. But as the minutes ticked by and the sounds continued, laughter, murmured voices, the occasional creak of the bed, her unease grew. And just as she began to tell herself she was overreacting, the mood shifted.

It started with a loud crash, sharp and sudden, like something had been knocked over. Lara bolted upright, her heart pounding. She strained to listen, every muscle in her body tense.

Then came the scream. High-pitched, panicked, and unmistakably Mia's. Lara was on her feet before she even realized it, her pulse roaring in her ears as she crossed the room in three long strides. She threw open her door, the cool night air from the hallway hitting her like a slap as she turned toward Mia's room.

"Mia?" she called, her voice trembling but loud. She pounded on the door with her fist. "Mia, are you okay? What's going on in there?"

Inside, she could hear crying. Mia's voice, broken and frantic, mixed with squeals of panic. Something thudded against the floor, and a muffled voice, too low for her to make out, barked something in response.

"Mia!" Lara shouted again, panic clawing at her chest. She pressed her ear to the door, trying to make sense of the sounds coming from inside. "Mia, open the door! It's me!"

More crying, then a loud crash, like furniture being upended. She heard Mia whimper. Lara's blood ran cold. The hallway stretched out in dim light, the kind that buzzed faintly overhead like a broken insect.

Lara stood outside Mia's door, her fist pounding against the cheap wood. The faded brass numbers nailed to the door, 203, shook with every blow, rattling in time with the thundering of her heart.

"Mia!" she shouted, her voice cracking with panic. The muffled sounds from the other side of the door, cries, squeals, something crashing, made her stomach churn.

Her body shook as she pressed her ear to the door, the cold surface sending a shiver down her spine. She could hear Mia crying, her voice high and frantic, mixing with Trent's low, growling tone. The words were indecipherable, but the anger in his voice was unmistakable.

"Mia, open the door!" Lara yelled again, her voice trembling. She pounded harder, her fist aching with the effort. "Let me in! Please!"

The crying grew louder, broken by sharp squeals and gasping breaths. Another crash echoed through the room, and Lara felt the blood drain from her face. Her pulse thundered in her ears, her hands trembling as she tried the doorknob. It didn't budge. The lock held firm.

"Mia!" she screamed, desperation clawing at her throat.

Adrenaline surged through her veins, hot and dizzying, as the thought hit her: she couldn't wait. She couldn't stand there, helpless, while her best friend was in danger. She took a step back, her heart pounding so hard it hurt. Her bare feet dug into the thin carpet as she braced herself, lifting her leg and slamming it against the door just below the handle.

The first kick sent a shock of pain up her leg, the door barely budging. The sound of wood splintering mixed with Mia's muffled sobs.

"Come on," Lara muttered under her breath, stepping back again.

She kicked harder this time, her muscles burning with the effort. The door groaned but held.

"Damn it," Lara hissed, her chest heaving. Her hands were shaking, her breaths shallow and frantic.

She glanced at the lock, at the thin, chipped frame of the door. She had to try again.

Summoning every ounce of strength she had, she lifted her leg and kicked one last time. The door flew open with a loud crack, slamming into the wall behind it.

The scene that greeted her knocked the breath from her lungs.

The room was chaos. The bedside lamp lay shattered on the floor, shards of glass glittering in the dim light. One of the chairs had been overturned, its legs splintered. The bed was a mess of crumpled sheets, twisted and stained with what looked like blood smeared across the mattress. A glass from the nightstand had been knocked over, its contents pooling on the carpet.

And there, in the corner of the room, was Mia. She was curled into a ball, her arms wrapped tightly around her knees as she rocked back and forth. Her top was still on, but her bottom half was bare, her legs trembling as she tried to tuck them beneath herself. Her dark hair hung in tangled strands over her face, shielding her from view.

"Mia," Lara whispered, her voice breaking.

Her friend didn't respond, didn't even look up. She was crying, deep, guttural sobs that made her entire body shake. Lara stepped into the room, her movements slow and hesitant, like she was walking through a nightmare. Everything felt hazy, the edges of the scene blurred and unreal.

"Get away from her!"

The voice snapped her out of her daze. She turned sharply to see Trent standing near the bed, his chest heaving, his face flushed with anger. His shirt was wrinkled, his hair disheveled, and there was a dark stain on his sleeve—blood.

"What the hell did you do?" Lara demanded, her voice shaking with fury.

Trent sneered, his lips curling into a twisted smirk. "This isn't what it looks like."

"It looks like you hurt her," Lara spat, stepping closer, her fists clenched. "Get out. Now."

Trent hesitated, his eyes flicking between Lara and the door. For a moment, she thought he might argue, but then he grabbed his jacket from the bed and stormed past her, shoving her shoulder as he went.

"You're crazy, both of you," he muttered, his voice venomous as he disappeared into the hallway.

Lara didn't watch him go. Her focus was on Mia.

She dropped to her knees in front of her friend, her hands trembling as she reached out. "Mia? It's me. It's Lara. You're safe now, okay? He's gone."

Mia flinched at the sound of her voice, her body curling tighter into itself.

"Mia, look at me," Lara said softly, her throat tightening. "Please."

Slowly, Mia lifted her head, her tear-streaked face coming into view. Her eyes were red and swollen, her lips trembling as she met Lara's gaze.

"I-I'm sorry," Mia whispered, her voice barely audible.

"No," Lara said quickly, shaking her head. "You don't have to be sorry. You didn't do anything wrong."

Mia sobbed, her body shaking as Lara wrapped her arms around her, pulling her close.

"It's okay," Lara murmured, her voice cracking as she held her friend. "You're okay. I've got you."

The room was still a disaster, the evidence of what had happened glaring and undeniable. But in that moment, all Lara cared about was the woman in her arms—the woman who needed her more than ever. And as the adrenaline slowly began to fade, a cold, sinking realization settled in Lara's chest.

9

The door had barely clicked shut behind Trent before Lara realized he wasn't leaving. She heard the thud of his boots in the hallway, too loud, too deliberate. The fine hairs on the back of her neck stood on end as a wave of menace seeped through the door. She turned, instinct kicking in, just as the door slammed open again, rebounding off the wall with a deafening crash.

"You think you can just waltz in here and mess with my business?" Trent growled, his voice slurred and dangerous as he staggered into the room. His leather jacket was gone now, revealing broad shoulders and a muscular build beneath his wrinkled t-shirt. His fists were clenched, his movements erratic with drunken anger.

"Get out," Lara snapped, stepping in front of Mia, who remained huddled in the corner. Her voice was steady, but her heart pounded, adrenaline surging through her veins. "You're done here. Leave."

Trent's eyes narrowed, his lips curling into a sneer. "You don't get to tell me what to do, lady. You're just some nosy little..."

"Leave," Lara said again, her voice rising as she stood her

ground. Her pulse hammered in her throat, but she refused to back down.

Trent took another step closer, his large frame looming over her. "Or what? You gonna call the cops? You don't want them poking around here, trust me."

Lara's jaw tightened. "Mia doesn't owe you anything. Whatever you think this is, it's over."

Trent let out a short, humorless laugh. "You don't know what you're talking about."

And then he lunged.

Lara barely had time to react before Trent's hands shoved her backward. She stumbled, her back slamming against the edge of the nightstand. The lamp toppled over, clattering to the floor. Pain shot up her spine, but she shoved it aside, instincts kicking in as she twisted out of his reach.

"Stay away from her!" Lara shouted, dodging as Trent swung an arm toward her. His movements were clumsy but forceful, and in the cramped space, every step felt like a collision waiting to happen.

Mia let out a small whimper from the corner, her knees drawn to her chest, her tear-streaked face pale and frozen in shock. Lara caught a glimpse of her, her heart twisting, but there was no time to think. Trent was coming at her again.

He grabbed her arm, his grip like a vise, and yanked her toward him. Lara fought back, her free hand striking out instinctively. Her palm slammed against his chest, but he barely flinched, his drunken strength overpowering her.

"You're gonna regret this," Trent hissed, his breath hot and sour against her face.

Lara twisted sharply, wrenching her arm free and stumbling toward the bed. Her eyes darted around the room, searching for anything, something she could use. Then she saw it: a half-empty beer bottle perched on the edge of the dresser.

She grabbed it without thinking, the glass cold and slick in her hand, and swung with all her might.

The bottle shattered against Trent's temple, sending shards of glass flying. He stumbled back with a roar of pain, his hands clutching his head as blood streamed down the side of his face.

Lara's chest heaved as she stared at him, the jagged neck of the bottle still clutched in her hand. The room felt impossibly small, the pungent metallic odor of blood everywhere.

"You bitch," Trent snarled, his voice raw with fury. He staggered forward, eyes wild, hands trembling as he reached for her.

Lara stepped back, her heart pounding so hard it felt like it might burst. "Stay back!" she shouted, holding the broken bottle in front of her like a shield.

But Trent didn't stop. He lunged again, clumsy but full of brute force. Lara barely had time to react before he was on her, his body slamming into her as she fought to push him away.

The bottle in her hand came down, reflex more than intention. The sharp edge sliced through fabric and flesh. Trent sucked in a sharp breath, stumbling back, his hands clutching his thigh.

For a moment, everything was still. The only sound was the harsh, uneven rhythm of their breathing.

Then Lara saw it—the dark stain spreading across Trent's jeans, blood pouring from the wound in gooey pulsing waves. Her stomach dropped, the realization hitting her like a freight train.

She'd hit his femoral artery.

"Shit," Lara muttered, her training kicking in as she dropped the bottle and stepped forward. "Trent, sit down. You're bleeding out ..."

But Trent shoved her away, his movements frantic as he staggered toward the door. "Get... get away from me," he gasped, his voice weak and slurred. His hand pressed uselessly against the wound, blood slipping through his fingers.

"Trent, listen to me," Lara said, forcing her voice to stay firm despite the panic clawing at her chest. "You need pressure on that wound, or you're going to..."

"Shut up!" he snapped, stumbling against the wall. His eyes were wide with fear now, his bravado crumbling as the color drained from his face.

Lara turned to Mia, who was still curled in the corner, her body trembling with silent sobs. "Mia, we have to go. Now."

Mia didn't move; her wide, tear-filled eyes locked on Trent's staggering form. "I... I can't..."

"Yes, you can," Lara said, crossing the room and grabbing her arm. She pulled her to her feet, steadying her as best she could. "Come on. We don't have time."

Mia nodded numbly, her legs wobbling beneath her as she let Lara guide her toward the door. They stepped over the shards of glass and the growing pool of blood, the room a blur of chaos and fear.

Lara snatched up their bags from her room, her hands trembling as she stuffed her belongings into the duffel. Every second felt like an eternity, her ears straining for the sound of footsteps in the hall.

When they finally reached the Impala, Lara threw their bags into the back seat and slid behind the wheel, her fingers shaking as she turned the key. The engine roared to life, and the car lurched forward, gravel spraying beneath the tires as they sped out of the lot.

Neither of them spoke as the bar disappeared in the rearview mirror, its flickering neon sign fading into the darkness. The only sounds were the roar of the engine and the ragged rhythm of their breathing.

Lara's fingers clung to the steering wheel, her mind racing to process what had just happened. Beside her, Mia sat rigid, arms wrapped tightly around herself, her gaze fixed on the dark road ahead.

The highway stretched endlessly before them; its surface illuminated only by the twin beams of the Impala's headlights. The night was eerily quiet now, the steady rumble of the engine the only sound filling the lull between them. Lara's grip on the wheel was ironclad, her knuckles pale and rigid, and the faint scent of blood lingered in the car, making her stomach twist.

Mia sat curled in the passenger seat, knees drawn to her chest, her body trembling visibly. Her arms were wrapped tightly around herself, breath hitching in uneven gasps as tears streamed down her face. The occasional sob broke free. Sharp, raw, and each one sent a painful squeeze through Lara's chest.

"Breathe, Mia," Lara said, her voice strained, quieter than usual. She kept her eyes on the road, jaw set tightly. "Just... breathe."

Mia nodded, but the tears didn't stop. She buried her face in her hands, muffling her cries as her shoulders shook. The normally chatty, upbeat Mia was gone, replaced by someone fragile, broken, teetering on the edge.

Lara swallowed hard, forcing her focus back on the road, but the sight of Mia in her peripheral vision kept pulling her attention. Her friend's pain was like an ache in her ribs, making it harder to breathe. The adrenaline that had carried her through the fight and escape was fading now, leaving only a gnawing ache of panic and guilt in its wake.

The Impala's headlights caught the reflective sign of a rest area up ahead, and without thinking, Lara flicked on the turn signal, pulling over onto the gravel shoulder. The car jolted slightly as it rolled to a stop, and Lara shifted into park, the engine idling softly.

"I can't," Lara muttered, pushing the door open and

stumbling out of the car. The cold night air hit her immediately, biting against her skin, forcing her to take a deep, shuddering breath. She leaned against the side of the car, body shaking as she doubled over, emptying the contents of her stomach onto the ground.

The harsh sound of retching filled the air, and for a moment, nothing else existed but the sick, churning feeling in Lara's gut. She braced herself against the car with one hand, the other on her knee as she gasped for air, tears pricking at the corners of her eyes.

When she finally straightened, she caught sight of her hands in the dim light of the car's interior. They were smeared with blood, dark and sticky, some dried, some still fresh. Her stomach turned again, but there was nothing left to bring up.

She scrubbed her hands against her jeans in a desperate, futile attempt to wipe the blood off, but it only smeared further. Her breaths quickened, chest tightening as the horror of what had happened crashed down on her again.

She'd hurt someone. Killed someone, maybe. And even though she'd had no choice, the reality of it made her feel like she was drowning.

"Lara?" Mia's voice was soft, hesitant, but hearing it snapped Lara out of her spiral.

She turned to see Mia leaning forward in the passenger seat, her tear-streaked face barely visible in the glow of the dashboard lights. Her hands trembled as she reached up to flip down the sun visor, the small mirror catching her reflection.

Mia sucked in a sharp breath, fingers brushing lightly over her face. Her bottom lip was split, swollen and bruised, a thin line of dried blood trailing down her chin. Her left eye was already swelling, the bruise forming in shades of angry purple and red.

"Oh my God," Mia whispered, voice trembling as her

fingertips grazed the bruise. Her reflection blurred as fresh tears welled up in her eyes.

Lara climbed back into the car, her movements slow and deliberate. She couldn't stop looking at Mia, at the way her hands shook as she traced the outline of her injuries, at the way her lips quivered as she stared at her own reflection.

"Mia," Lara said softly, her voice taut with emotion.

"He hit me," Mia whispered, her words barely audible. Her eyes dropped to her legs, trembling uncontrollably, the muscles spasming as though they had given up entirely. "He hit me, Lara. And he..."

She broke off, her hands flying to her face as another sob ripped through her.

"I know," Lara said, her voice cracking as she reached over and placed a hand on Mia's arm. "I know, Mia. I'm so sorry."

Mia shook her head, her sobs muffled by her hands. "I can still feel him. I can feel... everything." Her voice wavered, full of anguish and disbelief. "It hurts. My legs, my... everything hurts."

Lara swallowed hard, forcing down her own tears. "We're going to get through this," she said, her voice trembling but determined. "I promise you; we're going to get through this."

Mia lowered her hands slowly, her tear-streaked face turning toward Lara. "You saved me," she whispered, her voice breaking.

Lara shook her head, her grip on the steering wheel tightening. "No. I didn't save you. I should have stopped it before it got this far."

Mia didn't respond, her gaze drifting back to the mirror. She stared at her reflection for a long moment before flipping the visor back up, plunging the car into dim quiet once more.

The two women sat there in the idling Impala, the memory of what had happened smothering them like a suffocating blanket. Outside, the night stretched on, dark and endless, the quiet broken only by the faint rustle of wind through the trees. Without another word, Lara found Mia some clothes and helped her dress, sliding on jeans and a sweater, trying to be gentle so as not to cause any more pain to her friend's battered body.

And as the Impala finally pulled back onto the road, carrying them further away from the bar and the horrors they'd left behind, the only thing louder than the silence was the question neither of them dared to ask.

10

Mia was curled into herself, her arms wrapped around her knees as she stared blankly out the window. Her face was pale, her eyes swollen and rimmed with red. Every few minutes, she'd lift a trembling hand to touch her bruised eye or swipe at the tears that continued to fall silently.

Lara exhaled a shaky breath and flicked on the turn signal, pulling into the gravel lot of a rest area. The headlights illuminated an empty picnic table and a row of vending machines before cutting out as Lara turned off the car. The sudden quiet left only the faint sound of Mia's breathing and the rustle of her clothes as she shifted.

"Mia," Lara said softly, turning to face her. She hesitated, searching for the right words, but nothing about this situation felt like it had a right way. "We need to talk."

Mia didn't respond, her gaze fixed on the dark forest outside.

"Mia," Lara said again, her voice firmer this time. "We need to get you to a clinic. You need to be checked out."

That finally made Mia turn her head, her wide, fearful eyes meeting Lara's. "No," she said quickly, shaking her head. "No, I can't."

"Mia, listen to me..."

"No!" Mia's voice cracked as she sat up straighter, her hands gripping the edge of the seat. "I can't, Lara. I can't go to a clinic. I can't." Her breath hitched, and fresh tears spilled down her cheeks. "What if they... What if they call the police?"

Lara's chest tightened as she reached out, placing a gentle hand on Mia's arm. "Mia, that's exactly why we need to go. What happened to you, it's a crime. We need to report it."

But Mia shook her head harder, her whole-body trembling. "You don't understand. If the police find out, Dane will find out. And if he knows I was... I was drinking, and flirting with another man..." Her voice cracked, and she buried her face in her hands. "He'll never let me live it down. He'll use it against me. He'll say it's my fault."

Lara's stomach churned, anger flaring hot and sharp in her chest. Dane's name left a bitter taste in her mouth, and the thought of him adding to Mia's pain made her fists clench. But she forced herself to breathe, to focus on Mia, who was breaking apart right in front of her.

"Mia," Lara said gently, her voice steady despite the storm inside her. "This isn't your fault. None of it. You didn't ask for this. You didn't deserve this."

Mia didn't respond, her sobs muffled by her hands.

Lara leaned back in her seat, her mind racing. She knew she couldn't push too hard, not now, but she also couldn't ignore what she'd seen. There was something about Mia's behavior, her confusion, her sluggish movements, the way she kept blinking as if trying to clear her vision, that didn't sit right.

"Mia," Lara said softly, her tone shifting to something more clinical. "Look at me for a second."

Mia hesitated, then slowly lowered her hands. Her face was a mess of tears and bruises, her lip trembling as she met Lara's gaze.

Lara leaned closer, studying her carefully. "Your pupils..." she murmured, frowning. "They're uneven."

"What?" Mia asked, her voice barely above a whisper.

"Your pupils," Lara repeated, her stomach twisting as the realization dawned. "I think... I think you were drugged, Mia. I think Trent spiked your drink."

Mia's eyes widened, her breath hitching. "Drugged?" she whispered, the word falling from her lips like it didn't belong to her. "You think... he..."

Lara nodded, her jaw tightening. "It explains why you felt so out of it, why your legs are trembling. It's not just the alcohol, Mia. He planned this."

Mia's face crumpled, and she buried her head in her hands again. "Oh God," she whispered, her voice breaking. "Oh God."

Lara reached out, gripping her friend's shoulder firmly. "This is why we need to go to a clinic. They can test you, Mia. They can help."

Mia shook her head weakly, her voice muffled. "I can't. I can't, Lara. I just want to forget this ever happened."

Lara's chest ached as she looked at her friend, so small and fragile in the passenger seat. She wanted to fix this, to take away Mia's pain, but there was no way to undo what had happened. All she could do now, was be there for her, even if it wasn't enough.

After a long moment, Mia lifted her head, her tear-streaked face turning toward Lara. "What... what do you think happened to him?" she asked, her voice trembling. "Trent. What's going to happen to him?"

Lara hesitated, her hands tightening on the steering wheel. She hadn't wanted to think about Trent, about the blood pooling on the carpet of that dingy motel room. But the question hung in the air, demanding an answer.

"I don't know for sure," Lara said quietly, her voice barely above a whisper. "But if I hit his femoral artery... then he..." She trailed off, swallowing hard. "He probably didn't make it."

Mia's breath hitched, and she pressed her hand to her mouth, her eyes filling with fresh tears.

"I didn't mean for it to happen," Lara said quickly, her voice breaking. "I was just trying to protect you. I didn't... I didn't want him to die."

"I know," Mia whispered, her voice trembling. "I know, Lara. I just... I don't know what to do."

Lara reached over, gripping Mia's hand tightly. "We'll figure it out," she said firmly, though the fear in her chest made the words feel hollow. "We'll get through this. Together."

But as the Impala rolled back onto the dark highway, both women were haunted by the same unspoken fear: the knowledge that their lives had just changed forever, and there was no turning back.

The Impala's tires rolled over the asphalt, the sound steady and hypnotic as they sped down the empty highway. The dark sky above was speckled with faint stars, but the moon hung low, casting only the barest light on the landscape. Trees lined the road like silent sentinels, their branches swaying in the gentle night breeze. Every so often, the headlights caught the reflective gleam of a mile marker or the glint of an animal's eyes lurking in the woods.

Lara's eyes were fixed on the road ahead. The adrenaline that had fueled her escape from the motel was beginning to ebb, leaving behind a nauseating mix of fear and guilt. Beside her, Mia sat stiffly in the passenger seat, her knees drawn up to her chest, her arms wrapped tightly around them. She stared out the window, her reflection faintly visible in the glass. A ghostly image of swollen eyes, bruised skin, and trembling lips. Her breath came in shallow, uneven bursts, and every so often, her fingers twitched against her legs, like she was trying to hold herself together.

Mia finally broke the impasse, her voice barely above a whisper. "We're going to prison."

Lara's stomach clenched, her hands tightening on the wheel. "Don't say that."

"It's true," Mia said, her voice cracking. She turned to face Lara, her wide, tear-filled eyes glinting faintly in the dashboard light. "He's dead, Lara. You said it yourself. You hit his artery. And even if they find out what he did to me, they won't care. They'll just see... they'll think we're murderers."

Lara's chest tightened, a sharp ache spreading through her ribs. She kept her eyes on the road, unable to meet Mia's gaze. "Mia, we did what we had to do. I did what I had to do. He was going to hurt you, he already hurt you."

"And now he's dead," Mia said, her voice trembling. "He's dead, and we left him there, and when they find him..." She trailed off, her breathing quickening as panic set in. "Oh my God, Lara, what if they've already found him? What if the police are looking for us right now?"

Lara pulled the car over abruptly, the Impala skidding slightly as it came to a stop on the gravel shoulder. The sudden motion jolted both women, and the absence of sound that followed felt deafening.

Lara let out a shaky breath, her head falling forward to rest against the steering wheel. Her shoulders rose and fell with each uneven inhale.

"I didn't mean for it to happen," she whispered, her voice breaking. "I didn't mean to kill him, Mia. I just... I panicked. I was trying to protect you, and I wasn't thinking. I didn't even realize—"

Mia reached out, her hand brushing against Lara's arm. "Lara, I know. I know you didn't mean to." Her voice was soft, but it carried a desperation that made Lara lift her head to meet her gaze. "But that doesn't change what happened. He's dead, and it's because of us. And no one is going to believe it was self-defense. Not with the way things look."

Lara nodded slowly, the truth of Mia's words sinking in like stones dropping into her gut. Her training as a paramedic had taught her to stay calm under pressure, to make split-second decisions, to act without hesitation. But nothing could have prepared her for this, the sheer horror of taking a life, even in the name of protecting someone she loved.

"What do we do?" Mia asked, her voice breaking again. She wiped at her eyes with the back of her hand, smearing her tears. "What the hell do we do, Lara? I can't, I can't go to prison. I can't."

Lara leaned back in her seat, her eyes drifting to the dark woods beyond the road. The trees swayed gently, their shadows shifting and blending into the night. For a moment, the world outside the car felt distant, surreal, like a backdrop to a nightmare she couldn't wake up from.

"We put distance between us and the motel," Lara said finally, her voice steady but grim. "We keep moving. We don't stop unless we have to."

Mia frowned, her brow furrowing. "But where do we go? We can't just drive forever."

Lara hesitated, her mind racing. She thought of the map folded in the glove compartment, the one they'd used to plan their aimless road trip. She thought of the border, of the vast expanse of Canada just a few hours north.

"We cross into Canada," she said, the words tumbling out before she could second-guess them.

Mia blinked, startled. "You still want to go to Canada?"

"It's all I can think of," Lara said, her voice firmer now. "If we can get across the border, it'll buy us time. We can figure out what to do next once we're there."

Mia shook her head, her lips trembling. "Lara, that's insane. We don't even have a plan. What if they stop us? What if..."

"They won't," Lara interrupted, her tone sharp. "We don't have a choice, Mia. We can't stay here. You said it yourself. If the police find us, they're not going to believe us. So we go. We go now, and we figure it out along the way."

Mia stared at her, her eyes wide and full of fear. But there was something else there too. Trust, fragile and hesitant but undeniable.

"Okay," Mia said finally, her voice barely audible. She nodded, her hands gripping her knees tightly. "Okay. Canada."

Lara exhaled slowly. She shifted the car into drive, the engine rumbling softly as the Impala rolled back onto the highway.

The road stretched out before them, dark and endless, the horizon swallowed by shadow. Lara's hands tightened on the wheel; her jaw set as she focused on the path ahead.

They didn't speak again for a long time, both occupied by unspoken fears and unacknowledged truths. But as the miles ticked by, a fragile sense of determination began to take root. A shared understanding that they were in this together, no matter what lay ahead.

The night pressed on, the stars above cold and distant, and the Impala carried them forward, away from the life they'd left behind and toward an uncertain, uncharted future.

11

The first light of dawn seeped through the trees, casting soft, golden streaks across the Impala's fogged-up windows. The faint morning chill clung to the air, but the sun was beginning its slow climb, promising to melt away the frost that had settled overnight. Inside the car, the air was still, broken only by the occasional rustle of movement and the faint hum of crickets in the surrounding woods.

Lara opened her eyes first, blinking against the dim light. Her neck ached from the awkward position she had slept in, her head resting against the car's doorframe. She shifted, wincing as her stiff muscles protested. Beside her, Mia was curled into her side, her head tucked against Lara's shoulder, her breathing soft and uneven.

They had spent the night huddled in the back seat—too afraid to stop anywhere, too exhausted to keep driving. Sleep had finally overtaken their fear, and they had collapsed into each other, seeking comfort in shared warmth and proximity.

Lara gently eased herself away from Mia, careful not to wake her, and opened the car door. The crisp morning air hit her immediately, jolting her senses awake as she stepped out and stretched, her joints popping in protest. She ran a hand through her tangled hair, the memories of the night before filling her with dread.

Behind her, Mia stirred, blinking groggily as she sat up. Her hair was a mess, her face pale and drawn, the bruises on her eye and lip stark in the soft morning light. She wrapped her arms around herself, shivering slightly as the cool air crept into the car.

"Morning," Lara said softly, leaning against the car door. Her voice was rough from sleep and tension.

Mia offered a weak smile, though it didn't reach her eyes. "Morning."

Lara glanced at the horizon, where the sun's faint glow edged over the tops of the trees. "We still have a long way to go," she said, her tone measured. "The border's at least five hours from here, maybe more."

Mia nodded silently, her gaze dropping to her lap. Her fingers twisted the hem of her sweatshirt, fidgety and tense.

"We should clean up," Lara added, her voice softer now. "There's a river just up ahead. It'll help."

Mia hesitated, then nodded again, pressing her lips into a thin line.

They pulled off the road and parked near a dirt path that led down to the riverbank. The sound of rushing water reached them before the river itself came into view, its steady rhythm calm and unchanging. The sun had climbed higher now, casting golden light over the water as it flowed over smooth stones and fallen branches. The air smelled of damp earth and pine, fresh and crisp.

Lara led the way to the river's edge, her boots crunching softly against the pebbles. She knelt by the water, dipped her hands in, and shivered at the icy temperature. The blood on her skin, Trent's blood, had dried overnight, leaving her palms sticky and stained. She scrubbed at them furiously, her movements brisk and almost frantic, as if she could erase the memory along with the stain.

Behind her, Mia hovered hesitantly, arms wrapped around herself. She looked smaller than usual, her body hunched inward as if trying to disappear. Her gaze flicked to the water, then back to Lara. Her lips parted slightly before she pressed them together again.

"You need to wash too," Lara said gently, glancing over her shoulder. "It'll help."

Mia nodded, her cheeks flushing as she stepped closer to the water's edge. She glanced around nervously, her eyes darting to the trees as if expecting someone to be watching.

"There's no one here," Lara said, her voice soft but firm. "It's just us."

Mia hesitated, then slowly began peeling off her clothes. She shrugged out of her sweater first, then slid off her jeans, her movements slow and tentative. When she was down to her underwear, she paused, her hands hovering at her waistband.

Lara stood, her own shirt and pants already lying in a heap by the rocks. Without hesitation, she stepped into the river, the icy water rushing around her calves as she waded in up to her knees. "Come on," she said, her tone gentle but encouraging.

Mia looked at her, cheeks burning as her gaze darted away. Lara stood confidently in the water, her bare skin glowing in the morning light, the defined lines of her body strong and unashamed. The sight made Mia feel small and exposed, her own scars, both visible and invisible, suddenly magnified.

"You don't have to look," Mia muttered, barely audible.

Lara turned, giving her privacy as she began washing her arms and shoulders, the water biting at her skin. "I'm not looking," she said softly. "Take your time."

After a moment, Mia finally slipped off her underwear and

stepped cautiously into the water. The cold made her gasp, and she waded in slowly, the current tugging at her legs as she moved closer to Lara.

The two women washed in silent contemplation, the river's steady murmur filling the space between them. Mia knelt in the shallows, her hands trembling as she cleaned herself. Her groin ached, soreness radiating through her thighs, and she bit her lip to keep from crying out as she gently scrubbed away the dried blood.

Lara glanced at her briefly, her expression unreadable, then looked away again, focusing on rinsing her hair. The awkwardness of everything unsaid remained, but neither of them spoke.

When they finally stepped out of the river, the sun had risen higher, its warmth cutting through the morning chill. Lara grabbed a towel from the car and wrapped it around herself, shaking out her hair. Her skin was flushed from the cold water, but she felt cleaner, lighter—as if the river had taken some of the burden she carried.

Mia dressed quickly, her movements hurried and self-conscious. Her hands trembled as she pulled on fresh clothes, her wet hair plastered to her cheeks. When she finally turned to Lara, her swollen eye and bruised lip stood out starkly against her pale skin, but there was a faint steadiness in her gaze that hadn't been there before.

"Ready?" Lara asked, her voice low.

Mia nodded, though her fingers still twisted the hem of her sweatshirt. "Yeah."

Lara gave her a small, reassuring smile and opened the car door. They climbed back into the Impala, the morning sun glinting off the windshield as they pulled back onto the road.

The river faded into the distance behind them, its quiet solace replaced by the steady grind of the highway below. The journey ahead was long and uncertain, but for now, they had each other.

The highway leading to the border seemed to stretch on forever, a thin ribbon of asphalt slicing through the dense, towering evergreens. Their branches were thick and overgrown, casting deep shadows over the road despite the soft glow of the rising sun. Every so often, the trees parted, revealing fleeting glimpses of distant hills cloaked in mist or the glint of a hidden stream, but the landscape felt closed in, the walls of the forest becoming tighter the closer they got to the crossing.

Inside the Impala Lara's jaw was set, her gaze locked on the road ahead as though sheer focus alone could keep the panic at bay. Mia sat curled into the passenger seat, her knees drawn to her chest, her fingers fiddling with the hem of her sweatshirt in restless, anxious movements. Every shallow breath she took seemed to echo in the enclosed space, amplifying the gloom that had settled between them.

The border station finally appeared in the distance, its unassuming structure breaking through the tree line like a mirage. Lara's stomach twisted as the first signs of activity came into view: a low concrete building with large windows, a row of booths flanked by yellow barriers, and uniformed officers standing near their stations. A line of cars crawled toward the booths, each vehicle inching forward at an agonizingly slow pace.

Mia let out a shaky breath, her voice barely audible. "What if they stop us?"

"They won't," Lara said quickly, though her voice lacked the confidence she was trying to project.

The closer they got, the more suffocating the scene became. The cars ahead were a mix of locals and travelers, their bumpers plastered with faded stickers and license plates from various states. One SUV had a roof rack piled high with camping gear, while an old sedan in front of it had a dog sticking its head out of the back window, its tail wagging obliviously. Lara envied their normalcy, their unburdened purpose, as she eased the Impala into the queue.

The border building loomed closer, its design harsh and utilitarian. The windows reflected the morning light, making it impossible to see inside, and the officers stationed at the booths stood like statues, their expressions unreadable beneath the brims of their hats. A camera mounted on a nearby pole swiveled slowly, its lens sweeping the line of waiting cars like a silent, watchful eye.

Mia shifted in her seat, her movements stiff and jerky. "Lara... what if they ask too many questions?"

"They won't," Lara repeated, her tone sharper this time, though it was directed more at her own spiraling thoughts than at Mia.

Mia turned toward her, her bruised face stark in the pale light filtering through the windshield. "What if they don't believe us?" Her voice cracked, trembling with fear. "What if they..."

"Stop," Lara interrupted, cutting her off before she could finish the thought. Her gaze flicked to Mia briefly, her expression hard but not unkind. "We'll get through this. Just stick to the story and keep calm."

The line moved forward again, and Lara nudged the car closer to the booths. She could see the border officers more clearly now, the sharp creases of their uniforms, the way their eyes scanned each car with quiet scrutiny. Her chest felt tight, the air in the car growing heavier with every inch they moved closer.

When it was finally their turn, Lara eased the Impala up to one of the booths. The officer on duty was tall and broad-shouldered, his navy uniform pristine. His expression was neutral but serious, his dark eyes flicking between the car and a clipboard he held in one hand.

Lara rolled down the window, the mechanical whirring of the glass breaking the somber mood inside the car.

"Good morning," the officer said, his tone polite but firm. His eyes briefly swept over Lara before settling on Mia. They lingered on her bruised face a moment too long, and Lara felt her stomach twist.

"Morning," Lara replied, forcing a smile that she hoped didn't look as strained as it felt.

"Where are you headed today?" the officer asked, his gaze shifting back to Lara.

"Just a road trip," she replied, keeping her voice light. "We're planning to explore some of the national parks up north."

The officer nodded slightly; his expression unreadable as he leaned forward. "Passports, please."

Lara reached into the glove compartment, her hands trembling slightly as she pulled out their documents. She handed them over, her heart pounding as the officer flipped through the pages. Each movement felt slow, deliberate, like he was waiting for something to stand out, something to question.

Mia shifted nervously in her seat, her fingers digging into the hem of her sweatshirt. Her breaths were shallow, her body tense as the officer glanced at her again.

"Everything okay?" he asked, his tone casual but pointed.

Mia froze, her lips parting slightly as her gaze darted to Lara.

"She's fine," Lara said quickly, her voice steady. "She took a bad fall while we were hiking. Slipped on some rocks by a river."

The officer's brow furrowed slightly as he looked back at Mia. "Hiking, huh?"

Mia nodded stiffly, her voice barely above a whisper. "Y-yeah."

Lara could feel the tension radiating off her friend, and she jumped in again, trying to steer the conversation away. "It looks worse than it is," she said, forcing another tight smile. "She's stubborn and refused to stop until we finished the trail."

The officer's lips twitched, almost imperceptibly, as he handed the passports back. "Be more careful next time," he said, stepping back from the car.

"Thank you," Lara said, the relief in her voice almost audible as she rolled up the window.

She eased the Impala forward, her chest still tight as the car passed the barrier and rolled onto Canadian soil. Her hands gripped the wheel so tightly that her fingers strained, and her breath came in shallow gasps as she struggled to process what had just happened.

In the passenger seat, Mia let out a shaky sob, her body trembling as she pressed her hands to her face. "I thought... I thought he was going to stop us," she whispered, her voice cracking.

"Me too," Lara admitted, her voice quiet. She kept her eyes on the road, her jaw clenched. "But we made it."

The horizon stretched ahead of them, vast and uncertain, as they left the border and their sins behind.

12

The motel was the kind of place that whispered stories of weary travelers and forgotten moments. Its exterior was a faded yellow, the paint peeling in places, and the buzzing neon sign that read Vacancy flickered faintly against the twilight sky. The parking lot was empty except for the Impala and an old pickup truck parked near the manager's office. The only sound was of cicadas and the occasional creak of the motel's rusted sign swaying in the breeze.

Lara parked the car in the far corner of the lot, her shoulders tense as she scanned their surroundings. She could feel the unrelenting stress of the past but she forced herself to stay focused. Mia sat in the passenger seat, staring blankly out the window, her hands folded tightly in her lap.

"We'll stay here for the night," Lara said softly. "Just a few hours to rest, and then we'll keep going."

Mia nodded, but she didn't look at her. Her face was pale, her bruised eye a dark, angry purple that seemed to swallow what little color remained in her complexion. Her hair hung limply around her face, and her lips were pressed into a thin, trembling line.

Lara swallowed hard and opened her door. "Come on," she said, her voice firmer now. "Let's get inside."

The room was as unremarkable as the motel itself, two twin beds with faded floral comforters, a small table with a lamp, and a boxy TV perched on a stand in the corner. The air smelled faintly of must and cleaning supplies, and the carpet was worn thin in patches. Lara flicked on the light and dropped her bag onto the nearest bed. Mia lingered near the door; her arms wrapped tightly around herself.

"You can take the shower first," Lara offered, her voice gentle. "It might help you feel better."

Mia nodded again, her movements slow and mechanical as she stepped into the bathroom and shut the door behind her. The sound of running water filled the room a moment later, and Lara let out a shaky breath, sinking onto the edge of the bed.

She pulled out her phone, her thumb hovering over the screen. She didn't want to look, didn't want to know what might already be out there, but the need to stay ahead of whatever was coming was stronger than her fear.

The screen glowed as she opened a browser and typed in the name of the bar: *Pine Hollow Bar & Rooms, Saratoga*. Her stomach twisted as she hit search, the results loading with agonizing slowness.

The first few headlines made her heart drop:

"Local Man Found Dead in Barroom Altercation."

"Police Investigate Fatal Incident at Pine Hollow Motel."

"Trent Lanning, 37, Identified as Victim."

Lara's breath caught in her throat as she clicked on the first article. The details were sparse. Police had responded to reports of a disturbance, a man had been found dead in one of the motel rooms, and authorities were investigating the incident. There was no mention of suspects yet, but the words foul play jumped off the screen, sending a cold shiver down her spine.

She closed the browser quickly, her hands trembling as she set the phone aside. Her pulse raced, her chest tight, and she pressed her palms against her knees, forcing herself to breathe.

"It's fine," she whispered to herself, her voice barely audible. "They don't know it was us."

But the words felt hollow, and the knot in her stomach refused to loosen.

The bathroom door creaked open, and Mia stepped out, her hair damp and clinging to her face. She wore a clean pair of sweatpants and a loose hoodie, her arms wrapped tightly around herself as she shuffled toward the bed.

"You okay?" Lara asked, her voice soft.

Mia nodded, though her gaze didn't meet Lara's. "I'm just... tired."

Lara nodded, watching as Mia climbed into the bed nearest the window and pulled the comforter up to her chin. Her movements were slow and hesitant, as though she were trying to avoid disturbing the stillness of the room.

"Try to get some sleep," Lara said, though the words felt like a lie. She doubted either of them would find much rest tonight.

Mia didn't respond, her eyes already closing as she curled into herself. Lara sat back on her own bed, staring at the ceiling, looking for answers that weren't there.

It was well past midnight when Lara was jolted awake by a muffled cry. She sat up quickly, her heart racing as she turned toward Mia's bed. Her friend was tossing and turning, her face twisted in a grimace, her hands clutching at the blankets.

"No," Mia murmured, her voice trembling. "Please, no..."

Lara crossed the room in an instant, kneeling beside Mia's

bed, and placing a gentle hand on her shoulder. "Mia," she said softly, shaking her slightly. "Mia, wake up."

Mia's eyes snapped open, wild and unfocused, her breath coming in sharp gasps. She blinked rapidly, her gaze darting around the room before landing on Lara. Her chest heaved, and tears spilled down her cheeks as she sat up, clutching the blanket to her chest.

"It's okay," Lara said quickly, her voice soothing. "It was just a dream. You're safe."

Mia shook her head, her hands trembling as she wiped her face. "It wasn't a dream," she whispered, her voice breaking. "It happened. It... it was real."

Lara's chest ached as she sat beside her, wrapping an arm around her shoulders. "I know," she said quietly. "But he can't hurt you anymore. You're safe now."

Mia leaned into her, her body trembling as sobs wracked her frame. Lara held her tightly, her own eyes stinging as she tried to steady her friend. The reality of everything they'd been through, everything they'd done, pressed heavily on her, but she refused to let it break her. Not tonight.

The motel bathroom was cramped, its tile floor cold beneath their feet. The mirror above the sink was slightly warped, distorting their reflections and making them seem unfamiliar. Lara had risen early and headed to the nearest store to buy provisions for the next leg of the trip, and also, anything they needed to alter their appearance. She now stood in front of the mirror, a pair of scissors in hand, her expression tense as she studied her own reflection.

"This is going to be terrible," she muttered, running a hand through her damp hair from the quick shower she'd taken.

Mia sat on the closed toilet lid; a box of dark brown hair dye balanced on her knees. She watched Lara silently and fidgeted with the edge of the dye box, her movements slow and mechanical.

"It doesn't have to be perfect," Mia said softly, her voice still hoarse from crying. "Just... different enough."

Lara let out a short laugh, shaking her head. "Well, 'different' is about the only guarantee here." She raised the scissors and paused, glancing at Mia in the mirror. "You sure about this? I can cut yours first if you want."

Mia shook her head quickly, her gaze dropping to the floor. "No. I don't want to... I just want to dye it. I'll do mine after you."

Lara studied her for a moment, sickened by the sight of Mia's bruised, pale face. She wanted to push, to ask if Mia was okay. Not in the shallow way people asked out of politeness, but in a way that demanded an honest answer. But the words stuck in her throat, trapped by a knot of guilt and anger that had settled there since the night at the bar.

Instead, she turned back to the mirror, steeling herself as she grabbed a section of hair and brought the scissors up. The first cut was harsh, uneven, and far shorter than she'd intended. She winced but kept going, working her way around her head in erratic snips, the sound of the scissors slicing through the air filling the small bathroom.

Mia watched her work, her fingers tightening around the dye box.

"You're good at this," Mia said suddenly, her voice quiet, but with a faint, teasing lilt that surprised them both.

Lara glanced at her in the mirror, her eyebrows lifting. "Good? I look like I lost a fight with a weed whacker."

Mia's lips twitched into the faintest smile, and for a moment, the tension in the room eased. But then her gaze flicked back to the floor, and the heaviness returned.

When Lara finished, she stepped back from the sink,

running her hands through her uneven, choppy hair. It was shorter now, barely brushing her ears. The change made her feel exposed, but also lighter, as though she'd shed some of the baggage clinging to her.

"It's not great," she admitted, turning to Mia. "But it'll do."

Mia nodded, her expression unreadable as she stood and set the dye box on the counter. "I'll start mine now."

Lara stepped aside, watching as Mia opened the box and pulled out the plastic gloves and dye bottle. Her movements were slow, hesitant, as if each action required a deliberate effort. She didn't look at herself in the mirror, her gaze instead fixed on the sink.

"Need help?" Lara offered, keeping her tone light.

Mia hesitated, then nodded reluctantly. "Yeah. I can't see the back."

Lara took the dye bottle and began working it through Mia's hair. The chemical smell filled the room, making her eyes water, but she focused on the task, her fingers moving methodically through Mia's damp strands.

Mia stayed silent, her hands gripping the edge of the sink as Lara worked.

"I wasn't myself," Mia said suddenly, her voice barely above a whisper. "At the bar. That wasn't... I don't flirt like that. I don't drink like that. I don't..." She trailed off, her shoulders slumping.

Lara's hands paused for a moment before resuming. "I know," she said softly. "He drugged you, Mia. That wasn't your fault."

Mia shook her head, her knuckles turning white as she gripped the sink harder. "But I let him talk to me. I let him..." Her voice broke, and she took a shaky breath. "I should've known. I should've stopped it before it got that far."

Lara set the dye bottle down and turned her friend to face her, gently gripping her shoulders. "Stop," she said firmly, her gaze locking with Mia's. "You didn't let anything happen. He took advantage of you. He manipulated you, and he hurt you. That's on him, not you."

Mia's eyes filled with tears, and she looked down, her lip trembling. "I just... I don't feel like me anymore."

Lara pulled her into a hug, holding her tightly. "I know," she whispered. "But you're still here, Mia. You're still you. And we're going to get through this."

They stayed like that for a moment, the dye bottle forgotten on the counter, the harsh bathroom light buzzing overhead. When Mia finally pulled back, she wiped her eyes and nodded, her expression fragile but determined.

"Okay," she said softly. "Let's finish this."

By the time they emerged from the bathroom, the sun was fully up, casting warm light through the thin motel curtains. Lara's hair was shorter, messier, but it suited her in a way that felt oddly freeing. Mia's hair was now a rich, dark brown, the color bringing out her pale complexion and drawing attention away from her bruised eye.

Lara flopped onto one of the beds, her arms spread wide as she stared up at the ceiling. "Not bad for two amateurs," she said, her tone lighter than it had been all morning.

Mia sat on the edge of the other bed, her fingers brushing through her newly dyed hair. She looked different. Older, harder, but there was a faint glimmer of herself in her expression now, a tiny spark that hadn't been there before.

"Thanks," she said softly, glancing at Lara. "For everything."

Lara propped herself up on one elbow and gave her a small smile. "We're in this together, remember?"

Mia nodded, her gaze drifting to the window. The road ahead was still long and uncertain, but for the first time, it felt like they were taking steps toward reclaiming something, no matter how small.

13

The motel room was silent, save for the whir of the air conditioner, sputtering out warmth in uneven bursts. Lara was sprawled across one of the beds, idly flipping through an old paperback she'd found in the nightstand drawer. The scent of bleach and cheap detergent lingered in the air, mixing with the aroma of the coffee Lara had brewed earlier.

Mia sat cross-legged on the other bed; her newly dyed hair still damp from the shower. Her phone rested in her lap, the screen lighting up sporadically as notifications trickled in. She'd avoided checking it much since they'd left the bar, terrified of what she might see, but curiosity or perhaps inevitability had finally gotten the better of her.

The familiar ding of an alert broke through, and Mia's heart lurched in her chest. She hesitated, fingers hovering over the screen, before finally tapping to open the notification.

The headline hit her like a punch to the gut: "**Beloved Local Man Found Dead in Motel Altercation.**"

. . .

Her breath caught, her pulse thundering in her ears as she clicked the link. The article loaded slowly, the spinning wheel of buffering only heightening her growing sense of dread. When the text finally appeared, the words blurred together for a moment before snapping into sharp focus.

"Trent Lanning, 37, a well-known and respected member of the local community, was tragically found dead in a motel room late last night. Authorities have confirmed that Lanning was the victim of a violent altercation. No suspects have been named at this time, but police are urging anyone with information to come forward. Lanning, who was known for his charm and generosity, leaves behind grieving friends and family who remember him as a kind and selfless soul."

Mia's hand flew to her mouth, fingers trembling as she scrolled down, her eyes devouring every detail. There were quotes from supposed friends, describing Trent as "the kind of guy who'd give you the shirt off his back" and "a pillar of the community." The article portrayed him as a charismatic, beloved local figure, a man whose loss would leave a gaping hole in the hearts of those who knew him.

It was a lie. Every single word of it.

Mia's stomach churned, bile rising in her throat as her chest tightened painfully. She couldn't breathe, couldn't think. Her mind flashed with memories of that night, the way Trent had smiled at her, how his demeanor had shifted from charming to menacing, how his hands had grabbed her as if she were nothing more than an object.

"Mia?" Lara's voice broke through her spiraling thoughts.

Mia looked up, her wide, tear-filled eyes locking with Lara's concerned gaze. She didn't realize she was shaking until she saw Lara sit up, her book forgotten as she swung her legs off the bed.

"What's wrong?" Lara asked, her voice low and steady as she moved to Mia's bed. Her eyes flicked to the phone in Mia's hands. "What did you see?"

Mia opened her mouth, but no words came out. She simply handed Lara the phone, her fingers trembling as she pushed it toward her. Lara took it, brows furrowing as she scanned the screen.

The moment that followed was interminable. Lara's expression darkened, her jaw tightening as her eyes moved over the article. She read quickly but carefully, and when she finished, she exhaled sharply, her grip tightening on the phone.

"'Beloved local man,'" Lara said, her voice low, filled with barely contained anger. "Are they serious?"

Mia nodded, her throat constricting as she tried to speak. "They're... they're making him sound like some kind of hero," she whispered, her voice cracking. "Like he wasn't a monster."

Lara set the phone down on the nightstand, her hands curling into fists at her sides. "Of course they are. People like him always get the benefit of the doubt. He had everyone fooled."

"But what if..." Mia's voice faltered, her gaze dropping to her lap. "What if no one believes us? What if they find out what happened and think we're the villains?"

Lara knelt in front of her, her hands resting gently on Mia's knees. "Hey," she said softly, her tone steady yet firm. "Listen to me. We know the truth. You know what he did to you, what he was going to do. He wasn't some 'beloved local figure.' He was a predator, Mia. And we did what we had to do."

Mia shook her head, tears spilling down her cheeks. "But no one else will see it that way. They'll just think... they'll think I asked for it. That I deserved it."

Lara's chest tightened, a sharp ache spreading through her ribs. She wanted to tell Mia she was wrong, that the world would see the truth, but she couldn't bring herself to lie. Because Mia wasn't entirely wrong, there were people who would twist the story, who would blame her for what happened, who would paint her as complicit in her own assault.

But that didn't make it true.

"You didn't deserve what happened to you," Lara said firmly, her voice trembling with emotion. "None of this is your fault, Mia. None of it. And I don't care what anyone else thinks. I'll fight anyone who tries to say otherwise."

Mia let out a shaky breath, her tears falling faster. Lara reached up, brushing a strand of damp hair from her face.

"We're going to get through this," Lara continued, her voice softening. "We just need to keep moving. We stay ahead of this, and we stick together. Okay?"

Mia nodded weakly, her lip trembling as she wiped her face with the sleeve of her sweatshirt. "Okay," she whispered.

Lara stood, her expression hardening as she glanced back at the phone on the nightstand. The words of the article echoed in her mind, stoking the anger simmering beneath the surface. She didn't know how far the lie would spread, but she knew one thing for certain: they couldn't afford to let it catch up to them.

"Pack your stuff," Lara said, her tone sharp but not unkind. "We're leaving in fifteen."

Mia nodded, her movements slow and hesitant as she got to her feet. As she began gathering her things, Lara turned toward the window, staring out at the empty parking lot beyond the curtains.

The road ahead felt more uncertain than ever, but one thing was clear: they couldn't let the world's version of Trent's story become their undoing.

14

The phone on Dane's kitchen counter buzzed incessantly, the vibrations rattling against the stainless steel. He didn't pick it up immediately, instead pacing back and forth across the pristine tiles of the open-plan kitchen. His jaw was tight, and his fingers drummed against his leg in an irritated rhythm. The house was spotless, the counters gleaming under the overhead lights, but the tension in the air was anything but controlled. It was as though Mia was sending him a silent message by leaving the place in perfect order. Sterile.

He finally snatched up the phone, his thumb swiping across the screen to open a message thread. The last text he'd sent to Mia glared back at him: *Where the hell are you*? It was followed by several more messages, all unanswered, each more curt and demanding than the last. The timestamp of the most recent message, sent two days ago, triggered a fresh wave of anger through him.

"She thinks she can just disappear?" he muttered under his breath, his tone sharp and venomous.

He dialed her number again, holding the phone to his ear as he stared out the kitchen window at the neatly trimmed backyard. The ringing tone droned on, grating against his nerves, before finally going to voicemail. Her chipper, pre-recorded greeting played, a cruel contrast to the mute obstinance she was giving him.

"This is Mia. Leave a message, and I'll get back to you!"

Dane's lips twisted into a scowl as the tone beeped. He clenched his jaw, his grip tightening around the phone. "Mia, it's me. Call me back. Now," he snapped, before ending the call and tossing the phone onto the counter with a loud clatter.

He exhaled sharply, running a hand through his perfectly styled hair. This wasn't like her. Mia never ignored him, not for this long, not without telling him where she was going or what she was doing. She knew better than that.

Dane moved to the fridge, pulling out a beer and twisting the cap off with unnecessary force. He leaned against the counter, taking a long swig as his mind raced. He didn't like the uncertainty, the not knowing. Mia was supposed to be predictable, malleable. She didn't just vanish. He set the bottle down and grabbed his phone again, scrolling through his contacts until he found the number he was looking for. He pressed call, the line ringing twice before it connected.

"Sheriff's Department," a woman's voice answered crisply.

"Yes, I need to report a missing person," Dane said, his tone firm but measured, as though performing an unpleasant task that needed to be done.

"Can I have your name and the name of the missing person, sir?"

"Dane Carter," he said, straightening as he spoke. "My wife, Mia Williams, is missing. She's been gone for three days. She's not answering her phone, and I haven't heard from her."

There was a pause on the other end as the dispatcher typed. "And when was the last time you saw her?"

Dane hesitated, briefly weighing how much to reveal. "Three

days ago," he said. "She left home without saying where she was going. She's... been under a lot of stress lately."

"Stress?" the dispatcher repeated, her tone shifting slightly. "Can you clarify what you mean by that?"

Dane exhaled sharply, feigning concern. "She's been struggling mentally," he said carefully. "She's been having... episodes. She's not herself. I'm worried she might have done something reckless, or that she's in danger."

The dispatcher paused again, then continued, her tone professional. "Has Mia ever gone missing before, Mr. Carter?"

"No," Dane said quickly. "Never. This is completely out of character for her."

"And do you know if she might have traveled somewhere? Does she have any family or friends she might be staying with?"

Dane clenched his jaw, his mind briefly flicking to Lara. He hadn't thought about her in years, but she'd always been a bad influence on Mia, someone who encouraged her to believe she could do more with her life than what Dane had already given her.

"There's a friend she used to talk to," Dane said, his voice dripping with distaste. "Lara. I don't know her last name or where she lives now, but I think they've stayed in touch."

"Got it," the dispatcher replied. "We'll need a recent photo of Mia, along with any additional information you can provide—where she might go, any unusual behavior you've noticed. I'll send an officer out to take a formal statement."

Dane nodded to himself, his confidence returning. "I'll be here," he said curtly, before ending the call and setting the phone down. He stared at the counter, his mind already calculating his next move.

Meanwhile, at the Sheriff's Department, the report was entered into the system. The details were sparse, but the mention of Mia's supposed mental instability raised a red flag. The case was marked as unusual, and within hours, the information made its way into the FBI's missing persons database.

In an office filled with the quiet click of computer keyboards and the rustle of paperwork, Special Agent Julia O'Connor stared at the screen before her. The report about Mia Williams had just popped up, flagged for potential concern due to its unusual circumstances. She skimmed the details quickly, fiancée reported missing, no prior history of disappearing, described as mentally unstable.

O'Connor frowned, her instincts already on edge. There was something about the phrasing that didn't sit right with her. She tapped her pen against the desk, her sharp eyes narrowing as she clicked on the attached photo of Mia. The image showed a young woman with fair hair and a hesitant smile, her eyes soft yet guarded. O'Connor leaned back in her chair, her gut telling her there was more to this story than just a runaway fiancée.

She picked up the phone and dialed a number, her gaze still fixed on the screen. "Hey, it's O'Connor. I need a trace on Mia Williams. Possible interstate case. Let's see where this one leads."

The FBI's Regional Intelligence Unit buzzed with the kind of subdued chaos that came with chasing leads across jurisdictions. The murmur of agents on calls surrounded Special Agent Julia O'Connor who sat at her desk, her sharp eyes scanning the glowing monitor before her. The initial missing person report on Mia Williams was already beginning to expand into something larger, the pieces falling into place faster than anyone had anticipated.

Her phone vibrated against the desk, breaking her concentration. She grabbed it without looking, pressing it to her ear. "O'Connor."

"Agent O'Connor, this is Rogers at Border Patrol. We've flagged something on your missing person case," a voice on the other end said briskly. There was a faint crackle in the background, the sound of papers shuffling. "Looks like the individuals you're tracking crossed into Canada two days ago."

O'Connor straightened in her chair, her pulse quickening. "Two days? You're certain?"

"Yes, ma'am. Their passports were scanned at a border crossing near Sault Ste. Marie. They were driving an older-model Impala. The Canadian Border Services Agency has the record on file."

She leaned forward, typing quickly into her keyboard to pull up the details as she spoke. "No red flags at the time?"

"No, ma'am. The officer on duty noted the passengers, but there was nothing in the system when they passed through. A bruise on one of them was mentioned briefly, but they seemed calm enough not to raise suspicion."

Julia exhaled sharply, her jaw tightening. She hated missed opportunities, even when they weren't anyone's fault. "Alright. Send me everything you've got on the crossing, including surveillance footage if possible. I'll coordinate with CBSA from here."

"Already on it," Rogers replied. "You'll have it within the hour."

She hung up and immediately dialed another number, connecting her to a senior liaison officer at CBSA. It rang twice before a deep voice with a distinctly Canadian lilt answered.

"Sergeant Liam Dawson, CBSA."

"Sergeant Dawson, this is Special Agent Julia O'Connor with the FBI. I need your assistance on a case we're tracking. We believe two individuals involved in a possible homicide in the U.S. crossed the border into Ontario a couple of days ago."

There was a brief pause on the line before Dawson responded, his tone steady but curious. "You've got our attention, Agent. What can I do for you?"

Julia relayed the details quickly, her words clipped but precise. "We're looking for Mia Williams and Lara Edwards, both in their mid-thirties, traveling in a dark red Impala. We flagged their passports this morning and confirmed they crossed near Sault Ste. Marie. They're persons of interest in an active investigation."

Dawson didn't miss a beat. "Understood. We'll pull the logs and start running checks on possible locations. If they crossed there, they could be anywhere in northern Ontario by now. It's a lot of ground to cover."

"I know," Julia admitted, her voice tight. "But we can't afford to let this trail go cold. I'll send over their profiles, and we'll coordinate efforts from our side. Do you have any surveillance units in the area?"

"We do," Dawson replied. "But the terrain up here makes tracking difficult. There are plenty of small towns, motels, and backroads they could use to stay off the radar."

Julia's jaw tightened. "Just find me something. I don't care how small, anything that points to where they might be headed."

At CBSA's Ontario office, Sergeant Dawson hung up the phone and motioned to his team, who were gathered around a shared terminal in the corner of the open-plan office. The room was bright and utilitarian, with large windows overlooking the snowy streets of Sudbury.

"We've got two persons of interest flagged by the FBI," Dawson said, his voice calm but commanding. "Williams and Edwards. They're suspected of crossing into Canada at Sault Ste. Marie two days ago. Pull the footage from the crossing and get me their passport scans. I want every detail, down to the time stamps."

One of the officers, a younger man with neatly combed dark hair and an eager expression, nodded and began typing furiously at his station. "On it, sir. I'll have the surveillance feed in a few minutes."

Another officer, a woman in her early forties with sharp eyes and a no-nonsense demeanor, frowned slightly. "Do we know what they're wanted for?"

"Not yet," Dawson replied. "But the FBI doesn't call unless it's serious. My guess is we'll find out soon enough."

Minutes later, the younger officer called out, "Got it!" He clicked a few buttons, and the grainy footage from the border crossing appeared on the main screen. The timestamp confirmed it: two days ago, just before noon.

The camera showed the Impala pulling up to the booth, its dark red paint dusty from the road. Through the windshield, two women were visible, one behind the wheel, her short-cropped hair partially obscured by sunglasses, and another in the passenger seat, her face turned away from the camera. Even in the low-resolution footage, the tension in their posture was unmistakable.

"That them?" the female officer asked, leaning closer to the screen.

"Matches the descriptions the FBI sent over," Dawson confirmed. He crossed his arms, his sharp eyes narrowing as he studied the footage. "They're nervous. Look at how they're sitting, too stiff."

"And the one in the passenger seat," the younger officer

added, zooming in slightly. "Looks like she's got a bruise under her eye. Could be an injury, or it could be why they're running."

Dawson nodded, his mind already racing through possibilities. "Send this to Agent O'Connor. Let her know we've got visuals and the timestamp. I want the surrounding area checked, motels, gas stations, diners. They wouldn't have gotten far without stopping somewhere."

The officers scattered to their tasks, the buzz of activity in the room growing louder. Dawson leaned over the desk, his gaze fixed on the screen as the Impala rolled out of the booth and disappeared into the vast expanse of Ontario's wilderness.

Back at the FBI office, Julia's phone buzzed with an incoming email. She opened it immediately, her sharp eyes scanning the images and timestamp. Her stomach tightened as she studied the grainy footage, her instincts telling her this case was about to get much more complicated.

"Alright," she muttered to herself, pulling up a map of northern Ontario. "Let's see where you're hiding."

Leaning forward, Julia scrutinized the screen, trying to think the same way two women on the run would. Tapping into their psyche was vital. The mindset of two killers on the loose.

15

The road stretched endlessly ahead, a ribbon of gray cutting through the vast, untamed wilderness of northern Ontario. Towering evergreens lined the highway, their dense canopies blotting out the sun in patches, casting long shadows over the asphalt. The landscape was beautiful in a way that felt almost overwhelming. Its scale too vast to fully comprehend. It seemed to swallow them whole, reminding Lara of just how small they were and how far they still had to go.

Inside the Impala, Mia sat quietly in the passenger seat, her fingers twisting the frayed slash in the knee of her jeans. Her newly dyed hair was tucked behind her ears, and the bruise under her eye stood out starkly in the sunlight streaming through the windshield. She hadn't spoken much since they'd left the motel that morning, her reverie broken only by the occasional sharp intake of breath when her thoughts spiraled too far.

Lara stole a quick glance at her, hands gripping the wheel tightly. "You okay?"

Mia didn't look up. "Not really," she murmured, her voice barely audible.

Lara nodded, her jaw tightening. “We’ll stop soon. Get some food. Maybe stretch our legs.”

Mia nodded absentmindedly; her gaze fixed on the horizon. The road ahead stretched on, the miles passing with an almost hypnotic rhythm. The mood between them was strained, but neither woman had the energy to break it.

An hour later, they pulled into the gravel parking lot of a small roadside diner. The building was a squat, weathered structure with peeling red paint and a flickering neon sign that read, *Joan’s Diner: Home of the Best Pie in Canada*. A few pickup trucks and dusty sedans were parked out front, their drivers likely inside, enjoying a late lunch.

Lara turned off the engine and leaned back in her seat, releasing a slow breath. “Let’s grab something to eat,” she said, her voice gentle but firm. “You need to keep your strength up.”

Mia hesitated, her hands still fidgeting with her sweatshirt. “I’m not really hungry.”

“Doesn’t matter,” Lara replied, her tone softening. “We can’t afford to get weak. Let’s go.”

Mia nodded reluctantly, and the two women climbed out of the car. The air was cold and fresh, the sky above threatening snow. The diner's screen door creaked as they stepped inside, the warm, homey aroma of coffee and frying bacon wrapping around them like a comforting blanket.

The interior was cozy, with red vinyl booths and checkered tablecloths. A jukebox in the corner played an old Patsy Cline song, while the walls were adorned with faded photographs of the surrounding area—fishing trips, snowy landscapes, and smiling families. It was the kind of place that felt frozen in time, untouched by the chaos of the outside world.

A middle-aged waitress with short, curly hair and a warm smile approached, a notepad in one hand and a pot of coffee in the other. Her name tag read "Joan."

"Afternoon, ladies," Joan said cheerfully. "Grab a seat anywhere you like."

Lara and Mia slid into a booth near the window, the worn vinyl squeaking beneath them. Joan poured two mugs of coffee without being asked, setting them down with a smile.

"First cup's on the house," she said. "You two look like you've been on the road for a while."

Lara smiled faintly. "Something like that."

"Well, you're in the right place for a break," Joan said kindly. "Our pie's the best around. I'll bring you a couple of slices—on the house. You look like you could use it."

Mia's lips twitched into the faintest hint of a smile, but it didn't last. She nodded her thanks, her hands wrapped tightly around the coffee mug as if it were the only thing anchoring her.

Joan bustled off, returning a few minutes later with two plates of pie and a folded map. "Here you go," she said, setting everything down. "On the house, like I said. And here's an old map I keep behind the counter. It's not fancy, but it's reliable if you're headed west. Cell service can be spotty out here."

"Thank you," Lara said sincerely, her stomach tightening at the reminder of how far they still had to go.

Joan smiled and patted the edge of the table. "Take your time, ladies. Let me know if you need anything else."

When Joan walked away, Mia picked at the edge of her pie crust with her fork, her appetite clearly absent despite the generous slice in front of her. Lara watched her for a moment before leaning forward, her voice low.

"Mia, we need to talk about something," she said, her tone gentle but serious.

Mia looked up. Her expression wary. "What?"

"The phones," Lara said. "We need to ditch them."

Mia's eyes widened, her fork clattering against the plate.

"No," she said quickly, shaking her head. "Lara, I can't. What if Noah tries to call me? What if he needs me?"

Lara reached across the table, placing a steadying hand over Mia's. "Mia, listen to me. They can track us with those phones. The longer we keep them, the easier it'll be for them to find us."

"But Noah..." Mia's voice cracked, her breath hitching as her eyes filled with tears. "He's probably worried sick. What if he thinks I abandoned him?"

"You didn't abandon him," Lara said firmly, her grip tightening slightly. "You're doing this for him, to protect yourself, to make sure you can be there for him in the long run. But if they find us, Mia, you won't have that chance."

Mia shook her head, tears spilling over. "I can't just disappear from his life, Lara. He's all I have."

"And you're all he has," Lara said softly, her voice breaking slightly. "But if we're going to stay safe, we have to be smart. You can write him a letter, tell him you're okay. But we can't keep the phones."

Mia's shoulders slumped, the fight draining out of her as the truth of the situation settled over her. She nodded reluctantly, her fingers tightening around the coffee mug.

"Okay," she whispered. "But... I want to write to him before we do anything."

"Of course," Lara said gently. "We'll figure it out."

They sat in deep thought for a while, the din of the diner fading into the background as they both stared out the window at the endless road ahead. The wilderness stretched far and wide, a reminder of both the freedom and the danger that lay before them.

The animated conversation in the diner had faded to a low murmur as people ate, focused on their food. Joan stood at the counter, refilling coffee cups for a pair of elderly men who seemed like regulars, their voices soft and conspiratorial. The jukebox in the corner had gone quiet, leaving only the faint sound of a radio playing from the kitchen.

At first, it was just background noise, a barely noticeable mixture of static and voices.

Lara and Mia were finishing their pie, the tension from their earlier conversation still lingering. Mia picked at her plate, her fork tracing patterns in the half-eaten filling, while Lara scanned the map Joan had given them, her finger following the winding roads.

Then the broadcast changed.

"...investigation into the death of Trent Lanning continues. Authorities have identified Lanning as the victim of an apparent altercation at a local motel earlier this week. Police are now asking for anyone with information about the individuals seen leaving the scene to come forward..."

Lara froze, her finger halting mid-trail on the map. She looked up sharply, her eyes darting to Mia, who had gone pale. Her fork slipped from her hand, clattering against the plate.

"...Lanning, 37, was a respected figure in the community. Friends describe him as kind and generous, someone who always had time for those in need. The circumstances of his death remain unclear, but investigators are pursuing leads on two women believed to have been involved..."

Lara's chest tightened as the words washed over her. The heat of the broadcast crawled under her skin, the air around them suddenly suffocating. Her instincts screamed at her to move, to get out, to run.

Mia's breath hitched, her hands trembling as she reached for her coffee mug, her grip unsteady. "Lara..." she whispered, her voice shaking.

"Don't look," Lara muttered, her tone sharp but quiet. Her eyes flicked toward Joan, who was busy at the counter and didn't seem to notice the shift in the atmosphere. The other diners were chatting casually, paying no attention to the radio.

But it was only a matter of time.

"We need to go," Lara muttered under her breath, already reaching into her pocket for cash. She tossed a crumpled bill onto the table, more than enough to cover their meal, and grabbed the map. "Now."

Mia hesitated; her wide eyes filled with panic. "But..."

"Now, Mia," Lara hissed, standing abruptly and pulling Mia up with her. The sudden movement drew a glance from Joan, who raised an eyebrow but said nothing.

They walked quickly but deliberately toward the door, their movements careful and calculated to avoid drawing attention. The cold air hit them like a slap as they stepped outside, and Lara didn't stop until they reached the Impala. She unlocked the car with shaking hands, tossing the map onto the dashboard as she climbed into the driver's seat.

Mia slid into the passenger seat, her breath coming in quick, shallow gasps. "They're talking about us," she said, her voice breaking. "They know, Lara. They know it was us."

"They don't know it was us," Lara said firmly, starting the engine. The low rumble felt too loud in the stillness of the lot. "They're guessing. That's all. But we're not sticking around to let them figure it out."

She backed out of the lot, her eyes scanning the road for any sign of police cars or curious onlookers. The diner faded into the distance as they sped away.

By nightfall, they had left the highway and were deep in the forest, parked in a small clearing off a dirt road that looked barely used. The trees towered above them, their dark branches blotting out the stars. The only sounds were the distant calls of owls and the faint rustle of leaves in the breeze.

Lara had spread a blanket on the ground near the car, and they sat huddled together, the night's chill seeping into their bones. The scent of pine filled the air, mingling with the faint smoke curling from the small campfire Lara had built. Its flickering light cast long, shifting shadows on the trees, making the forest feel both alive and threatening.

Mia stared into the fire; her arms wrapped tightly around her knees. She hadn't spoken much since they'd left the diner, her mute state felt more stubborn than usual. In the firelight, her face looked even paler, the bruised eye and swollen lip stark against her skin.

Lara leaned back on her hands; her gaze fixed on the flames. "You okay?" she asked quietly, though she already knew the answer.

Mia didn't respond at first, her gaze unfocused. Then she let out a shaky breath, her voice barely above a whisper. "I don't think I've ever been okay."

Lara frowned, sitting up straighter. "What do you mean?"

Mia's hands tightened on her knees, her knuckles turning white. "Dane," she said, the name dropping into the stillness like a stone in water. "He... he's been like this for years. Controlling everything. My money, my time, my... my life."

Lara's stomach twisted, anger flaring in her chest. "Mia..."

"He didn't hit me," Mia cut in, her voice sharp and brittle. "Not at first. That came later. It started small, comments about my clothes, about my friends. Then he'd tell me I was wasting money on stupid things or that I didn't need to work because he'd take care of me."

She let out a bitter laugh, the sound hollow. "Except he wasn't taking care of me. He was keeping me trapped."

Lara's fists clenched at her sides, the firelight flickering in her eyes. "Why didn't you tell me?"

"I couldn't," Mia whispered, her voice breaking. "He cut me off from everyone. He made me think it was my fault, that I wasn't good enough, that I didn't deserve better. And I believed him. For so long, I believed him."

Tears streaked down her face, catching the firelight, and Lara moved closer, wrapping her in a tight hug. Mia clung to her, her body trembling as she sobbed into Lara's shoulder.

"You didn't deserve any of that," Lara said fiercely, her voice shaking. "None of it. And you don't have to believe him anymore, Mia. You're out. You're free."

Mia shook her head, her sobs muffled against Lara's jacket. "I don't feel free. I feel... I feel like I'm still running. From him, from everything."

Lara pulled back just enough to meet her eyes, gripping Mia's shoulders. "You're not just running," she said firmly. "You're moving toward something better. We both are. And we'll figure this out, together. I promise."

Mia nodded weakly, her tears slowing but not stopping. The forest seemed to close in around them, shadows stretching longer as the fire crackled softly. As the night wore on, the two women sat side by side, their pasts looming like dark specters behind them. The fire had burned down to glowing embers, casting faint, flickering light over the clearing. The forest around them was dark and still, the towering trees standing like silent sentinels beneath the night sky. Mia sat huddled on the blanket, knees drawn to her chest, arms wrapped tightly around herself. Her face was turned away from the fire, her gaze lost in the darkness but it was clear she wasn't really seeing anything.

Lara watched her, worry tightening in her chest. She wanted to say something, to pull Mia back from wherever her mind had drifted, but she didn't know how to bridge the distance that had suddenly opened between them.

Then, softly, Mia spoke. "I can't stop seeing his face."

Lara straightened, her pulse quickening. "Trent?" she asked quietly.

Mia nodded, her breath hitching as tears spilled down her cheeks. "It's like... flashes. Pieces. I can't remember everything, but it's enough. The way he looked at me. The way he..." She broke off, her voice cracking.

Lara moved closer, her hand hovering over Mia's arm before finally resting there, light but steady. "Mia," she said gently, her voice filled with quiet urgency. "You don't have to do this right now."

"I need to," Mia whispered, her gaze still locked on the shadows. "I need to remember. Because I feel like... if I don't, it's going to eat me alive."

Lara nodded, her grip tightening slightly in silent support. She stayed quiet, waiting, giving Mia the space to speak when she was ready.

Mia's voice was barely more than a whisper when she began again. "I remember the smell of him. Beer and cigarettes. His breath was right in my face, and I couldn't move. I couldn't... my body wouldn't listen to me." She shuddered, clutching her knees so tightly her knuckles turned white. "He kept saying things, but it's all a blur. I just remember feeling... dirty. Small. Like I was nothing."

Lara swallowed hard, a sharp pang of anger flaring in her chest. But she kept it contained, not wanting to overwhelm Mia. "He was a monster," she said quietly. "What he did to you was unforgivable. None of it was your fault."

Mia shook her head, her tears falling faster now. "But I let him talk to me. I let him buy me a drink. I..."

"You didn't let him do anything," Lara interrupted, her voice firm but gentle. "He took advantage of you. He drugged you. That's on him, Mia. Not you."

Mia let out a shaky breath, her shoulders sagging as if the sum of the words was too much to bear. "I thought Dane was bad," she murmured after a long pause, her voice barely more than a whisper. "But Trent... he was worse. And now, I don't know how to make sense of any of it."

Lara frowned, her grip on Mia's arm tightening slightly. "What do you mean? Dane was bad too, Mia. You said so yourself."

Mia nodded slowly, her gaze dropping to the blanket beneath her. "I stayed with Dane because of Noah. I told myself it was for him—that he needed a stable home, even if it wasn't a happy one. But deep down, I knew it wasn't right. Dane... he's controlling. Manipulative. He made me feel like I was nothing without him, like I couldn't survive on my own." Her voice faltered, barely holding together. "He's no better than Trent. Not really."

Lara's chest ached at the rawness in Mia's voice, at the way her friend seemed to be unraveling right in front of her. She reached out, pulling Mia into a tight embrace. "You're not nothing, Mia," she said fiercely, her voice trembling. "You're stronger than you think. You're here. You got away. And I'm not going to let anyone hurt you again."

Mia clung to her; her sobs muffled against Lara's shoulder. They sat like that for a long time, the fire crackling softly in the background, the night closing in around them.

But even as Lara held Mia, offering comfort and strength, a quiet voice in the back of her mind whispered a truth she didn't want to face, their differences ran deeper than she liked to admit. Mia had stayed with Dane for Noah, had endured years of control and manipulation for the sake of her son. Lara couldn't imagine making that kind of sacrifice, couldn't fathom tying herself to someone like Dane for any reason.

It wasn't a judgment, not really. But it was a distance—an unspoken divide between them, one she wasn't sure how to bridge.

When Mia finally pulled back, her face streaked with tears, she looked at Lara with an expression that was equal parts gratitude and sorrow. "Thank you," she whispered, her voice raw.

Lara nodded. Her own throat tight. "Always," she said simply.

They sat in contemplation after that, the fire dwindling to glowing embers. The forest around them was still, the night sky stretching vast and endless above. And as the honesty of their conversation settled over them, they both felt the fragile thread of their bond pulling tighter. Imperfect, strained, but unbreakable.

The morning sun hung low over the vast prairie, painting the horizon in muted yellows and oranges. The landscape stretched endlessly in every direction, the fields barren except for patches of wild grass swaying in the gentle wind. To Mia, the openness felt exposing, like there was nowhere to hide, no trees or hills to shield them from the watchful eyes of the world.

She sat slumped in the passenger seat of the Impala, her body aching after a restless night in the woods. Her legs were cramped, her head throbbed faintly, and the gnawing hunger in her stomach felt like claws tearing at her insides.

Lara didn't look much better. Her cropped hair was messy, dark circles shadowed her eyes, and her hands gripped the wheel so tightly her knuckles turned white. She stared at the empty road with a fierce determination that made Mia uneasy. The awkwardness between them was broken only by the low hum of the car's engine.

"We need food," Lara said at last, her voice breaking the quiet. It was flat, matter of fact, but the tension beneath it was unmistakable.

Mia didn't answer right away. Her eyes remained fixed on the horizon, where a tiny building was beginning to take shape against the blur of the prairie. As they drew closer, it resolved into a small, weathered gas station with a single pump and a faded red sign that read *Jed's Pitstop: Friendly Service*! in peeling letters.

The parking lot was gravel, and only one other vehicle was there, a battered old pickup truck parked near the pump, its bed piled high with rusted tools and dented cans.

"I know," Mia murmured finally, her voice barely audible. "But we don't have any money."

Lara didn't reply. Her lips pressed into a thin line as she turned into the lot and parked near the side of the building, away from the truck.

The gas station itself was unremarkable—a squat, weathered structure with a tin roof and a smudged glass door. A single neon OPEN sign buzzed faintly in the window, but the place looked like it had seen better days.

Lara shut off the engine and leaned back in her seat, letting out a slow breath. For a moment, she stared at the building, her expression unreadable. Then she unbuckled her seatbelt and opened the door.

"Stay here," she said curtly, stepping out before Mia could respond.

"What are you doing?" Mia's voice was sharp with suspicion.

But Lara was already walking away, her boots crunching

against the gravel as she headed toward the pickup truck. The driver, a burly man in a plaid shirt and baseball cap, was inside the gas station, chatting with the cashier. Through the smudged window, Lara could see his large hands gesturing animatedly as he laughed at something the cashier said.

Lara's stomach growled loudly, and she clenched her fists at her sides. They needed food, gas, anything to keep them moving. She glanced at the truck's passenger seat through the rolled-down window and spotted a battered leather purse resting there.

Her heart pounded, instincts screaming at her to keep moving, to think this through. But hunger and desperation clouded her judgment, narrowing her focus to a single point.

Her hands trembled as she reached through the window, the smell of grease and old upholstery hitting her nostrils as her fingers closed around the purse's strap. It felt heavier than she expected, the faint jingle of loose change echoing in her ears as she pulled it free. Every sound seemed amplified—the crunch of gravel beneath her boots, the low rhythm of conversation inside the building, the faint rustle of the wind.

Lara straightened quickly, clutching the purse tightly as she walked back to the car. Her pulse pounded, her breath coming in shallow bursts. She didn't look back at the truck, didn't check to see if the driver had noticed. She couldn't afford to.

Mia sat bolt upright in the passenger seat, her wide eyes filled with disbelief and fury as Lara climbed in.

"What the hell, Lara?" Mia hissed. Her voice low but sharp. "You stole that?"

Lara tossed the purse onto the console between them, her hands shaking as she gripped the steering wheel.

"We didn't have a choice," she said shortly, turning the key in the ignition.

"We didn't have a choice?" Mia repeated, her voice rising.

"Are you serious right now? You just stole from someone! What if they come after us? What if they call the police?"

"They won't," Lara said tightly, backing the car out of the lot.

She glanced toward the gas station, her heart leaping into her throat as the driver stepped onto the porch, his eyes scanning the parking lot. She pressed harder on the gas pedal, the Impala kicking up a cloud of dust as they sped onto the highway.

Mia let out a frustrated laugh, throwing up her hands. "Oh, sure, because no one will notice their purse is gone while we drive away in a car that screams suspicious! This is insane, Lara!"

"Do you think I wanted to do that?" Lara snapped, her voice sharp and defensive. She shot a brief glance at Mia, her expression hard but strained. "You think I enjoyed it? We're out of money, Mia. We're starving. What do you want me to do, sit here and wait for us to keel over from hunger?"

"I want you to *think*!" Mia shot back, her voice trembling with anger. "We're already running from the police, and now you're adding theft to the list. This isn't survival, Lara. This is reckless!"

"Reckless would be doing nothing," Lara countered, her grip tightening on the wheel. "Reckless would be sitting here and waiting for everything to catch up to us. I did what I had to do to keep us going."

Mia shook her head, pressing her trembling hands against her temples. "Every time we do something like this, we're digging ourselves deeper. We're making it harder to ever come back from this."

"Maybe there's no coming back," Lara said flatly, her voice cold. "Maybe we're past that point already."

The words hit Mia like a slap, her breath catching as she

turned to stare at Lara. She wanted to argue, to shout, but Lara's words settled over her like a stone—too heavy to lift.

The Impala roared down the empty road, the prairie stretching endlessly before them. The purse sat between them, its presence like a third passenger, a silent witness to the widening gulf between them.

16

Detective Joel Barnes leaned back in his creaky office chair, the dim light of his desk lamp casting shadows across the faint lines on his face. A steaming cup of coffee sat untouched beside an open file; its contents spread haphazardly across the desk. The manila folder bore bold black letters: *Persons of Interest: Mia Williams and Lara Edwards.*

The case had landed on his desk that morning, passed down from a higher division with a request to assist the FBI in tracking the two women. The facts were sparse, the details murky, but there was enough to pique his interest—two women on the run, crossing into Canada after an alleged altercation in the U.S. that had left one man dead.

He flipped through the documents again, pausing at the photos. Mia's bruised face stared back at him; her dark eyes filled with something he couldn't quite name. Fear? Resignation? Lara's image was less telling. A sharp, unreadable gaze that seemed to challenge anyone who dared to look too closely.

Joel sipped his coffee, his mind turning over the inconsistencies in the case. The women's profiles didn't match the narrative the FBI was subtly pushing, that they were cold-blooded killers. The man they'd allegedly left dead, Trent Lanning, was described as a *beloved figure*, but Joel had seen enough cases to know that public perception rarely told the whole story. And the bruise on Mia's face… that didn't sit right with him either.

"Detective Barnes."

The voice cut through his thoughts. He looked up to see Officer Nadia Torres standing in the doorway, a tablet in hand. Her expression was as sharp as her pressed uniform.

"We've got something," she said.

Joel gestured for her to enter. "What is it?"

Torres stepped inside, swiping at the screen as she approached. "Border patrol flagged their crossing two days ago at Sault Ste. Marie. They've been off the grid since, but there was a report from a gas station near Winnipeg this morning. A truck driver claims someone stole his purse from his vehicle while he was inside paying for gas."

Joel leaned forward, his brow furrowing. "And you think it's them?"

"Timing lines up," Torres said, setting the tablet on the desk. Grainy security footage from the gas station began to play, showing a dark red Impala pulling into the lot. The video was choppy, but the two women were clearly visible—one behind the wheel, the other in the passenger seat.

The footage skipped ahead, cutting to a figure, Lara, approaching the truck. The angle wasn't great, but Joel could see her lean into the window before quickly retreating to the car.

Moments later, the truck driver emerged from the station, glancing around in confusion before climbing into the truck only to realize what had happened.

Joel frowned as he studied Lara's movements. "She doesn't

look like a seasoned criminal," he murmured, half to himself. "That was impulsive. Desperate."

Torres nodded. "The truck driver said the purse didn't have much, just some cash, a credit card, and his ID. He's already reported the theft, but he's not pressing charges. Said he felt sorry for them."

"Did he see anything else? Did they say anything to him?"

"Nothing. They were gone before he even realized it was missing."

Joel leaned back in his chair, rubbing a hand over his stubbled jaw. "They're running on fumes. No phones, no credit cards, stealing cash to get by. If they're this desperate, they'll have to make more mistakes."

"They're headed west," Torres said. "We're flagging motels and diners along Highway 1. If they keep driving, they'll hit the Rockies soon. That'll limit their options."

Joel nodded, his mind already spinning through possibilities. He picked up the photos of Mia and Lara again, studying them closely. "Anything on Trent Lanning? Anything that explains why they might've been involved in what happened to him?"

Torres hesitated. "Nothing solid yet. The FBI's report paints him as a stand-up guy, but..." She trailed off, her expression skeptical.

"But you don't buy it," Joel finished for her.

"No, sir. Something feels off. If these women were just thrill-seekers or criminals, why didn't they run before things escalated? And the bruises on Mia... She doesn't look like someone who walked away unscathed."

Joel tapped his fingers on the desk, his instincts pulling him in the same direction. "There's more to this than what we're seeing," he said quietly. "People don't just snap without a reason.

If Trent Lanning was the kind of man they say he was, why did this happen?"

Torres tilted her head. "Think it's worth digging into his background?"

Joel's lips twitched into a faint, humorless smile. "Always is. Start with locals, friends, family, coworkers. See if there's a history of complaints, rumors, anything that paints a different picture. And keep an eye on those credit cards and the stolen cash. If they use either, I want to know immediately."

Torres nodded, gathering her tablet as she turned toward the door. "On it, Detective."

When she was gone, Joel leaned back again, the room settling into ominous quiet. He stared at the photos on his desk, his thoughts a whirlwind. There was a story here, buried beneath layers of fear and desperation, and he wasn't going to stop until he uncovered it.

"Alright, Mia and Lara," he muttered, his gaze lingering on their faces. "Let's see where this road takes us."

17

The road was changing. The flat, endless prairie that had stretched across Manitoba and Saskatchewan was giving way to something grander. The air was cooler, fresher, as the Rockies loomed on the horizon, their snow-capped peaks piercing a hazy sky. The Impala climbed steadily along winding roads flanked by dense pine forests and sheer cliffs plunging into rushing rivers far below.

Mia sat in the passenger seat; her hands clasped tightly in her lap. She hadn't spoken in hours, but the tension radiating off her was impossible to miss. Her eyes flicked toward the glove compartment, where her powered-down phone lay tucked away, as if she could wish it back to life with just her thoughts. Her lips parted a few times, but the words caught in her throat before they could form.

Finally, Mia spoke. "Lara, I need to talk to Noah."

Lara's grip tightened on the steering wheel. "Mia, we've been over this."

"He's my son!" Mia snapped, her voice cracking. "He must be worried sick. He doesn't know where I am, if I'm okay... I can't just leave him like this."

Lara sighed heavily and pulled the car into a small overlook off the highway. She shut off the engine and turned to face Mia, frustration and compassion warring in her expression.

"I know you want to talk to him. I get it, Mia, I really do. But you know what will happen if you call. The police are monitoring every line connected to Dane, including Noah's. If you reach out, they'll trace it, and we're done. Is that what you want?"

Mia's eyes filled with tears. Her hands trembled as she wiped them on her jeans. "I just want him to know I'm okay," she whispered. "I don't want him to think I abandoned him."

Lara's voice softened. "He knows you love him, Mia. And one day, you'll explain all of this to him. But right now, the best thing you can do for Noah is stay safe. If they catch us..." She trailed off, but the unspoken words pressed between them, raw and terrifying.

Mia turned her head, staring out at the mountains in the distance. Her shoulders slumped as she pressed her forehead against the cool glass of the window. "I hate this," she muttered. "I hate all of it."

"You think I don't?" Lara's reply came sharper than she intended. She exhaled shakily, gripping the steering wheel as if to steady herself. "You think I don't want to call Emily and tell her everything? Ask her what I should do next, just to hear her voice?"

Her voice wavered, and she shook her head, forcing herself to push past the lump in her throat. "But I won't. Because it's not about what we want anymore. It's about surviving."

The wind rustled through the trees, and somewhere in the distance, a river murmured over the rocks. When Mia finally spoke again, her voice was barely a whisper. "I miss him so much."

Lara swallowed hard. When she answered, her voice was quiet but steady. “I know,” she said. “I know.”

Later that evening, the Impala’s headlights carved a path through the deepening darkness, illuminating the narrow dirt road ahead. They were miles from the highway now, the forest closing in on either side, dense and impenetrable. When Lara spotted a sign for a small artist’s retreat near Jasper they’d decided it was worth investigating.

The cabin appeared suddenly, its warm glow flickering through the trees. It was small but inviting, with a sloping roof and smoke curling lazily from a stone chimney. A rusty pickup truck sat out front, its bumper plastered with faded stickers.

Lara eased the Impala to a stop a short distance away. She glanced at Mia, who hovered beside her, eyes moving anxiously between the trees.

The cabin door creaked open. A woman stepped onto the porch; her gray-streaked braid draped over one shoulder. She looked to be in her sixties, her weathered face etched with lines of a life spent outdoors. Her gaze was steady, kind, but cautious.

“Can I help you?” she called out, her voice carrying easily over the quiet night.

“We’re just passing through,” Lara said, keeping her tone cautious, friendly, but not too eager. “We saw the sign for the retreat and thought… maybe you had a place we could rest for the night.”

The woman studied them for a long moment, her sharp gaze lingering just enough to make Lara’s pulse quicken. Then she nodded. “I’m Sandy,” she said, stepping aside and motioning them forward. “You look like you could use a hot meal.”

Mia exhaled, relief softening the tight lines of her face. Lara hesitated a beat longer before nodding. “Thank you.”

Inside, the cabin was warm and cluttered, shelves overflowing with books, pottery, and half-finished sculptures.

Paintings leaned against the walls, bold strokes of color standing in striking contrast to the shadowed forest beyond the windows. The scent of wood smoke and something rich and savory filled the air, wrapping around them like a well-worn quilt.

Sandy moved easily through the small kitchen, setting two steaming bowls of stew in front of them at the table. As they ate, her sharp eyes flicked between them, reading the tension in their shoulders, the gaps between their words.

"You're running from something," she said finally, her voice calm but certain.

Lara stiffened, her spoon halting midway to her mouth. "Why would you say that?"

"Because I've been there," Sandy said simply. She lowered herself into the chair across from them, folding her hands on the table. "I left an abusive husband twenty years ago. Took my daughter and ran. We ended up here, and I've been helping women like me ever since."

Mia's eyes welled with tears, and she set her spoon down, her appetite forgotten. "How did you do it?" she asked, her voice unsteady. "How did you start over?"

Sandy's smile was faint, touched with both sorrow and resilience. "One step at a time," she said. "It wasn't easy, and there were moments I wanted to give up. But I kept going because I knew staying wasn't an option."

Sandy's words seemed to breathe new life into Mia, who nodded slowly, her fingers tightening around her bowl. But Lara couldn't shake the unease creeping up her spine as she caught Sandy's eyes flick toward the small TV in the corner. The news played silently, and for the briefest moment, a photo of Mia and Lara flashed on the screen before disappearing. A jolt of fear shot through Lara's chest.

Sandy turned back to them. Her expression carefully

neutral. "You can stay the night," she said. "But tomorrow, you need to move on."

Lara nodded, though every instinct screamed at her to stay on guard. "Thank you," she said, forcing a smile. "We really appreciate it."

As the evening wore on, the fire crackled in the hearth, shadows deepening around them. Lara stared into the flames, the gravity of their situation beating down on her. How much longer could they keep running before the world finally caught up?

Lara sat on the edge of the bed in Sandy's cabin, her gaze fixed on the glowing embers in the fireplace across the room. The warmth was comforting, but it did little to loosen the tight knot in her chest. From her seat, she caught Sandy's subtle glances toward the muted television in the corner, where a looping news segment had just flashed Mia's and her own faces onscreen.

The tension in Sandy's shoulders didn't escape Lara. The older woman was kind, Lara could see that, but there was something else beneath her warmth. Hesitation. Maybe even fear. She was trying to hide it, but not well enough for someone as on edge as Lara to miss it.

Mia, seated at the table with a blanket draped over her shoulders, didn't seem to notice. She was lost in thought, her fingers tracing a crack in the woodgrain. Exhaustion and vulnerability were etched into every line of her face, and Lara couldn't blame her. They were both running on fumes, the severity of their situation taking its toll mentally.

"Thank you," Lara said, as she met Sandy's eyes. Her tone was steady, but her gaze carried an unspoken question: *Do you know who we are*?

Sandy's lips curved into a faint, practiced smile, one that didn't quite reach her eyes. "You're welcome," she said softly, moving toward the kitchen counter. She pulled open a drawer with slow, deliberate movements and took out an envelope. For a moment, she hesitated before turning back to them.

"I don't know where you're headed," she said, placing the envelope in front of Mia, "but take this. It's not much, but it'll help."

Mia's head snapped up; her expression startled. "We can't..."

"You can," Sandy interrupted gently but firmly. "I've been where you are. Sometimes, you need a little help to keep going."

Lara rose to her feet, her muscles coiled with tension. "Why are you doing this?"

Sandy's gaze softened as she met Lara's eyes with quiet understanding. "Because I know what it's like to be desperate, to feel like the world is closing in on you." She paused, her voice dropping to a near whisper. "And because everyone deserves a chance to start over."

Lara's throat tightened. She gave a small nod, unwilling to say more. Picking up the envelope, she felt the faint weight of cash inside before slipping it into her pocket.

"Thank you," Mia said, her voice trembling.

Sandy reached out and briefly squeezed Mia's hand. "Be careful," she said, her tone laced with meaning. "The world can be cruel, but it can also surprise you. Trust your instincts."

They left the cabin at dawn, the Impala slicing through the early morning mist as they headed westward toward the Rockies. With each passing hour, the jagged peaks loomed closer, the landscape growing more rugged and wild. The crisp air carried the scent of woodsmoke and pine, and the road wound through dense forests that felt untouched by time.

Mia was unusually quiet, her hands clasped tightly in her lap as she stared out the window. Lara stole occasional glances at her, noting the tension in her jaw and the restless way her fingers fidgeted. She wanted to say something, to reassure her, but the words wouldn't come.

It was just after noon when they spotted him. A young man stood by the side of the road near Banff, a large backpack slung over one shoulder and a cardboard sign in his hand that read: *Vancouver or anywhere west*! He was tall and lean, his sun-kissed skin and tousled blond hair giving him a carefree look. His smile was easy, confident, as he waved at the Impala, his other hand gripping the strap of his pack.

Lara slowed but didn't stop, her eyes narrowing as she sized him up. "Hitchhiker," she muttered.

"Should we pick him up?" Mia asked, her voice hesitant.

Lara hesitated, her grip tightening on the wheel. Mia glanced back at the young man, uncertainty flickering across her face. "But he looks harmless. And maybe he knows the area."

Lara sighed, her instincts warring with practicality. They couldn't afford to draw attention to themselves, but they also couldn't risk alienating someone who might help or at the very least, not hurt their chances.

She pulled over, rolling down the window as the man jogged up to the car.

"Thanks for stopping," he said, flashing a charming smile. His voice was warm, friendly, with a slight lilt that hinted he wasn't from the area. "I'm Benji. Headed west to Vancouver. Mind if I hitch a ride?"

Lara studied him, her expression unreadable. "We're not going all the way to Vancouver."

Benji shrugged, unfazed. "Anywhere along the way works for me. I'm not picky."

Lara glanced at Mia, who gave a small nod, then turned back to Benji. "Fine," she said, her tone clipped. "Get in."

Benji slid into the backseat, tossing his pack onto the floor. "Thanks, ladies. I owe you one."

Lara didn't respond, her eyes flicking to the rearview mirror as she started the car. Mia offered a small, hesitant smile, which Benji returned with an easy wink.

"So, what brings you two out here?" he asked, leaning forward slightly. "Road trip?"

"Something like that," Lara said curtly, her tone making it clear the conversation wouldn't go much further.

Benji, however, didn't seem deterred. "Well, whatever it is, you've picked a hell of a route. These mountains are something else, huh?"

Mia nodded. Her voice soft. "They're beautiful."

Benji grinned. "You said it. Nothing like a bit of natural beauty to get the creative juices flowing. I'm an artist, by the way. Heading to Vancouver to find some inspiration."

Lara's gaze sharpened in the mirror. "An artist?"

"Yeah," Benji said, leaning back with an easy smile. "Painter, mostly. Landscapes, portraits, that kind of thing. Though lately, I've been thinking about branching out. You know, trying something new."

Mia offered a polite nod, but Lara remained silent, her instincts on high alert. There was something too smooth about Benji, too practiced in his charm. She couldn't put her finger on it, but she didn't trust him, not yet.

As the Impala wound through the mountains, Benji kept the conversation light, weaving tales of his travels and cracking jokes that drew nervous laughter from Mia. But Lara's focus stayed on the road and the stranger in her backseat. Her mind raced through the possibilities.

Because if there was one thing Lara knew for certain, it was that appearances could be deceiving.

18

The Impala rolled steadily along the winding roads of the Rockies, flanked by towering peaks streaked with snow. Pine trees stretched endlessly, their dark green spires cutting sharply against the cloudless blue sky. Waterfalls tumbled over jagged cliffs. The landscape was breathtaking. A postcard-perfect scene that felt almost surreal after days of tension and fear.

In the backseat, Benji lounged with one leg crossed over the other, his head resting lazily against the window as he watched the scenery blur past. His backpack sat neatly at his feet, and a thin woven leather bracelet caught the sunlight as it circled his wrist. Dressed in a faded flannel shirt and worn jeans, he had the look of a drifter, yet there was something about him, an easy charm, a relaxed confidence that subtly shifted the air in the car.

"So," Benji said, with a casual drawl. "I'm guessing you two aren't from around here."

Lara glanced at him in the rearview mirror, the faintest hint of a smile tugging at her lips. "What gave it away?"

"Maybe the license plate," Benji said with a grin, nodding toward the dashboard. "Or the fact that you're trying to blend in and failing miserably."

Mia let out a soft laugh, the sound surprising even herself. It had been weeks since she'd laughed, and for a brief moment, the pressure on her chest felt a little lighter. Benji caught her reaction and winked, his smile widening.

"Don't worry," he said, leaning forward slightly. "I'm not exactly a local either. Grew up in Ontario, but I've been bouncing around for years. Never could stay in one place."

"What brought you out here?" Mia asked, her voice tentative but laced with curiosity.

Benji shrugged, his gaze drifting back to the mountains. "Inspiration, I guess. There's something about this place... It's raw, you know? Untouched. Makes you feel small in the best way."

Lara nodded, her gaze flicking briefly from the road to the mirror, meeting his eyes. "I can see that."

"What about you two?" Benji asked, his tone light but laced with curiosity. "What's got you driving through the middle of nowhere?"

"Just a road trip," Lara said smoothly, her voice carefully neutral.

Benji didn't push, sensing the boundary in her tone. Instead, he shifted his attention to Mia, who was still gazing out the window, her fingers absently tracing patterns on her jeans.

"You're quiet," he said gently. "What's your story?"

Mia hesitated, her fingers stilling. "Not much of one," she said finally, her voice barely above a whisper. "Just... trying to figure things out."

Benji nodded, his expression thoughtful. "Aren't we all?"

The miles slipped by with conversation flowing more easily as the sun climbed higher in the sky. Benji told them about his travels, nights spent camping under the stars, a stint working on an organic farm in British Columbia, and his brief but disastrous attempt at bartending in Montreal. His stories brimmed with humor and warmth, his voice carrying an infectious enthusiasm that made even the most mundane details feel captivating.

Lara found herself relaxing in his presence, her grip on the wheel easing as tension bled from her shoulders. Even Mia seemed lighter, her guarded posture softening as she asked him about his art and favorite places to visit. It was a rare moment of reprieve—an illusion of normalcy in a life that had been anything but.

"Banff's beautiful, but wait until you hit Jasper," Benji said, leaning forward slightly. "The glaciers up there are unreal. Like something out of a dream."

"Sounds amazing," Mia murmured, a note of wistfulness in her voice.

"It is," Benji agreed. He leaned back again, tilting his head as he studied her. "You should paint it."

Mia blinked, caught off guard. "I'm not an artist."

"Could've fooled me," Benji said with an easy grin. "You've got the eyes for it."

A flush crept up Mia's neck as she turned back to the window. Lara smirked, a hint of amusement in her voice. "Careful, Benji. Flattery won't get you far."

Benji's grin widened. "Who says I'm flattering? I'm just calling it like I see it."

The drive continued, the sun casting golden light over the landscape as mountain shadows stretched long across the valleys. For a while, they rode in easy companionship, the only sounds the rattle of the engine and the occasional chirping of birds outside.

It wasn't until they stopped at a roadside rest area to stretch their legs that the fragile sense of peace shattered. While Lara refilled the car's water jug at a nearby spigot and Mia sat on a bench, gazing at the mountains, Benji wandered over to a payphone mounted on the rest stop wall. Above it, a bulletin board displayed local announcements and clippings, one of which caught his eye.

His easy smile faltered as he read the bold headline:

"American Fugitives Suspected in Motel Death: Dangerous Duo May Be Hiding in Canada."

The grainy black-and-white photos beneath the headline were unmistakable. Mia's bruised face. Lara's sharp, wary gaze. The article framed them as cold, calculated criminals.

Benji stepped back, his smile fading entirely. He glanced toward the car, where Lara wiped her hands on a rag, her gaze sharp and watchful. Mia was watching him too but remained on the bench, her hair stirring gently in the breeze.

When Benji returned to the car, his usual charm remained intact, but Lara caught a flicker of something else in his eyes—doubt, perhaps, or curiosity. She said nothing, but her grip on the steering wheel tightened slightly as they pulled onto the road.

The easy camaraderie they had shared earlier lingered, but an undercurrent of tension settled in. Lara couldn't shake the feeling that the fragile balance between them had begun to shift.

The Impala rolled steadily along the highway, winding through a valley framed by towering peaks. The snow-dusted summits shimmered in the late afternoon sun; their grandeur impossible to ignore. But inside the car, the mood was anything but serene.

Benji sat in the backseat, uncharacteristically quiet, his usual easy smile absent as he stared out the window. In the passenger seat, Mia leaned slightly toward the door, her fingers twisting a loose thread on her jacket. Lara kept her eyes on the road, her expression unreadable, but the tension in her jaw betrayed her unease.

She hadn't missed the way Benji had stiffened when he got

back into the car at the rest stop, nor the faint shift in his demeanor since. Something had changed. He hadn't said anything outright, but Lara's instincts were on high alert.

It was Mia who finally broke the quiet. "We need to drop you off soon," she said quietly, her voice firm but not unkind.

Benji's head snapped up, his brows knitting together. "What? Why?"

Lara sighed, her fingers tightening around the steering wheel. "This isn't personal, Benji. We just... we need to keep moving. And it's better if you're not involved with us."

"Involved in what, exactly?" Benji asked, his tone edged with suspicion. "You've been dodging that question since I got in the car."

Lara glanced at him in the rearview mirror, her gaze steady but guarded. "Let's just say we've got things to work through, and it's safer for everyone if we do it alone."

Benji leaned back, crossing his arms over his chest. "You know, you two are really bad at hiding things. Whatever you're running from it's all over your faces."

"Benji..." Mia started, but he cut her off.

"I'm not an idiot, Mia," he said, his tone softer but insistent. "I saw the news at the rest stop. The story about the two women on the run from the States." He let the words settle before adding, "It's you, isn't it?"

Mia's breath hitched. Her eyes darted to Lara, but Lara kept her focus on the road. The lack of words was answer enough.

Benji let out a low whistle, shaking his head. "Damn. I knew something was up, but I didn't think it was that."

"Look," Lara said finally, her voice calm but firm. "You don't need to worry about us. We're not dangerous."

"I believe you," Benji said, surprising them both. He leaned forward slightly, his gaze earnest. "But you're in over your heads, and you know it. Whatever happened back there you're not going to outrun it forever."

"We're not looking for advice," Lara said flatly.

Benji held up his hands in mock surrender, leaning back again. "Alright, alright. Just thought I'd say my piece." He hesitated before adding, "You're doing what you think you have to. I get that."

They dropped him off at a small roadside café just outside Jasper, a weathered wooden sign out front advertising *homemade pies and coffee*. Benji climbed out with his pack, then turned back to look at them one last time.

"Good luck," he said, his tone sincere. "I mean that."

Mia gave him a small, tentative wave, while Lara offered only a curt nod. As the Impala eased back onto the road, Mia twisted in her seat, watching Benji disappear into the café, a faint pang of regret tugging at her chest.

"He was nice," she said softly.

"He was trouble waiting to happen," Lara countered, her tone clipped.

Mia frowned but didn't argue. Instead, she rested her head against the window, her thoughts drifting as the mountains towered around them.

Later that evening, as they wound through a dense stretch of forest, the faint crackle of the radio filled the car. Lara had switched it on out of habit, letting the low murmur of news and static serve as a distraction. But as the signal cleared, a report caught their attention.

"...The story of two American women suspected in the death of Saratoga local Trent Lanning has taken an unexpected turn. While authorities continue to pursue leads, social media has erupted in support of the women, with many portraying them as symbols of defiance against abusive men. The hashtag #StandWithThem has gone viral, sparking a wave of personal stories from women across North America about their own experiences with abuse and control."

Mia sat up straighter, her eyes wide. "Did you hear that?"

Lara nodded grimly, her knuckles tightening around the wheel. The broadcast continued, the anchor's voice laced with both curiosity and intrigue.

"Some users have even launched crowdfunding campaigns to raise money for the women, despite the lack of confirmed details about the case. Others are urging authorities to reconsider their approach, arguing that the women may have acted in self-defense."

Mia's lips parted, her shock giving way to something resembling hope. "They're on our side," she murmured, almost disbelieving. "People actually believe us."

Lara shook her head, her jaw tightening. "They don't know us, Mia. They're creating a story that fits what they want to believe. That doesn't mean they know the truth."

"But it's not all lies," Mia pressed. "Trent was a monster. Dane is, too. Maybe this is our chance to show people what we've been through."

Lara sighed; her gaze fixed on the road ahead. "Or it's just another opportunity for the media to twist everything further. The truth doesn't matter to them, Mia. It's all about the story."

Mia looked away, her excitement dimming but not disappearing entirely. "Maybe... but maybe it's enough that someone's listening."

Lara's nodded then focused her eyes on the road ahead, her mind racing with the implications of the broadcast.

19

The gravel crunched beneath the Impala's tires as they pulled into the small campground. Nestled deep in the woods, the site consisted of rustic cabins scattered around a central clearing, where a fire pit and weathered picnic tables sat beneath a canopy of towering pines. The late afternoon sun filtered through the branches, casting warm golden light, but the long shadows creeping across the ground lent the place an air of quiet isolation.

Lara eased the car to a stop near the office, a modest building with peeling white paint and a hand-painted sign that read *Whispering Pines Campground: Cabins & RV Hookups*. A row of wind chimes dangled from the porch, their faint, discordant tinkling carried on the breeze

Mia leaned forward, scanning the cabins with wary eyes. "Do you think this is safe?" she asked quietly, her voice edged with exhaustion and unease.

"It's as safe as anywhere else," Lara replied, her tone clipped. "We need rest, Mia. A shower. Real sleep. We can't keep going without stopping."

Mia nodded reluctantly, her fingers twisting the hem of her sweatshirt. She hadn't argued with Lara's decision to come here, but the unease in her posture was unmistakable.

The cabin they rented with Sandy's money was one of the smallest on the site, set slightly apart from the others. A simple, weathered structure with a slanted tin roof, it had a single front window and a wooden porch that groaned beneath their footsteps. The door let out a sharp squeak as Lara pushed it open, revealing a dim interior that smelled of aged wood and the faint, lingering traces of past visitors.

Inside, the main room was sparsely furnished: a small table with two mismatched chairs, a battered loveseat near the fireplace, and a twin bed tucked into the corner. A narrow door led to a tiny bathroom with a cracked mirror and a rust-streaked sink. It wasn't much, but it was shelter, and for now, that was enough.

Lara dropped her bag onto the loveseat and turned to Mia, who lingered in the doorway, arms wrapped tightly around herself. "Do you want to wash up first?" Lara said gently. "I don't mind."

Mia nodded but didn't move. Her gaze drifted toward the single bed, her face pale and drawn. "I'll go in a minute," she murmured, barely audible.

Lara didn't push. Instead, she turned to unpack what little they had, pulling out the few clothes and toiletries they'd managed to keep. The quiet of the cabin unsettled her, the absence of noise amplifying the tension between them.

Eventually, Mia disappeared into the bathroom, and the sound of running water filled the space. Lara sat at the table, staring out the window as the trees swayed gently in the breeze. Everything settled onto her shoulders, the enormity of what they were doing, the uncertainty of what lay ahead.

When Mia emerged, her damp hair clung to her face, her skin scrubbed raw. She looked fragile, almost childlike. Wrapping herself in the blanket from the bed, she curled up on the loveseat, pulling her knees to her chest. Her eyes were red-rimmed, and she avoided Lara's gaze.

"I can't stop thinking about Noah," she said finally, her voice cracking. "What's he going to think of me when he finds out about all this? How am I supposed to explain any of it to him?"

Noah. Just his name sent a flood of images through Mia's mind, his lanky frame sprawled across the couch, guitar in hand; the way he'd spend hours in the garage, fine-tuning his skateboard until it was just right; the crooked grin that always hinted at some private joke.

At seventeen, Noah was already taller than her, built like his father but with Mia's fair hair and hazel eyes. He had an effortless sense of style, oversized hoodies, ripped jeans, sneakers that always seemed just a little too clean for a teenager.

He was grounded in a way Mia often envied. Confident but never cocky, Noah moved through the world with an ease beyond his years. He was popular without trying, the kind of kid who could drift between cliques without ever fully belonging to one. One afternoon, he'd be skateboarding at the park with the guys; the next, he'd be helping his friend Casey rehearse lines for the school play.

Music was his passion. His room was always cluttered with guitar picks, sheet music, and a secondhand keyboard he'd found at a yard sale and insisted on buying. He loved old-school rock, a taste he'd picked up from Mia, though he never missed a chance to tease her about her love for cheesy '80s ballads.

"I'll make you a playlist," he'd say with a smirk, plugging his phone into the speaker. "You need some better influences."

But what Mia cherished most about Noah was his heart. He

had a quiet kind of kindness, an instinct to protect the people he cared about. She'd never forget the day he stepped between her and Dane, his voice steady despite the tremor in his hands.

"You don't get to talk to her like that," he'd said, his stance unwavering.

That moment had both terrified and filled her with pride.

Mia's fingers tightened around the blanket bunched in her lap. "I just... I don't want him to hate me," she murmured, her voice trembling. "He's all I have, Lara. What if this ruins everything?"

Lara leaned forward, resting her elbows on the table. "You don't have to explain anything right now," she said carefully. "Noah loves you, Mia. He'll understand—maybe not right away, but he will."

Mia let out a bitter laugh, shaking her head. "Will he? What if he thinks I'm just like Dane—selfish, controlling... a coward?"

"You're nothing like Dane," Lara said firmly, leaving no room for argument. "You left because you had to. Because staying would've destroyed you. And Noah might not understand now, but he will someday."

As night fell, the quiet of the cabin settled heavier around them. Mia sat at the table, her gaze distant, her thoughts consumed by Noah. She could see him in her mind's eye, his easy smile, the way his hair always fell into his face no matter how many times he pushed it back.

She thought of the way he used to hug her when he was little, his small arms tight around her neck as he whispered, "You're the best, Mom."

The cabin was quiet, save for the occasional creak of wood settling in the cool night air. The fire in the small hearth had burned low, its faint glow casting restless shadows across the walls. Lara sat on the edge of the bed, elbows resting on her knees, staring into the dying embers.

Mia was still curled up in the loveseat, a blanket draped over her shoulders, absently tugging at a loose thread on the hem. Neither of them spoke. The atmosphere felt fragile, stretched thin over the space of everything left unsaid.

Then came the knock.

Soft but deliberate, it echoed through the stillness of the cabin. Both women froze, eyes snapping toward the door. A single beat passed. Then another. Their hearts pounded in unison.

Lara rose slowly, her movements careful, controlled. She crossed to the small window by the door, peering through the warped glass.

The dim porch light flickered, casting uneven illumination over the figure outside, a man, lean and scruffy, his thick coat worn and weathered. His hands were buried in his pockets, his stance restless as he shifted his weight from foot to foot.

Taking a deep breath, Lara cracked the door open, keeping her body between the stranger and the room behind her. "Can I help you?"

The man offered a hesitant smile, his features rough but not unkind. Strands of gray threaded through his dark hair, and the deep lines on his face suggested a life spent on the road. "Sorry to bother you," he said, his voice gruff but polite. "I'm in one of the other cabins and ran out of matches for my stove. Thought I'd see if you had some to spare."

Lara studied him carefully, every instinct on high alert. His eyes met hers with a sincerity that felt genuine, but she refused to let her guard down. "Give me a minute," she said, her tone measured.

She eased the door shut just enough to turn to Mia, who had straightened in her seat, the blanket clutched tightly around her shoulders. "Matches?" Lara asked quietly.

Mia nodded, standing and moving to the small kitchenette,

where a tin of matches sat beside the stove. She handed them to Lara, her hands trembling slightly. "Be careful," she whispered.

Lara nodded and turned back to the door, opening it wider but still keeping herself positioned between the man and the cabin's interior. "Here," she said, extending the tin. "We'll need them back."

The man took the matches with a grateful nod. "Of course," he said. "Just need to get the fire going. I'll bring them back once I'm set."

Lara didn't respond, watching as he stepped off the porch and disappeared into the darkness. She lingered by the door, listening for any sign of trouble, but the only sound was the faint rustle of trees in the night breeze. Finally, she shut the door and locked it, double-checking the latch.

"That was weird," Mia murmured, still clutching the blanket as she sank back onto the loveseat.

"He seemed harmless," Lara said, though her gaze remained fixed on the door. "But we can't be too careful."

Mia nodded. Her expression tight with unease. "Do you think he knows?"

"No," Lara said firmly, though a flicker of doubt crossed her mind. "He's just another drifter. Probably here for the same reason we are, to stay out of sight."

Later, they climbed into the narrow bed together, the blankets rough but warm against the night chill. The cabin's small size left little room for space between them, but neither seemed to mind. Mia curled onto her side, facing the wall, her shoulders hunched as if trying to make herself smaller, to disappear.

Lara lay on her back at first, staring up at the ceiling, her thoughts a relentless blur of everything that had happened and everything still ahead.

Mia's voice broke, soft and trembling. "I miss him so much, Lara. Every second, it hurts. It's like there's this piece of me missing, and I don't know how to get it back."

Lara turned onto her side, propping herself up on one elbow to look at Mia. Her friend's face was partially buried in the pillow, but Lara could still see the tears streaking her cheeks, the way her body trembled with barely suppressed sobs.

"You're stronger than you think," Lara murmured, resting a light hand on Mia's shoulder. "Noah knows how much you love him. He's going to be okay, Mia. And so are you."

Mia let out a shaky breath, her tears falling harder now. "I don't know if I can do this, Lara. I feel so broken. I can't stop seeing Trent's face, hearing his voice... feeling him." Her voice cracked, and she pressed her face deeper into the pillow, as if trying to disappear.

Lara's chest tightened, a familiar ache rising in her throat. She didn't have the words to erase Mia's pain, but she could offer her presence, her steadying touch. Gently, she stroked Mia's shoulder, tracing slow, soothing circles over the fabric of the blanket.

"You're not alone," Lara whispered. "I'm here. We'll get through this together."

Mia's breathing slowed, her sobs fading as Lara's touch and words wrapped around her like a cocoon. She shifted slightly, leaning into Lara's hand as if it were the only anchor she had in a storm-tossed sea.

"Thank you," Mia whispered, her voice barely audible.

Lara didn't reply, her own throat was too tight to speak. Instead, she kept up the soothing motion, her fingers tracing slow, reassuring circles until she felt Mia's body relax, her breathing evening out as sleep finally took hold.

Lara remained awake a little longer, her hand resting lightly on Mia's shoulder, her mind churning over their situation. But as the fire dwindled and dark corners deepened in the small cabin, exhaustion finally pulled her under.

For the first time in days, the two women slept, held in the fragile sanctuary of each other's warmth, the world outside kept at bay, if only for a little while.

20

The morning chill seeped into the cabin, curling around the small room's corners and settling over everything like a damp fog. Lara stirred first, the ache in her back from the narrow bed pulling her reluctantly into consciousness. The embers in the fireplace had long since gone cold, and her breath puffed out in faint clouds as she sat up and rubbed her arms.

Beside her, Mia was still asleep, her face half-buried in the pillow. Her dark hair spilled over her shoulder, messy and tangled, and her expression was soft in a way that made Lara's chest ache. She looked younger like this, the lines of worry and exhaustion smoothed away in sleep. But even in the stillness, there was something fragile about her, like glass that had been cracked too many times and was holding together by sheer will.

Lara swung her legs over the edge of the bed, her feet hitting the cold wooden floor. She reached for her jacket, pulling it on against the chill, and crossed the room to the small pile of firewood stacked near the hearth. The sight of it made her pause, brow furrowing. The matches. The drifter hadn't returned them.

With a low sigh, Lara glanced toward the window, where the

faint light of dawn was just beginning to filter through the trees. She didn't want to wake Mia, not yet. Mia needed rest, needed just one more moment of peace before reality came crashing down again. And maybe, just maybe, Lara could fix this small thing without adding another worry to their already overflowing pile.

The air outside was sharp and biting, the kind of cold that stung her lungs as she stepped onto the porch. The trees loomed tall and still, their branches heavy with frost. The campground was quiet, the other cabins tucked into the shadows of the forest. Only a faint trail of smoke from one of the chimneys hinted at life nearby.

Lara shoved her hands into her pockets as she made her way down the gravel path toward the cabin where the drifter had said he was staying. The closer she got, the more she noticed the small details, the uneven footprints in the frost-covered ground, the empty soup can perched on a tree stump, the faint scent of burnt wood hanging in the air.

She knocked on the door, her fist rapping lightly against the weathered wood. The sound echoed faintly, but no response came. She knocked again, harder this time, and called out, "Hey! You there?"

Nothing.

Lara frowned and pressed her ear to the door. The cabin was silent, its small window dark and empty. She tried the doorknob, but it didn't budge. Something in the back of her mind alerted her, a mix of annoyance and unease as she stepped back and surveyed the area. There was no sign of the drifter, no indication that anyone had been there recently.

"Dammit," she muttered under her breath, kicking at a loose stone on the path. She lingered a moment longer, her breath puffing in the air as she scanned the trees, half-expecting him to appear from the shadows. But the forest remained still, and after a moment, she turned and made her way back to her cabin.

When Lara stepped inside, the cabin was still cold, the firewood stacked uselessly beside the unlit hearth. She shrugged off her jacket and glanced toward the bed, where Mia was now sitting up, her blanket wrapped around her shoulders.

"Did you find him?" Mia asked, her voice croaky.

Lara shook her head, running a hand through her hair. "No. He's gone."

Mia frowned, her hands tightening on the edge of the blanket. "Gone? He didn't bring the matches back?"

"Nope." Lara crossed the room to the small table where their belongings were piled. "Guess he decided not to keep his word."

As she reached for the envelope of money Sandy had given them, Lara's hand froze. The space where the envelope had been, was empty. She blinked, her heart skipping a beat as she searched the table, shuffling through their things with increasing urgency. But it wasn't there.

"What's wrong?" Mia asked, her tone sharp with worry.

"The money," Lara said, her voice low and tight. "It's gone."

Mia's eyes widened, and she threw off the blanket, rushing to Lara's side. "What do you mean, gone? Are you sure?"

Lara didn't answer immediately, her hands moving frantically now, checking the floor, the chairs, even the small shelf near the door. But there was no sign of the envelope. It was as though it had vanished.

"It was here," Lara said finally, her voice trembling with a mix of anger and disbelief. "I know it was here last night."

Mia's face paled, her hands trembling as she clutched the edge of the table. "You think... you think he took it?"

Lara straightened, her jaw tightening. "Who else could it have been? He must have broken in here. Snuck in while we slept but I swore I locked the door. It must be him. Maybe he did bring the matches back, opened the door and saw the envelope and took a chance, and now he's gone."

Mia sank into one of the chairs, burying her face in her hands. "Oh my God," she whispered. "What are we going to do?"

Lara didn't answer, her gaze fixed on the window as a cold, hard realization settled over her. The drifter had played them, taking advantage of their desperation and trust. And now, with their funds gone, their fragile sense of security had been ripped away.

The cabin felt colder than ever and for the first time in a long time, Lara didn't have an immediate answer.

She slammed her fist onto the table, the sound sharp and startling in the small, frigid cabin. "This is exactly why I said we shouldn't trust anyone, Mia! How could you not see this coming?"

Mia flinched but quickly straightened in her chair, her eyes narrowing. "Excuse me? I didn't invite him in, Lara! I made him stay by the door while you handed over the matches like it was nothing."

"And you didn't say a damn thing to stop me," Lara snapped, her voice rising. "God, Mia, you just sit there and let things happen, like you're waiting for someone else to fix it all for you."

Mia's face flushed, and she shot up from her seat, the blanket slipping to the floor. "You don't get to put this all on me!" she spat, her voice trembling with anger. "You think you're so much better, so much smarter, but you're not. You just hide behind this wall of yours, like nothing can touch you. At least I try to trust people, Lara. At least I try to believe there's still good out there."

"Good out there?" Lara repeated, sarcasm lacing her voice as she gestured toward the door. "Does this feel like good to you? He stole from us, Mia. That money was all we had, and now it's gone because you..."

"Because I what?" Mia interrupted, stepping closer. Her

voice cracked, but she didn't back down. "Say it, Lara. Go on. Tell me how I ruin everything, how I always make things worse."

Lara opened her mouth, but the words didn't come. The fury on her face softened just enough to let something else slip through—something raw and vulnerable. She turned away, raking a hand through her hair as she paced the small room.

"You don't ruin everything," Lara said finally, her voice quieter but no less tense. "You just... you don't think things through. You act on emotion, and it gets us into trouble."

"And you don't act at all unless you've overthought every possible outcome," Mia shot back, her eyes blazing. "You're so damn cautious, Lara. You second-guess everything, everyone, and it's exhausting."

Lara stopped pacing and turned to face her. "That caution is the only reason we're still here, Mia. If I wasn't careful, we'd already be in a jail cell or worse."

"Maybe we wouldn't be in this mess at all if you weren't so afraid to let people in," Mia said, her voice dropping to a quieter, sharper tone. "You act like nothing can touch you, like you don't feel anything, but it's a lie. You're just scared, scared to care, scared to hurt."

Lara's jaw tightened, her fists clenching at her sides. "You think I don't care? You think I don't feel anything?" Her voice was low, almost a growl. "I feel everything, Mia. Every mistake, every decision we've made, every time I look at you and see how much this is breaking you. Don't you dare tell me I don't care."

Mia's breath hitched, and for a moment, the room felt charged. Lara's chest rose and fell with labored breaths, her eyes locked on Mia's, daring her to say more.

"You never say it," Mia said finally, her voice trembling but steady. "You never admit it. You just... bury everything under this armor of yours and hope no one notices. But I see you, Lara. I see the cracks."

Lara stepped closer, her presence overwhelming in the small space. "You think I'm the one hiding? What about you, Mia? You act like the victim, like everything happens to you, but you never take responsibility for anything. You let Dane control you, you let Trent..." She stopped, the name catching in her throat, and for a brief moment, her gaze softened, betraying the truth of her words.

Mia's eyes filled with tears, her hands trembling at her sides. "Don't," she whispered, her voice barely audible. "Don't you dare say his name."

Lara exhaled sharply, raking a hand through her hair. "I'm sorry," she said, her voice low and rough. "I didn't mean..."

"Yes, you did," Mia cut in, her voice cracking, but her gaze didn't waver. "You always mean it, Lara. You just don't like what it says about you."

Silence followed as their words settled over them and the room like a storm cloud. Neither moved, their breaths uneven, their emotions raw and exposed.

And beneath the anger, beneath the hurt and exhaustion, something else lingered, something unspoken yet undeniable. The space between them felt smaller, the air charged with a tension that wasn't just born of their fight.

Lara's gaze softened as it lingered on Mia's tear-streaked face, and Mia's breath hitched when she caught the glimmer of something in Lara's eyes, something tender, something painful.

But neither of them acted on it. Neither dared cross that invisible line, not here, not now. The hard facts of their circumstances pressed too heavily, leaving no room for anything but survival.

"I'll figure something out," Lara said finally, her voice quiet but firm. "We'll figure something out. But right now, we need to focus."

Mia nodded, wrapping her arms tightly around herself as

she turned away. Her tears fell silently, shoulders shaking as she sank onto the loveseat.

Lara watched her for a moment longer, her own emotions clawing at her chest, before turning toward the window. Frost clung to the glass, catching the pale morning light and casting faint shadows across the room.

They were both breaking, piece by piece, yet they held on—barely. The fire that had once burned so brightly between them now smoldered, unresolved but still there, waiting for the moment it would either ignite or extinguish for good.

21

Detective Joel Barnes sat at his desk in the quiet station, the fluorescent lights casting a pale sheen over the stacks of papers and photographs before him. The soft background noise of activity, phones ringing, the occasional burst of laughter, barely registered. His focus was locked on the file splayed open on his desk: Dane Larson.

The man's smug face stared back at him from the photo clipped to the corner of the report. A sharp suit, slicked-back hair, and a carefully curated public persona screamed success. But Joel had seen too many men like Dane, men who wore their respectability like armor, concealing the rot beneath. And now, after hours of combing through records and piecing together fragments of a story, Joel's instincts told him that Mia Williams had been running from far more than just the fallout of a crime.

He leaned back in his chair, rubbing a hand over his stubbled jaw. It had taken hours of backchanneling and sifting through sealed records, but he'd finally found it: a restraining order, filed nearly two decades ago, by a woman named Lindsey Carver. She had accused Dane of being controlling, manipulative, and increasingly violent during their two-year relationship. The restraining order had been granted, but Lindsey moved out of state shortly after, her allegations quietly buried by Dane's legal team and connections.

Joel tapped his pen against the desk, the rhythmic clicking echoing in his head. He flipped through the rest of the file, scanning emails, phone records, and Dane's statements to authorities. The pieces were beginning to align, and they painted a picture Joel couldn't ignore. Mia wasn't just running. She was escaping.

But there was pressure. There was always pressure. His superiors wanted results, and the directive was clear—apprehend Mia and Lara, not unravel the complexities of their lives. The women were fugitives. A man was dead. The narrative was simple, clean, easy to sell to the public. But the truth was rarely simple, and Joel knew it.

Joel wasn't the type to shy away from hard truths. He'd been on the force for nearly two decades, cutting his teeth on the gritty streets of Montreal before transferring west to quieter precincts. At forty-four, he carried the scars of his career in the lines etched around his eyes and the occasional stiffness in his knee from an old injury. But it was the cases that never left him—the faces of the victims, the ones he couldn't save that weighed the heaviest.

He had a daughter, Emily, who lived with her mother in Vancouver. Divorce hadn't been part of the plan, but it had come all the same, the slow unraveling of a marriage frayed by late nights at the station and the emotional toll of the job. Emily was twelve now, a bright, headstrong kid who loved soccer and had a knack for asking questions that made Joel wonder if she saw right through him. He called her every weekend without fail, and when her laughter filled the phone line, it was the only thing that reminded him why he kept doing this work.

But this case, it was getting under his skin in a way he hadn't anticipated. Maybe it was Mia's bruised face staring out from the grainy surveillance footage. Maybe it was the way Lara's eyes held a fierce protectiveness that Joel recognized in himself, the way he'd do anything to shield Emily from harm. Or maybe it was just the gnawing feeling that there was more to this story than anyone was willing to see.

He reached for his coffee, now lukewarm and bitter, and took a sip as he stared at Dane's file. The restraining order wasn't the only thing he'd found. There were whispers, anonymous complaints from neighbors, police reports that went nowhere, incidents that painted Dane as a man who thrived on control. A man who would see Mia's attempt to escape as a personal affront.

Joel exhaled sharply and set the coffee down with a dull thud. "She's not a criminal," he muttered. "She's a victim."

"Talking to yourself again, Barnes?" Officer Nadia Torres leaned against the doorframe; a folder tucked under her arm. Her sharp eyes took in the mess of papers on his desk before landing on him. "Find something?"

"More like confirmation," Joel replied, gesturing toward the file. "Dane Larson isn't the upstanding citizen he pretends to be. Restraining order from an ex, sealed police reports all pointing to a history of abuse."

Torres raised an eyebrow and crossed the room to glance at the papers. "Does it change anything? As far as the higher-ups are concerned, she and her friend are still fugitives. They want us focused on bringing them in, not dissecting their lives."

"It changes everything," Joel said firmly. "If she's running from him, if he's been controlling her all this time, then this isn't just about what happened at that bar. It's about survival."

Torres studied him for a moment, her expression unreadable. "You really think the brass cares about that?"

"No," Joel admitted, leaning back in his chair. "But I do."

She nodded, her mouth pulling into a tight line. "Just be careful, Barnes. You dig too deep, and you might not like what you find."

"Story of my life," he said with a dry smile.

Torres left, and Joel returned to the file, his mind spinning. He knew the system wasn't perfect. He knew it didn't always protect the people who needed it most. But he also knew he couldn't ignore what he'd found.

Mia Williams wasn't a monster. She was a woman backed into a corner, fighting to protect herself and if Joel's instincts were right, her son. And Lara Edwards? She wasn't just an accomplice. She was a shield, a protector, the kind of person Joel would want in his corner if he were ever in a fight for his life.

As the clock ticked into the early hours of the morning, Joel made a decision. He would keep digging, keep piecing together the truth, no matter how inconvenient it was to the narrative his superiors wanted to sell. Because if there was one thing he'd learned in his years on the force, it was that the truth mattered —even when no one else wanted to see it.

The Impala roared to life in the pale dawn light, gravel crunching beneath its tires as Lara guided it back onto the winding road away from the campsite. The cabin and the drifter who had stripped them of their money faded into the distance, swallowed by the dense pine forest. Lara's hands gripped the wheel tightly, her jaw set in a grim line as she stared straight ahead. Beside her, Mia sat tense, her fingers knotting and unknotting the loose threads of her sweatshirt sleeve.

Neither of them spoke for miles. The tension in the car was

like a storm cloud that refused to break. Outside, the world stretched wide and empty, the vast wilderness of northern Canada unfurling in endless waves of trees and snow-covered mountains. The road was narrow, flanked by frost-covered grasses and occasional bursts of rocky outcroppings that seemed to rise out of nowhere.

The Yukon lay ahead—a sprawling, untouched expanse that felt both like a promise and a punishment. The air here was sharper, cleaner, biting through the cracked window that Lara had opened just enough to keep herself awake.

"I can't believe we didn't pay," Mia said finally, her voice small, as if she were afraid to say it out loud.

Lara scoffed, her eyes still on the road. "We didn't have anything to pay with, Mia. And I wasn't about to stick around and explain that to someone."

Mia looked down at her hands, her fingers twisting the edge of the blanket draped over her lap. "I hate this," she whispered. "I hate stealing. I hate running."

Lara glanced at her briefly, her expression softening just enough to let a hint of guilt slip through. "I know," she said quietly. "I hate it too."

The miles slipped by, the rhythmic chug of the engine the only sound as they drove deeper into the Yukon. The landscape grew wilder, the trees thicker and darker, their branches heavy with snow. A river snaked alongside the road for a stretch, its icy surface glittering in the weak sunlight. The beauty of it all was almost painful and a stark reminder of how far removed they were from the lives they'd once lived.

"You remember that time we went camping during spring break?" Mia asked suddenly, breaking the stillness.

Lara's lips twitched into a faint smile. "The time you forgot the tent poles?"

Mia let out a soft laugh, the sound surprising both of them. "It wasn't my fault! You were supposed to pack them."

"And you were supposed to double-check," Lara shot back, her smile growing. "We ended up sleeping in the back of your old Jeep, remember?"

Mia nodded. Her smile tinged with nostalgia. "And you spent the whole night complaining about the smell of the gas can."

"It was awful," Lara said, her voice lighter now. "But we still managed to make s'mores on the campfire."

"With a coat hanger because we forgot skewers," Mia added, laughing again.

For a moment, the tension between them eased, replaced by the warmth of a shared memory. The enormity of their reality didn't disappear, but it lessened just a little as they clung to the fleeting joy of simpler times.

But as the hours stretched on, the worry crept back in. The road narrowed further, winding through valleys and cutting along steep cliffs that plunged into icy ravines. The sun dipped lower, casting long shadows across the land, and the vastness of the wilderness began to feel an enemy.

Mia stared out the window, her breath fogging the glass as she traced patterns on it with her finger. Her voice, when she spoke, was barely above a whisper. "Do you ever think we made the wrong choice?"

Lara didn't answer right away.

"No," she said finally, her tone firm. "We did what we had to do."

"But what if..." Mia's voice cracked, and she turned to face Lara, her eyes glistening with unshed tears. "What if we'd gone to the police? What if we'd told them the truth?"

"And then what?" Lara snapped, her frustration bubbling to

the surface. “Let them paint us as killers? Let them twist everything into a story that fits their narrative? You think they would’ve believed us, Mia? You think Dane would’ve let them?”

Mia shrank back, her tears spilling over. “I just... I don’t know how we keep doing this,” she said, her voice breaking. “Every day, it feels like we’re losing more of ourselves. I don’t even know who I am anymore.”

Lara’s chest tightened, her anger fading as quickly as it had come. She sighed, her voice softening.

“I know it’s hard. I know it feels impossible. But you’re still you, Mia. You’re still the woman who danced barefoot in the rain during that thunderstorm in college. The one who always beat me at Scrabble, even though you pretended you didn’t care about winning.”

Mia let out a shaky laugh, wiping at her eyes. “That was because I kept a dictionary under my bed.”

Lara smiled faintly; her gaze soft as she glanced at her. “You’re stronger than you think. You’ve made it this far, and you’re going to keep going.”

Mia nodded, her tears slowing, though her shoulders still trembled. The road stretched on ahead of them, the vast wilderness rising and falling in an endless rhythm. It was beautiful, yes, but it was also bleak and a reminder of just how alone they were in a world that seemed determined to swallow them whole.

As night fell, the Impala’s headlights sliced through the darkness, illuminating the road ahead. The lack of talk between them was obvious but not hostile, each woman lost in her own thoughts. And though the path before them was uncertain, one thing was clear: there was no turning back now. They had crossed a line, and the lives they’d left behind were no longer within reach.

Lara glanced at Mia, who had drifted into an uneasy sleep,

her head resting against the window. Her bruised face was still, her features softened by the shadows. Lara's heart ached for her —for everything she had endured, for everything she had lost. And though she didn't say it out loud, she made a silent promise: she would protect Mia.

22

The frost-covered ground crunched beneath their boots as Lara and Mia moved through the dense wilderness. The forest around Whitehorse was vast, its towering trees stretching endlessly in every direction, their trunks gnarled and ancient. The air was biting, sharp and clean. Filling their lungs with each shallow breath. They had ventured out early that morning, driven by hunger and the slim hope of finding something edible, berries, perhaps, or even small game, though neither had any idea how to hunt.

Mia hugged her jacket tighter around herself, her teeth chattering despite her best efforts to stay warm. "I don't know why we thought this was a good idea," she muttered, kicking at a rock half-buried in the dirt.

"We need food," Lara said simply, her tone clipped as she scanned the trees ahead. "Sitting in the car isn't going to make it magically appear."

Mia sighed, her breath curling in the cold air. "Yeah, well, at least the car isn't freezing."

Lara didn't reply, her focus shifting as something caught her eye through the trees. A structure, barely visible in the distance, its weathered wood blending seamlessly with the surrounding forest. She stopped, squinting. "Wait," she said, pointing. "Do you see that?"

Mia followed her gaze, her brows furrowing. "What is that? A cabin?"

"Looks like it." Lara adjusted the strap of her backpack and quickened her pace. "Come on."

As they drew closer, the structure came into sharper focus. It wasn't quite a cabin in the traditional sense. It was smaller, more like a shack, its wooden planks weathered and warped from years of exposure. The roof sagged slightly in the middle, patched in places with sheets of tin that gleamed faintly in the weak sunlight. A crooked chimney jutted from one side, a thin wisp of smoke curling upward, proof that someone was inside.

Lara and Mia exchanged a wary glance.

"Do you think it's abandoned?" Mia asked, her voice hushed.

"The smoke means someone's there," Lara replied. "But I doubt it's crowded. Let's see."

They approached cautiously. Their footsteps soft against the frozen earth. The door was slightly ajar, revealing a dim interior lit only by the soft glow of a fire. Lara raised a hand and rapped her knuckles lightly against the wooden frame.

"Hello?" she called, her voice firm but not aggressive.

For a moment, there was nothing. Then, light, deliberate footsteps approached from inside. The door creaked open wider, revealing a woman who looked like she had stepped out of a storybook.

She was tall and willowy, with long dark hair streaked with silver that cascaded down her back in loose waves. Her skin was sun-kissed despite the season, her high cheekbones accentuating eyes so vividly green they seemed to glimmer like emeralds in the firelight. She wore a patchwork sweater over a long skirt, her feet bare despite the cold.

"Well, this is unexpected," she said, her voice warm and lilting, like a melody. Leaning casually against the doorframe, she rested one hand lightly on the wood. "You're a long way from town."

Lara straightened; her hands buried in her jacket pockets. "We're just passing through," she said evenly. "Saw the smoke, thought maybe..." She trailed off, unsure how to finish.

"Thought maybe I'd invite you in?" The woman finished for her, a small smile tugging at the corner of her mouth. She stepped back, gesturing toward the fire. "Come on, then. No sense standing out there freezing to death."

Mia hesitated, glancing at Lara for reassurance. Lara gave a slight nod, and together, they stepped inside.

The shack was a hodgepodge of mismatched furniture and eclectic trinkets, every inch radiating warmth despite its rough exterior. A small wood-burning stove crackled in the corner, casting flickering light across the room. Shelves lined the walls, crammed with jars of preserves, books, and what looked like handmade pottery. An old quilt draped over a lopsided couch, and the floor was layered with rugs that appeared handwoven. The air carried the faint scent of pine and something sweet, lavender, maybe.

"Don't mind the mess," she said, closing the door behind them. "I don't get visitors often, now, my name's Patricia, and who would you two be?"

"It's nice," Mia said softly, her eyes roaming over the space. She ran her fingers along the edge of the quilt, marveling at the intricate stitching. "Oh, and I'm Mia and this is Lara," she nodded in Lara's direction.

"Nice," Patricia repeated with a laugh, her green eyes twinkling. "That's generous of you." She moved to the stove, grabbing a metal kettle and setting it over the heat. "I was just about to make tea. You drink tea?"

Lara nodded. "Sure."

"Good." Patricia busied herself with the kettle, her movements graceful and unhurried. "So, what brings you out this way? You don't exactly look like locals."

Lara and Mia exchanged a quick glance before Lara spoke carefully. "Just... traveling. Trying to see as much of the wilderness as we can."

Patricia smiled knowingly but didn't press. "Well, you've certainly picked the right place. Nothing but wilderness out here."

As the tea brewed, Patricia handed them each a mismatched mug, her expression curious but kind. She sat cross-legged on the rug, her posture relaxed, as if she had all the time in the world.

"You've been here a while?" Lara asked, nodding toward the walls lined with jars and trinkets.

"Long enough," Patricia replied, her tone light but evasive. "Off the grid suits me."

Mia tilted her head, studying the woman. "Why stay out here? Don't you get lonely?"

Patricia's smile faltered slightly, her gaze dropping to the steaming mug in her hands. "Sometimes," she admitted. "But some things are worth the trade-off."

A quiet moment settled between them, the fire's gentle crackle filling the space. Lara studied Patricia, her instincts picking up on the subtle shifts—how her fingers tightened around the mug, the flicker of something guarded in her eyes. Patricia was running, just like they were.

"Well," Patricia said suddenly, her smile returning, though it didn't quite reach her eyes, "you're welcome to warm up here for a while. No sense braving the cold until you're ready."

Lara nodded. Her gratitude genuine but cautious. "Thanks."

As they sat by the fire, sipping tea and exchanging fragments of their stories, the wilderness outside seemed to grow darker, the trees like silent sentinels. Patricia's warmth and generosity offered a brief reprieve, but Lara couldn't shake the feeling that this shack, this woman, held more secrets than met the eye.

And as Mia's laughter intertwined with Patricia's lilting voice, Lara's gaze drifted to the window, her mind racing with questions. Even in this fleeting moment of respite, the wilderness like their pasts, felt inescapable.

The firelight flickered against the cabin's rough-hewn walls, casting warm, uneven patterns that danced with every pop and crackle of the wood stove. Patricia leaned back against the couch, legs folded beneath her, emerald-green eyes soft with understanding as she watched Mia absentmindedly trace circles along the rim of her empty mug.

"You should stay the night," Patricia said suddenly, her voice gentle but firm.

Mia's head snapped up, and Lara stilled, her eyes narrowing slightly as she studied Patricia.

"It's not safe to keep moving in the dark," Patricia continued, as if sensing Lara's hesitation. "This place is off the grid, no electricity, no phones. No one's going to find you here if you don't want to be found."

Moments stretched between them, the invitation hanging in the air like a lifeline offered by a stranger they weren't sure they could trust. But there was something about Patricia, the quiet certainty in her voice, the way her smile asked for nothing in return, that made refusal difficult.

Lara held her gaze for a moment longer before nodding. "Thank you," she said finally, her voice measured but sincere. "We appreciate it."

Patricia's smile was warm, absent of expectation. "You can take the loft," she said, gesturing toward the wooden ladder leading up to a small platform beneath the slanted roof. "It's not much, but the blankets up there are warm, and the fire should keep it cozy."

As night settled in, the three women sat together by the fire, the warmth of the cabin easing the tension that had gripped Lara and Mia for days. Patricia's presence was steadying, her easy laughter, the unhurried way she spoke about life in the wilderness, making the space feel almost... safe.

Mia leaned back against the couch, tucking her legs beneath her. The firelight flickered in her eyes, but there was a sadness there, a mournful demeanor she couldn't shake.

"I miss my son," she said quietly, the words slipping out before she could stop them.

Patricia's expression softened. "How old is he?"

"Seventeen," Mia murmured, her voice thick with emotion. "Noah. He's... he's everything to me. Works hard, gets his grades, is kind and respectful, my world really. He's the reason I got up every morning."

Patricia nodded. Her gaze thoughtful. "He sounds like a good kid."

A small, wistful smile ghosted across Mia's lips. "He is. Smart, kind... way more put together than I ever was at his age." But the smile faded just as quickly. Her fingers tightened around the edge of her sleeve. "But I can't call him. I can't even let him know I'm okay."

Her voice cracked, and she turned her head away, swiping at the tears that slipped down her cheeks. Lara shifted in her seat, her hand twitching as if she wanted to reach out—but she didn't. Instead, she sat still, her expression tight with unspoken pain.

"You can still talk to him," Patricia said softly.

Mia frowned, glancing up. "How? I can't call. I can't text."

Patricia leaned forward, resting her elbows on her knees. "Write him a letter," she said simply. "Pour it all out. Everything you're feeling, everything you wish you could say. And when I go into town next week, I'll post it for you."

Mia blinked, her mouth parting as if to argue, but no words came. She glanced at Lara, who was watching Patricia with cautious curiosity, then back at Patricia, who held her gaze with quiet encouragement.

"It's not the same as hearing his voice, or he, yours," Patricia said gently, "but it's something. And sometimes, when you're carrying too much, writing it down helps lighten the load."

Mia swallowed hard, her hands tightening in her lap. "You'd really do that? Send it for me?"

"Of course," Patricia said, as if the question were absurd. "What's a stamp between friends?"

The word friends hung in the air, both comforting and bittersweet. Mia nodded slowly, her throat tight as she whispered, "Thank you."

Patricia disappeared into the kitchen, returning moments later with a battered notebook and a pen. She handed them to Mia with a wink. "Start with 'Dear Noah.' The rest will come."

Mia took the notebook with trembling hands, her fingers brushing over the worn cover. The fire crackled softly in the background as she flipped it open, the blank page staring back at her, a quiet challenge.

She hesitated, the pen hovering just above the paper, before finally pressing it down.

Dear Noah, she wrote, the letters shaky but determined. I miss you more than I can put into words...

Lara watched from her seat, her heart aching at the raw emotion etched into Mia's face. Across the room, Patricia leaned casually against the counter, arms crossed, her gaze steady with quiet understanding. There was something about her, something unspoken yet undeniable. She carried her own burdens, her own reasons for retreating to the middle of nowhere. But whatever her story was, she wasn't offering it, and Lara didn't ask.

Instead, she let herself relax just for a moment. The cabin was warm, the fire steady, and for the first time in days, it felt like they weren't completely alone.

Time passed, the soft scratch of Mia's pen filling the room. Her words poured out in a messy scrawl, each line a release, a confession, a quiet plea. By the time she set the pen down, her eyes were red, but something in her expression had shifted. Lighter. As though she'd finally let go of the guilt she'd been carrying.

Patricia's voice was gentle. "Feel better?"

Mia nodded, clutching the notebook to her chest. "Yeah," she said, her voice hoarse. "I do."

Patricia's smile was warm, her emerald eyes soft with understanding. "Good. Now get some rest. Tomorrow's a new day."

Lara helped Mia up the ladder to the loft, where the blankets were thick and surprisingly soft. They settled in, the firelight flickering against the low ceiling, casting faint, shifting shadows. Mia curled into Lara's side, her breath slowing as exhaustion finally pulled her under.

Lara stayed awake a little longer, her gaze drifting to the window where the night stretched endlessly beyond the glass. She didn't trust easily, didn't want to trust Patricia. But here, with Mia's head resting against her shoulder and the warmth of the cabin wrapped around them, she let herself believe just for a moment that maybe they weren't completely lost.

23

The forest was unnaturally still, the kind of silence that made every twig snapping underfoot sound like a gunshot.

It was early morning and Patricia stood on the porch of her shack, arms loosely crossed over her chest, watching as the police cruiser crept up the narrow dirt path to her home. Its tires crunched over frost and gravel, sending up wisps of dust, while red and blue lights fractured against the snow-dusted trees, a kaleidoscope of tension. The scene felt charged, as though the forest itself was holding its breath.

She cast a glance toward the edge of the woods, where the Impala had been parked just last night. The car had been hidden somewhere deep in the forest as planned. Lara and Mia would have followed an old, logger track that Patricia had described, hoping it would remain unseen for a few days at least and give them time to get away. Unfortunately, it looked like someone had spotted it and clearly remembered its make and plate. Patricia pressed her lips into a thin line. She leaned against the doorframe with a practiced ease, projecting an air of calm even as her heart pounded, every instinct screaming at her to stay composed.

The cruiser rolled to a stop, and two officers stepped out. The older of the two, a gruff-looking man with a huge mustache and the kind of demeanor that screamed career cop adjusted his belt as he approached. The younger officer, barely out of training by the look of him, followed closely, his hand resting nervously on the butt of his holstered weapon. The tension in his posture made Patricia's stomach twist. Men like him made mistakes, and mistakes with weapons rarely ended well.

"Mornin'," the older officer called, tipping his hat slightly. "You Patricia?"

"That's me," she replied, her tone light, almost bored. "What can I do for you gentlemen?"

The officer pulled a notepad from his pocket and flipped it open. "We're looking for two women. Travelers, by the looks of it. They were spotted in a red Chevy Impala which has been found not far from here. Someone thought they might've stopped by your place."

Patricia tilted her head, feigning thoughtfulness as her pulse quickened. "Can't say I've seen anyone like that. Just me out here, minding my business."

The younger officer frowned, his gaze flicking around the yard. His fingers tensed briefly on his holster, a reflex that didn't go unnoticed by Patricia.

"A hunter said he saw the car parked here."

Patricia arched a brow, giving him a look equal parts amusement and annoyance. "Did he, now? Funny. I didn't see any car. And I think I'd notice something like that."

The older officer's eyes narrowed slightly, his expression hardening, though his tone remained polite. "Mind if we take a look around?"

Patricia shrugged, stepping aside with a nonchalance she didn't feel. "Suit yourself. Not much to see, though."

Inside the shack, the officers moved methodically, checking

every corner, every crevice. Patricia stood near the stove, her hands resting lightly on the countertop, her expression carefully neutral. She knew they wouldn't find anything. Mia and Lara had slipped away just before dawn, leaving no trace behind.

The younger officer hesitated near the loft ladder, his gaze lingering on the rumpled blankets. "Someone's been up here," he muttered, his voice low and suspicious.

"Just me," Patricia said smoothly, her tone laced with faint humor. "And if you're worried about the bed being messy, well, I don't make it every day. Perks of living alone."

The older officer exchanged a glance with his partner before stepping outside. He reached for his radio, his voice low but sharp. Patricia couldn't make out the words, but the clipped tone sent a shiver down her spine.

She followed him onto the porch, arms crossed tightly against the chill, although the cold was the least of her concerns.

"Anything else I can help you with?" she asked, keeping her voice calm, though it took effort to steady it.

The officer studied her for a long moment, suspicion clear in his eyes. "If you see anything or anyone, you let us know."

"Of course," Patricia said, flashing a polite smile that didn't reach her eyes. "Wouldn't dream of doing otherwise."

As the cruiser pulled away, Patricia leaned against the railing, watching until it disappeared down the dirt path. Then she exhaled slowly, her hands gripping the wood so tightly her knuckles turned white. She didn't know how much longer she could keep this up, but for now, she'd done her part.

Less than an hour later, the quiet of the forest shattered as more vehicles arrived. SUVs, tactical vans, and unmarked cars poured down the narrow path like a flood, their occupants moving with practiced precision. The SWAT team emerged, their black uniforms stark against the muted wilderness. Their movements were sharp, their faces obscured behind tinted visors. The clamor of voices and the metallic clink of weapons being readied turned the peaceful clearing into a war zone.

Officer Ted Grayson, the same gruff man who had questioned Patricia earlier, stood at the edge of the chaos, his radio crackling with instructions. "We need to search the surrounding area," he barked. "They couldn't have gone far."

"Hold off on that," a new voice cut in.

Joel Barnes stepped out of one of the SUVs, his breath visible in the cold air. His jacket was zipped up tight, the badge clipped to his belt catching the light as he approached Grayson.

Grayson turned, his expression sour. "And you are?"

"Detective Joel Barnes," Joel replied, flashing his credentials. "I'm leading the investigation into these two women."

Grayson sneered; his tone laced with disdain. "With all due respect, Detective, we've got a job to do. These women are killers. They need to be brought in before anyone else gets hurt."

Joel's jaw tightened, his eyes narrowing. "They're not killers," he said evenly, though his voice carried an edge. "And unless you want this turning into a national headline about a botched manhunt, we're going to handle this carefully. No need to go crashing through the woods like we're chasing armed terrorists."

Grayson scoffed, gesturing toward the SWAT team assembling nearby. "They stabbed a man and left him to bleed out. That's dangerous enough for me."

Joel stepped closer, his voice lowering but losing none of its intensity. "And they were attacked by that man. You've seen the reports, Grayson. Don't turn this into a witch hunt."

Grayson bristled, but before he could respond, Joel turned toward Patricia, who stood on the porch, arms crossed, her expression unreadable.

"Patricia, is it?" Joel asked, his tone calm but authoritative.

"That's right," she said, tilting her head slightly. "And you are?"

"Detective Joel Barnes," he said. "I believe you might've seen two women.... travelers. Did they stop here?"

Patricia's lips curved into a faint smile, though her eyes betrayed nothing. "Can't say I have. Like I told the other officers, it's just me out here."

Joel studied her carefully, his sharp instincts picking up on the way she held herself, relaxed, but guarded. "If you do see them," he said softly, his voice losing its edge, "I'd appreciate it if you let me know."

Patricia's smile didn't falter, but something in her eyes shifted, a flicker of defiance buried beneath her polite facade. "Of course, Detective," she said smoothly. "But like I told the others, there's nothing here."

Joel lingered, his gut telling him there was more to this woman than she let on. But pressing her wouldn't get him anywhere. Not yet.

As the SWAT team prepared to fan out into the forest, Joel's mind raced. The women were out there, somewhere in the vast wilderness. And if they didn't make a mistake soon, it might already be too late to find them.

As the last police SUV disappeared down the narrow dirt path, its tires kicking up a cloud of frost and gravel, Patricia stood motionless on the porch, her gaze lingering on the spot where they had vanished. The tension in her shoulders slowly eased as the forest reclaimed its quiet, the distant crackle of radios and voices fading into nothing.

She slipped a hand into the pocket of her patchwork sweater, her fingers brushing against the soft edge of the envelope tucked inside. Pulling it out, she turned it over gently, her thumb tracing the faint impression of Mia's hurried handwriting scrawled across the front: Noah Williams.

A wistful smile flickered across her lips as she held it close, the firelight reflecting the warmth in her green eyes.

"Don't worry, sweetheart," she murmured to the empty air. "I'll make sure it reaches him, when the time is right."

With that, she tucked the letter back into her pocket, her resolve firm as she stepped inside and shut the door, leaving the wilderness to its secrets once more.

24

The wind howled through the endless expanse of wilderness, its icy breath cutting through even the thickest layers of clothing. Snow crunched beneath their boots as Mia and Lara trudged along the narrow trail, their breaths coming in shallow, visible puffs in the frigid air. The vast stretch of Alaska's border loomed somewhere ahead; a shadowy promise shrouded in the dim light of winter dusk. The world around them felt infinite, the only sound the rustle of pine branches and the occasional distant crack of ice shifting under its own weight.

Mia shivered violently, clutching her jacket tighter around herself. Her face was pale, her lips chapped and trembling as she fought against the cold that seeped into her very bones. Lara glanced at her; exhaustion carved into the lines of her face. She was no stranger to pushing through fatigue, but this was something else entirely—this was survival, raw and unrelenting.

"We need to stop," Lara said finally, her voice hoarse from disuse. She scanned the surrounding trees, searching for some semblance of shelter, a rocky outcrop, a dense thicket to block the wind, anything. "We're not going to make it if we keep going like this

Mia nodded wordlessly, too tired to argue. Her legs felt like lead, each step heavier than the last, and the hunger gnawing at her stomach was a constant, dull ache. She stumbled slightly, her foot catching on an exposed root, and Lara was there in an instant, steadying her with a firm grip.

"Hey," Lara said softly, her eyes searching Mia's face. "You okay?"

"I'm fine," Mia lied, though the tears glistening in her eyes told a different story. She swiped at them angrily, her voice breaking as she added, "I just...I can't do this anymore, Lara. I can't."

"Yes, you can," Lara said firmly, her tone leaving no room for doubt. She slid an arm around Mia's shoulders, pulling her close. "We've come too far to stop now. Just a little longer, okay? We'll find somewhere to rest."

They finally found a small hollow at the base of a rocky hill, sheltered on one side by a jagged outcropping of stone and on the other by a cluster of snow-laden trees. It wasn't much, but it was enough to block the worst of the wind. Lara cleared away some of the snow with her boots, creating a patch of bare ground where they could sit.

Mia sank down immediately, wrapping her arms around her knees as she huddled against the rock. Lara dropped beside her, their shoulders pressed together, sharing what little warmth they could. Time stretched between them, laden with everything they'd endured and the uncertainty of what lay ahead.

"I don't think I've ever been this cold," Mia whispered, her voice barely audible over the wind.

Lara let out a faint, humorless laugh. "Me neither."

Mia turned her head slightly, her gaze lingering on Lara's profile. Her face was pale, her cheeks raw from the wind, but her eyes were steady, determined even in the face of exhaustion.

"How do you do it?" Mia asked quietly. "How do you keep going?"

Lara shrugged. Her breath visible in the cold air. "I don't know. I guess I just... don't let myself think about stopping. If I stop, if I let myself feel how tired I am, how scared..." She trailed off, shaking her head. "I can't let myself go there."

Mia looked down at her hands, her fingers trembling as she rubbed them together for warmth. "I wish I could be like you."

Lara turned to her, her eyes softening. "You're stronger than you think, Mia. You've been through hell, and you're still here. That's not nothing."

Mia swallowed hard. Her throat tight. "Sometimes it feels like nothing. Like I'm just... taking up space, dragging you down."

"You're not dragging me down," Lara said firmly, her voice cutting through the cold. "We're in this together, okay? I need you as much as you need me."

Mia's breath hitched, her chest tightening at the sincerity in Lara's voice. She nodded, tears spilling over as she whispered, "Thank you."

The wind howled around them, the cold biting at their exposed skin. Lara shifted slightly, wrapping an arm around Mia's shoulders and drawing her closer. Mia leaned into her, resting her head against Lara's shoulder, and for the first time in days, the tension in her body began to ease.

The closeness, the warmth of their shared presence, was a fragile comfort in the midst of the storm. Mia tilted her head up, her gaze meeting Lara's, and for a moment, the world seemed to still. There was something in Lara's eyes, something raw, unspoken, but undeniably there.

Without thinking, Mia leaned in, her lips brushing against Lara's in a tentative, trembling kiss. It was soft, hesitant, a question more than a statement. Lara froze for a moment, caught off guard, then responded, her hand coming up to cup Mia's cheek as she deepened the kiss.

It wasn't perfect, nothing about their lives was, but it was real, and in that moment, it was enough. When they pulled away, their breaths mingling in the cold air, neither spoke. They didn't need to. They shared an understanding that words couldn't capture.

Lara rested her forehead against Mia's, her hand still cradling her cheek. "We're going to get through this," she whispered, her voice steady despite the tears glistening in her eyes. "I promise."

Mia nodded, her own tears falling freely now. "Okay," she whispered back. "Okay."

The wind howled around them, but in their small hollow, they held onto each other, their shared warmth a fragile barrier against the cold. The road ahead was still uncertain, still dangerous, but for the first time in a long time, they didn't feel entirely alone.

The wind howled around them, carrying with it the biting chill of the wilderness, but in their little hollow, a different warmth began to spread. Lara's forehead rested against Mia's. For a moment, neither moved, the reality of what had just happened settling over them like the faint glow of dawn breaking over a frozen landscape.

Mia pulled back slightly, just enough to see Lara's face. Her lips parted as if she wanted to say something, but the words wouldn't come. Her cheeks were flushed, not just from the cold, and her eyes were wide, uncertain, but soft. Vulnerable.

"Lara," she whispered, her voice trembling like the leaves clinging stubbornly to the branches above them. "I..."

"Don't," Lara cut her off gently, her voice low but firm. Her hand was still on Mia's cheek, her thumb brushing against her chilled skin. "You don't have to explain."

Mia searched her face, her emotions swirling like a storm, fear, confusion, but also something she hadn't felt in so long she almost didn't recognize it. Hope.

"I wasn't expecting that," she admitted, her voice barely audible over the wind. "I didn't mean..."

"Neither did I," Lara said, her lips curving into a faint, almost rueful smile. "But... I'm not sorry."

Mia blinked, her breath catching in her throat. "You're not?"

Lara shook her head, her gaze steady despite the pounding of her heart. "No. I think... I think I've been trying not to feel anything for so long, and then you..." She stopped, struggling for the right words. "You make me feel, Mia. Even when it's messy. Even when it's hard."

Mia's chest tightened, her tears spilling over again though this time, they weren't from fear or despair. "I don't know what I'm doing," she admitted, her voice cracking. "I've been so lost for so long. I don't know how to feel anything good anymore."

Lara let out a soft laugh, the sound warm despite the cold. "Join the club."

They both laughed then, brittle at first, but it grew, filling the space between them like sunlight breaking through a storm. It wasn't much, but it was enough to ease the tension, to remind them that even in the darkest moments, there was still room for light.

As their laughter faded, Mia leaned her head against Lara's shoulder, her body relaxing into the warmth and solidity of her presence. "This is crazy, right?" she asked, disbelief threading through her voice. "Everything about this. Us."

Lara rested her chin lightly against Mia's hair, her arms tightening around her. "Yeah," she said quietly. "It's crazy. But maybe that's why it makes sense."

Mia tilted her head up, her eyes meeting Lara's. "You think so?"

Lara nodded. Her gaze steady. “When everything else is falling apart, maybe the only thing that makes sense is holding onto the one person who’s still here.”

Mia’s throat tightened, her tears threatening to spill over again. She reached up, covering Lara’s hand where it rested on her shoulder. “You’ve been there for me more than anyone ever has,” she said, her voice trembling. “And I don’t know how to thank you for that.”

“You don’t have to,” Lara murmured. “You’ve been there for me too, whether you realize it or not.”

Mia stared at her, emotions so raw and exposed she didn’t know how to hold them all. “I don’t deserve you,” she whispered, barely audible.

Lara’s lips curved into a soft smile, and she leaned down, pressing a gentle kiss to Mia’s forehead. “You deserve more than you think, Mia. You always have.”

The sentiment was warm, comforting. They sat like that for a long time, huddled together against the cold, their shared warmth a fragile but unbreakable bond.

As the stars began to appear in the sky above them, Mia shifted slightly, her gaze drifting upward. “Do you think there’s a way out of this?” she asked softly, her voice laced with both hope and fear.

Lara followed her gaze, her own thoughts a tangled mess of uncertainty and determination. “I don’t know,” she admitted. “But I know we’ll figure it out. Together.”

Mia nodded, her hand still resting over Lara’s. “Together,” she echoed—a quiet promise.

And as the night deepened and the cold pressed in, they held onto each other, their growing feelings a flicker of light in the vast, unyielding darkness.

25

Joel Barnes sat at his desk in the dimly lit precinct, the pressure from his superiors bearing down on him like an anvil. The glow of his laptop screen reflected off his glasses as he replayed the latest news segment about Mia and Lara for what felt like the hundredth time. The anchor's voice was sharp, clinical, describing them as fugitives, violent and unpredictable.

He rubbed the bridge of his nose, exhaling a slow, frustrated breath. "They're not killers," he muttered, his voice barely above a whisper.

Enquiries had turned up some interesting facts about the victim, a supposedly upright member of society who according to the bartender that served Trent and Mia that night, was known amongst females in the town as a predator. He had a reputation for treating women roughly but used his connections wisely, namely his uncle who was the mayor and his brother, the deputy sheriff. Victims had given up making complaints about him because it resulted in witch-hunts and even now, they were scared to tell their stories for fear of reprisals.

A knock on the doorframe drew his attention. Nadia Torres leaned against it, arms crossed, a skeptical look on her face.

"Talking to yourself again?" she quipped, though there was no humor in her tone.

Joel leaned back in his chair, the leather creaking under his weight. "If it gets through to someone, maybe it's worth it," he said dryly.

Torres stepped inside, closing the door behind her. "You're not seriously thinking about going public with this, are you?"

Joel raised an eyebrow, his expression sharp. "Someone has to. They're being hunted like animals. If they feel like there's no way out, they'll do something desperate. I don't want to be responsible for that."

Torres sighed, her posture softening slightly. "You really think they'll listen to you? That they're sitting in some cabin, watching the six o'clock news?"

"No," Joel admitted, running a hand through his hair. "But if they hear it somehow, if they know someone out there sees them as more than just criminals, it might make a difference."

Torres didn't reply right away. She studied him, her sharp eyes narrowing. "You really believe they're victims."

Joel's jaw tightened. "Because they are. Mia's running from an abusive man who had complete control over her life. And Lara? She's trying to protect her. If we back them into a corner, we'll be proving them right, proving that the system doesn't care about people like them."

Torres nodded slowly. Her expression unreadable. "Good luck convincing the brass of that."

Later that day, Joel stood in the station's small press room, staring at the microphone in front of him. The local news crew was already setting up, their equipment humming softly in the background. He adjusted his tie, his nerves fraying at the edges as he rehearsed his message in his head.

"Detective Barnes," a gruff voice cut through his thoughts.

Joel turned to see Captain Grayson striding toward him, his face like a storm cloud. "What the hell is this?"

Joel straightened, squaring his shoulders. "I'm making a public plea," he said simply. "Urging them to surrender peacefully."

Grayson's lips curled into a sneer. "Peacefully? These women stabbed a man to death and ran. You think they deserve 'peaceful'?"

"They were defending themselves," Joel shot back, his voice steady but firm. "And the man they stabbed? He was a predator. The evidence is clear."

Grayson took a step closer, lowering his voice. "The evidence is simple; two women killed a man and left him to bleed out. The rest is noise. We're not here to coddle them, Barnes. We're here to bring them in."

"And what happens when we do, huh?" Joel challenged, his eyes narrowing. "You think a jury's going to care about the nuances of their situation? You think the media circus won't paint them as monsters? If we don't give them a chance to come in willingly, this ends badly for everyone."

Grayson's stare was cold, unyielding. "You're letting your emotions cloud your judgment, Detective. Stand down."

Joel's fists clenched at his sides, but he forced himself to stay calm. "I'm trying to prevent this from escalating. We owe them that much."

Grayson snorted, shaking his head. "What we owe them is justice. You want to play the hero? Fine. But this isn't your call."

Despite Grayson's interference, Joel managed to record a brief statement. Standing before the cameras, he kept his tone measured, his words carefully chosen.

"Mia Williams and Lara Edwards," Joel began, his voice steady. "If you're out there, I want you to know we're listening. I know it feels like the world is against you, like there's no way out. But there is. Surrendering doesn't mean giving up. It means giving yourselves a chance to tell your story, to show the truth of who you are."

He paused, meeting the camera head-on. "I know you're scared. I know it feels like no one believes you. But I do. And I'll do everything in my power to make sure you're treated fairly. Please don't let fear drive you into a corner. You deserve more than this."

A hush settled over the room as he stepped away from the microphone. He hadn't expected applause, but the absence of any reaction still stung. From the doorway, Grayson watched, his expression unreadable. But Joel didn't need to hear the man's words to know exactly what he was thinking.

Back in his office, Joel slumped into his chair, exhaustion settling over him like a blanket. He stared at his phone, the screen dark and silent, and wondered if his words would ever reach the two women he was trying so hard to protect. Somewhere out there, Mia and Lara were still running, their lives unraveling with every mile. He didn't know if they had heard him.

But he hoped more than anything that they had. Because if they didn't come in soon, Joel knew he might not be able to stop what was coming.

By morning, his plea was everywhere. News outlets dissected his words with the precision of a scalpel, slicing them into fragments and twisting them to fit their own narratives. The more conservative networks splashed Mia and Lara's faces across their screens, branding them as dangerous fugitives who had seduced public sympathy. Anchors spoke with sharp-edged disdain, calling them manipulative, their every move calculated to evade justice.

"A tragic tale of trust betrayed," one host declared solemnly.

"These women have exploited the kindness of strangers to further their escape."

Other outlets swung the pendulum in the opposite direction, casting Mia and Lara as tragic figures caught in a relentless battle for survival. Grainy photos of Mia's bruised face and Lara's steely, protective stance played on an endless loop, interspersed with tearful testimonials from so-called experts on trauma and domestic violence.

"These women are symbols of defiance," a morning show anchor declared with unflinching confidence. "They represent the countless victims silenced by the very systems meant to protect them."

And then there was social media—an all-out battleground.

Hashtags like #RunMiaRun and #JusticeForTrent trended simultaneously, each one igniting its own war in the comment threads. Some users posted images of bruised fists and black eyes, sharing their own stories of survival, hailing Mia and Lara as heroines. Others played armchair detective, scrutinizing every detail of the case, branding the women as grifters, manipulators, and murderers.

Joel sat in his office, watching the coverage with a sinking feeling in his gut. He'd tried to humanize them, to remind the world that they weren't villains or martyrs, just two people caught in an impossible situation. Instead, they had become symbols. Distorted. Dehumanized. Their stories no longer their own.

Across the border, in a small grocery store on the outskirts of a quiet Canadian town, Patricia stood in front of a rack of newspapers. Her sharp green eyes flicked over the headlines, her stomach twisting as familiar faces stared back at her.

"On the Run: The Fugitive Women Capturing a Nation's Attention."

Beneath it, a smaller subheading posed the question: "Abused Victims or Calculating Criminals?"

Patricia's lips pressed into a thin line as she snatched the paper from the rack, flipping through the pages. The article inside rehashed every known detail of the case, spinning theories about the women's motives and speculating on their whereabouts. Dramatic phrases leapt off the page, "a modern-day Bonnie and Clyde" and "a story that has divided the nation."

Her stomach churned. Their suffering had been twisted into entertainment.

She could almost hear Lara's voice, sharp and defiant, pushing back against this narrative. She imagined Mia, quiet and overwhelmed, shrinking under the glare of so much scrutiny.

Patricia's heart ached for them. They were out there somewhere, cold, hungry, hunted, while strangers dissected their lives from the comfort of their living rooms. Patricia folded the newspaper under her arm and made her way to the register, her thoughts all over the place. The young cashier gave her a friendly smile as he rang her up, but she barely noticed. Her mind was elsewhere, replaying the brief time she'd spent with Mia and Lara, the raw vulnerability in their eyes, the quiet desperation in their voices.

Back at her cabin, Patricia set the newspaper on the counter and pulled the envelope from her pocket, the one addressed to Noah Williams. She held it delicately, her thumb brushing over the slightly smudged ink of Mia's handwriting. She could still hear Mia's voice, trembling as she spoke of her son, her love for him shining through layers of fear and exhaustion.

Patricia sank into the small wooden chair by the window, the envelope still in her hands. Outside, the forest was quiet, snow falling softly, blanketing the world in a deceptive calm. She thought about the women. Their bravery, their pain. She thought about how they had clung to each other in her cabin, how Lara's sharp protectiveness balanced Mia's quiet fragility. And she thought about Noah. A boy she'd never met yet already felt connected to through the words his mother had poured onto paper.

"I'll keep it safe," Patricia murmured, her voice barely audible over the fire's steady crackle. "Until the time is right."

She tucked the envelope into a drawer, closing it carefully as though the fragility of its contents might shatter. Then she stood, her jaw set with quiet determination. Whatever happened next was beyond her control. But this, this she could control. She could make sure Mia's voice reached her son when the world finally quieted enough for him to hear it.

Patricia glanced at the newspaper one last time before folding it and tucking it into the firewood basket. It didn't deserve space on her counter. The truth wasn't in those headlines, no matter how loudly they shouted. The truth was in that letter, in the love Mia had for her son. And Patricia vowed to carry it carefully, until the time was right.

26

The town was smaller than they'd expected. A cluster of tired buildings leaning into one another, as if barely able to withstand the relentless wind sweeping in from the water. The air carried the sharp tang of salt and rust, and a cold drizzle seeped from the slate-gray sky, soaking into their clothes and chilling them to the bone.

In the distance, the ferry terminal loomed, its hulking white shape tethered to the dock. Even from here, Mia could see the long line of cars and pedestrians queued up to board. It might as well have been a thousand miles away.

Mia pulled her jacket tighter, shivering as they ducked into the shadow of a narrow alley between a closed diner and what looked like an abandoned hardware store. Every step sent a dull ache through her legs; the soles of her boots were worn thin from days of walking. Her stomach growled loud enough to make Lara glance over.

"You okay?" Lara asked, her voice low and tight.

Mia nodded, but the truth lodged in her chest. She wasn't okay, not even close. She was starving, freezing, and so exhausted she could barely think straight.

Her reflection in the cracked diner window confirmed what she already knew: she looked as bad as she felt. Pale skin, limp, unwashed hair, clothes hanging off her frame like they belonged to someone else.

"What's the plan?" Mia asked, her voice hoarse.

Lara leaned against the damp brick wall; arms crossed as she stared out at the street. Rain dripped from her dark hair, clinging to her face, but her eyes remained sharp and calculating despite the deep shadows beneath them.

"We need tickets for that ferry," she said, her voice steady. "Which means we need money."

Mia swallowed hard, her stomach twisting. "We don't have money, Lara."

"I know." Lara's jaw tightened. She turned to look at Mia, and for a fleeting moment, her expression softened just enough to remind her that beneath all that steel, Lara was just as scared as she was.

"Stay here," Lara murmured. "I'll figure it out."

Mia's brow furrowed, unease prickling at the back of her neck. "What do you mean, 'figure it out'? What are you going to do?"

Lara didn't answer right away. She pulled up her hood, her gaze flicking to the street as if she were already mapping out her next move.

"Just stay out of sight," she said finally. "I'll be back."

"Lara..." Mia started, but Lara cut her off.

"I'll be back," she repeated, her voice firm. "Don't do anything stupid. And whatever you do, don't let anyone see you."

Mia opened her mouth to argue, but the look in Lara's eyes stopped her. It wasn't anger—it was something rawer, something desperate.

She swallowed hard, nodding reluctantly. "Okay."

Mia watched as Lara slipped out of the alley, vanishing into the rain-soaked street with a quiet confidence that made her wonder if she'd done this before. The thought unsettled her, but there was no time to dwell on it.

She turned and sank down behind a rusting dumpster, the cold metal biting into her back as she hugged her knees to her chest.

The alley reeked of rotting food and decay, the kind of place that made her skin crawl, but it was safer than being out in the open. She rested her head on her knees, her breath curling in the frigid air, and tried to ignore the gnawing ache in her stomach.

Rain pattered against the pavement, punctuated by the occasional rumble of a passing car. Nearby, a seagull let out a shrill cry, its wings flapping as it swooped down to scavenge for scraps. The town felt both alive and abandoned, a strange mix of movement and decay. The buildings were weather-beaten, their paint peeling, their windows clouded with grime. Even the people who passed by seemed worn down, their heads bowed against the wind, their faces etched with a weariness that came from more than just a long day.

Mia's thoughts drifted to Noah, as they so often did. She pictured him at home, sitting at the kitchen table with his laptop, earbuds in, his hair falling into his eyes the way it always did when he was focused. He'd push it back absently—just as she used to when he was little—and the memory made her chest ache. Was he thinking about her? Was he worried? Or had Dane already poisoned him against her, twisting the truth until Noah didn't know what to believe?

Tears pricked at her eyes, and she pressed her face harder against her knees, willing them away. She didn't have time to cry, not here, not now. But the thought clung to her, gnawing at her like the hunger in her belly.

What if I just turned myself in? The thought came unbidden, sharp and unwelcome. It wasn't the first time it had crossed her mind, but now, sitting here in the freezing rain with no money, no food, and no plan, it felt more tempting than ever. At least then, Noah would know she was alive. At least then, she wouldn't have to keep running.

But then, there was Lara. Lara, who had fought so hard to protect her, who had carried them both even as the strain threatened to break her. Turning herself in would mean betraying her—leaving her to face this nightmare alone.

And that was something Mia couldn't do.

The minutes dragged on, each one stretching unbearably until Mia lost all sense of time. Her legs cramped from being curled up for so long, and she shifted uncomfortably, casting another glance toward the mouth of the alley, half-expecting to see Lara emerging from the rain. But the street remained empty.

She squeezed her eyes shut, her fingers digging into her knees as the downpour seeped through her clothes, leeching the last remnants of warmth from her body. The cold was merciless, creeping into her bones, tightening around her like a vice. She tried to focus on her breathing, to stop herself from spiraling but fear lingered just beneath the surface, waiting to swallow her whole.

A sudden noise shattered the quiet, a distant shout, followed by the muffled thud of hurried footsteps. Mia's heart shot to her throat. She pressed herself tighter against the dumpster, holding her breath as she strained to listen. But the sounds faded as quickly as they had come, swallowed by the rain.

Finally, Lara emerged from the shadows, her hair plastered to her face by the relentless drizzle, a fistful of crumpled dollar bills clutched tightly in her hand. Her eyes flicked around the alley before locking onto Mia, who remained huddled behind the dumpster, knees drawn to her chest. Without a word, Lara crouched in front of her and held out the money, her jaw rigid with a tension that made Mia's stomach twist.

"Where did you get that?" Mia whispered, concern threading through her exhaustion. Her weary eyes searched Lara's face, trying to piece together what she wasn't saying.

"Don't ask." Lara's reply was sharp, but her hands trembled slightly as she shoved the bills into her pocket. Her tone softened just enough as she added, "We needed it, okay? Let's go. You need food, and I'm not arguing about it."

Mia hesitated, her gut screaming at her to push for answers. But the gnawing hunger in her belly and the deep ache in her limbs won out. She nodded reluctantly, pulling herself to her feet as Lara reached out, steadying her with a firm grip.

Together, they stepped out of the alley, the diner's neon sign glowing through the foggy gloom ahead.

The diner was the kind of place that had seen better decades. Its vinyl booths cracked, its laminate tables sticky despite the persistent scent of lemon cleaner hanging in the air. A faded chalkboard behind the counter listed the day's specials in smeared handwriting, the words "Meatloaf Monday" barely legible.

Warmth wrapped around them as Mia and Lara stepped inside, a jarring contrast to the cold, wet world outside. A dozen pairs of eyes flicked toward them, wary and brief, before quickly looking away.

The bell above the entrance jingled as the door swung shut, and Mia shivered, the dampness clinging to her skin making her feel colder than she should. She scanned the room, taking in the handful of patrons hunched over coffee mugs and plates of greasy hash browns. No one seemed overly interested in them, but the tension in her shoulders refused to ease.

Lara led the way to a booth in the back corner, her stride purposeful despite the exhaustion etched into her face. Mia followed silently, her stomach twisting as the scent of fried bacon and fresh-brewed coffee wrapped around her like a cruel taunt. They slid into the booth, the cracked vinyl groaning beneath them. Lara immediately grabbed the menu, her eyes darting over it as if memorizing the prices.

"*We'll just share something*," she muttered, more to herself than to Mia. "*Eggs and toast, maybe*. Cheap and filling."

Mia nodded numbly, placing her hands on the table to keep them from trembling. Her nails were dirty, her skin raw and dry, and she resisted the urge to tug her sleeves down to hide them.

The waitress, an older woman with graying hair and a kind but tired face approached with a pot of coffee in one hand and a pad of paper in the other. She gave them a quick once-over, her gaze lingering just a second too long on their worn clothes before offering a polite smile.

"*What can I get you girls*?" she asked, her voice as warm as the coffee she poured into the mugs in front of them.

"Just eggs and toast," Lara said quickly, folding the menu and sliding it to the edge of the table. "*Thanks*."

The waitress nodded, her expression softening. "I'll be right back."

As she walked away, Mia wrapped her hands around the mug, letting the heat seep into her frozen fingers. She lifted it to her lips, the bitter liquid burning her throat in the most satisfying way. For a brief moment, she allowed herself to feel human again, warm, fed, sheltered. Even if it wouldn't last.

The moment shattered when the radio behind the counter crackled to life, cutting through the low murmur of the diner with the sharp, clipped voice of a news anchor.

"Authorities are continuing their search for two women believed to be connected to a fatal stabbing in the United States. Sources confirm that a SWAT team has been deployed to assist in the manhunt, which has now crossed into Canadian territory..."

Mia froze, her coffee mug trembling in her hands. She didn't dare look at Lara. She didn't need to. Lara's sudden stillness, the rigid set of her shoulders, told her everything.

The anchor's voice droned on, each word tightening like a noose around Mia's throat.

"...described as armed and dangerous, the suspects are considered a threat to public safety. Anyone with information is urged to contact authorities immediately..."

Lara moved first. Without a word, she slid out of the booth, her movements swift but controlled. She grabbed her mug and downed the rest of her coffee in a single gulp, then tossed a crumpled bill onto the table.

"Let's go," she murmured, her voice low but firm.

Mia followed without question; her legs stiff as they made their way to the door. The other patrons watched them, but no one spoke, their curiosity overshadowed by an unspoken discomfort. As the bell jingled behind them, Mia couldn't shake the feeling that each step they took left a trail for someone to follow.

The walk to the port felt endless, the drizzle turning to sleet as they trudged along the narrow road. The air reeked of brine and diesel, the sound of waves slapping against the docks growing louder with every step. Mia's chest tightened as they neared the terminal, her gaze flicking nervously to the clusters of people milling about with suitcases and backpacks.

Lara's pace quickened; her focus locked on the ticket counter just inside the small terminal building. Fluorescent light spilled onto the pavement, streaking the wet ground in pale yellow. Mia hesitated, lingering in the shadows at the building's edge, her heart pounding as she watched Lara disappear inside.

Minutes crawled by like hours. The cold seeped deeper into her bones, her damp clothes clinging like a second skin. She shifted her weight from one foot to the other, unease twisting in her stomach. Finally, Lara emerged, pale and drawn, her hands empty.

"It's gone," she said, her voice hollow. "The ferry's gone."

They walked to the dock's edge, their footsteps muffled against the wet wood. The ferry was little more than a distant shape now, its lights faint and flickering on the horizon. The water between them and their escape stretched endlessly, dark and unyielding, and for the first time, their situation felt truly inescapable.

Mia stared after it, her breath hitching as tears blurred her vision. The ferry grew smaller and smaller, its shape dissolving into the mist until it vanished, swallowed by the vast expanse of the sea.

Lara stood beside her, jaw tight, fists clenched at her sides. She didn't speak, but the tension radiating from her was palpable. An unspoken admission that this was a blow they might not recover from. The wind howled around them, carrying the scent of salt and failure. Mia wrapped her arms around herself, shivering as she fought to keep the tears at bay. But it was no use. They slipped free, tracing silent paths down her cheeks as she stood there, watching the ferry vanish into the unknown.

Lara shifted slightly, her shoulder brushing against Mia's in the faintest gesture of solidarity. They didn't speak, didn't need to. The reality of their situation sinking in like the cold seeping into their skin.

And as the waves lapped at the dock's edge, relentless and indifferent, they stood in silence, their dreams of escape drifting further and further away, leaving them stranded in a world they no longer recognized.

27

The road out of town was empty, save for the occasional rusted car abandoned on the shoulder or a scattering of trash caught in the wind. The drizzle had turned into a steady rain, soaking through their already-damp clothes and clinging to their skin like a second, colder layer. Behind them, the town disappeared into the mist that clung low to the trees, while ahead, the mountains loomed dark and jagged against the gray sky.

Lara walked in front, shoulders squared against the chill, each step purposeful despite the exhaustion tugging at her limbs. Her boots crunched against the gravel. The sound eerily loud in the quiet of the wilderness. Mia followed a few paces behind, arms wrapped tightly around herself, head bowed against the rain. Every step sent a fresh ache through her legs, her stomach hollow with hunger, but she didn't complain. There was no point.

The farther they walked, the narrower the road became, the trees seeming closer until it felt as if the forest were swallowing them whole. A thick fog clung to the ground, swirling around their ankles as if it had a mind of its own.

"How much farther?" Mia asked after what felt like hours, her voice barely audible over the rain.

Lara glanced back. Her face unreadable beneath the hood of her jacket. "Not far," she said, though the doubt edging her tone betrayed her.

Mia nodded, not trusting herself to speak. She kept her gaze on the ground, watching the way water pooled in the uneven cracks of the road, her thoughts drifting to the letter she'd written to Noah. She could still see it clearly in her mind. The shaky handwriting, the way her fingers had trembled as she folded it into the envelope.

Dear Noah, she'd written, the words coming easier than she'd expected once she started. *I need you to know how much I love you. How much I've always loved you, even when I haven't been able to show it.*

Her chest tightened, breath hitching as she imagined him reading it, his brow furrowing the way it always did when he was upset. She wondered if Patricia had sent it yet, if Noah had held it in his hands, if he understood how desperately she wished she could have been better for him. A sob threatened to escape, but she swallowed it down, forcing herself to focus on the present, on the endless road and the woman walking ahead of her, who had given up just as much to be here.

The road ended abruptly, giving way to a narrow dirt path that cut into the base of the mountains. The terrain was rough, the ground uneven and slick with mud, and the incline steeper than either of them had anticipated. Mia hesitated, her gaze tracing the trail as it vanished into a dense wall of fog.

"Are you sure about this?" she asked, her voice trembling with something more than just the cold.

Lara turned to her, expression hard but not unkind. "Do we have another choice?"

Mia shook her head, biting her lip as she fought back the panic threatening to consume her. "No," she admitted quietly.

"Then we keep moving," Lara said, her voice firm but steady. She stepped onto the trail, her boots sinking slightly into the wet earth. "One step at a time."

Mia followed, her legs trembling with the effort of climbing, her lungs burning as the altitude took its toll. The rain turned to sleet as they ascended, icy pellets stinging her face and hands, but she didn't stop. She couldn't. The alternative was unthinkable.

The mountains were both beautiful and unforgiving, their peaks shrouded in mist, their slopes treacherous and unyielding. As they climbed, the trees thinned, giving way to rocky outcrops and patches of frozen ground that crunched beneath their boots. The wind howled through the valleys, carrying a bone-deep chill that made Mia's teeth chatter despite the scarf wrapped tightly around her face.

Lara paused at the crest of a hill, hands on her knees as she caught her breath. She glanced back at Mia, her brow furrowing as she took in the way Mia's shoulders shook, her face pale and drawn. "You okay?" she asked, her voice rough with exertion.

Mia nodded, though the truth was written all over her face. She wasn't okay. None of this was okay. But there was no room for weakness, not here, not now. "I'm fine," she said, though the words felt hollow even as they left her lips.

Lara didn't push her, didn't say anything more. She just reached out a hand, and when Mia took it, she held on tightly, pulling her up the last few feet of the incline.

By the time night fell, the sleet had turned to snow, the flakes swirling around them in a chaotic dance that made it nearly impossible to see more than a few feet ahead. The trail had all but vanished, leaving them to navigate by instinct and sheer determination. Every step felt heavier than the last, their bodies screaming for rest, for warmth—for anything but this endless climb.

Mia stumbled, her knee buckling as she caught herself against a rock. Lara was there in an instant, slipping an arm around Mia's waist to steady her.

"I've got you," she said, her voice softer now, her strength unwavering even as exhaustion threatened to pull her under.

"I don't think I can do this," Mia admitted, her voice barely more than a whisper. Tears streamed down her face, freezing on her cheeks before they could fall. "I don't think I can make it."

"Yes, you can," Lara said fiercely, her grip tightening. "We're almost there. Just a little farther."

Mia nodded, though her heart felt as heavy as the pack on her back. She thought of Noah again, his laugh, his smile, the way he used to wrap his arms around her and tell her everything would be okay. She clung to that memory like a lifeline, using it to push herself forward when every part of her wanted to collapse.

As the snow thickened, the wind howled louder, and the mountains loomed higher, the fragile thread of hope they clung to began to fray, threatening to snap with every passing moment.

Mia's legs burned with every step, her boots slipping on the snow-covered rocks as they pressed deeper into the wilderness. The mountains stretched endlessly, their jagged peaks cutting into the steel-gray sky. Snow blanketed the ground in a treacherous layer of ice, slowing their progress to a painful crawl. Every breath Mia took felt sharp, like inhaling shards of glass, and her fingers were numb despite the gloves she wore.

Lara walked a few steps ahead, her focus unyielding as she scanned the path for any semblance of shelter. The desperation of their situation hung between them, unspoken but palpable. Every now and then, she glanced back to make sure Mia was still following. Her jaw was tight, her eyes shadowed with exhaustion, but she didn't falter.

"We'll rest soon," Lara said, her voice barely audible over the wind. "I just need to find somewhere safe."

Mia nodded, though every part of her body screamed for her to stop. The hope she'd clung to earlier, fragile as it was, had begun to unravel with every freezing gust of wind and every aching step. She thought again of Noah, of the letter she'd written, and wondered if he'd ever read it. The thought was the only thing keeping her moving.

The trail curved sharply, revealing a narrow ledge that clung to the mountainside. Below them, the valley stretched endlessly, a vast expanse of white dotted with clusters of pine trees and shrouded in mist. Mia hesitated, her stomach twisting as she looked down at the steep drop, but Lara extended a hand, steady and unwavering.

"You've got this," Lara said, her voice firm yet reassuring.

Mia swallowed hard, her heart pounding as she took Lara's hand and stepped onto the ledge. The wind lashed at her face, threatening to throw her off balance, but Lara's grip was strong, anchoring her. Step by step, they edged along the precarious path, their breaths shallow, their movements cautious.

When they finally reached the other side, Mia collapsed onto a rock, her body trembling from more than just the cold. Lara knelt beside her, pulled a bottle of water from her pack, and pressed it into Mia's hands.

"Drink," Lara said, her tone leaving no room for argument.

Mia obeyed, the cold water soothing her parched throat even as a shiver ran through her. She looked up at Lara, her voice unsteady as she asked, "How much longer can we do this?"

Lara didn't answer right away. She sat down beside Mia, her gaze fixed on the horizon where the sun dipped below the mountains, casting the snow in hues of soft pink and gold.

"As long as we have to," she said finally, her voice quiet but resolute.

~

Back in town, the diner was eerily quiet, its usual buzz of conversation replaced by the sharp voices of police officers and the static crackle of their radios. The waitress, the same older woman who had served Mia and Lara hours earlier, stood behind the counter, her hands twisting nervously in her apron as she answered their questions.

"They came in for a bit," she said, her voice trembling slightly. "Eggs and toast, that's all they had. Didn't say much. Looked... tired."

Detective Joel Barnes stood nearby, arms crossed, listening intently. His sharp eyes swept the room, noting every detail, the half-empty coffee cups still sitting on the corner table, the damp footprints trailing out the door. His gut twisted, frustration and unease gnawing at him.

They were close. Too close.

"Which direction did they go when they left?" Joel asked, his tone calm but urgent.

The waitress hesitated, her eyes flicking toward the door as if the answer might still be out there. "I don't know," she admitted. "They didn't stay long. Paid cash, kept their heads down. Seemed... nervous."

"Did they talk to anyone?" another officer asked, pen poised over his notepad.

"No," she said quickly. "Just each other. And even then, not much."

Joel's jaw tightened, his mind racing as he pieced together the fragments of information. They were running on instinct, making decisions out of desperation. That much was clear. But where would they go from here? The ferry was the logical choice, but if they didn't have tickets...

"Check the terminal," Joel said, turning to one of the officers. "If they made it onto that ferry, I want confirmation. If they didn't, find out where they went next."

The officer nodded and hurried out the door.

Joel turned back to the waitress. "Thank you," he said, his voice softer now. "If you remember anything else, anything at all, please call me."

She nodded, though unease still lingered in her expression. Joel couldn't blame her. Things like this didn't happen in quiet towns like this.

Stepping outside, he was met with a blast of cold wind, sharp enough to steal his breath. He pulled his coat tighter, his gaze sweeping the darkening streets. The sun was setting, stretching long shadows across the wet pavement, and he couldn't shake the feeling that time was slipping through his fingers.

They were out there—somewhere in the wilderness—and with every passing moment, the odds of finding them alive grew slimmer.

28

The snow was endless, a white curtain that blurred the edges of the world and muffled all but the howling wind. Each step felt heavier than the last, the cold seeping into their bones, draining what little strength they had left. Lara trudged forward, her breath escaping in short, uneven puffs, her legs burning from the relentless climb. Every so often, she glanced back at Mia, who lagged a few steps behind, her face pale and drawn.

"We can't keep going like this," Lara said at last, her voice barely carrying over the wind. She stopped, turning to face Mia, whose shoulders sagged with exhaustion. "We need to stop. Just for a little while."

Mia nodded wordlessly, her lips trembling as she fought back tears. She buried her hands deeper into her jacket pockets, her fingers numb despite the gloves. Lifting her gaze, she stared up at the mountains towering above them, their jagged peaks swallowed by the swirling snow. A pang of hopelessness stabbed through her chest.

Lara scanned the landscape, her sharp eyes narrowing as she spotted a cluster of rocks forming a shallow alcove at the base of a hill. It wasn't much, but it was better than nothing. "Over there," she said, nodding toward it. "It'll block the wind."

Mia didn't reply, but she followed as Lara led the way, her boots slipping on the icy ground. When they reached the rocks, Lara knelt, brushing away the snow with stiff fingers to carve out a small space for them to huddle. She glanced up at Mia, her voice softer now. "Come here. You're freezing."

Mia hesitated, arms wrapped tightly around herself, before finally sinking down beside Lara. The cold stone beneath her seemed to leech what little warmth she had left. Without hesitation, Lara wrapped an arm around her, pulling her close. Mia let out a shaky breath, her body trembling against Lara's.

They sat for a while, the snow piling up around them, the wind howling like a wounded animal. Lara's arm tightened around Mia, her fingers brushing lightly against her shoulder, an unspoken reassurance that she wasn't alone. But Mia couldn't stop the tears that slipped down her cheeks, hot against her freezing skin.

"I'm so sorry," Mia whispered, her voice barely audible. She buried her face in Lara's shoulder, her tears soaking into the fabric of her jacket. "For all of it. For dragging you into this mess. For everything."

Lara stiffened slightly, her jaw tightening. "Mia, don't," she said, her voice low but firm.

"I mean it," Mia insisted, her voice cracking. She pulled back just enough to meet Lara's eyes, her own shimmering with guilt and pain. "If I hadn't gone off with Trent, if I'd just listened to you..."

"Mia, stop," Lara interrupted, her tone sharper now. She cupped Mia's face with both hands, her fingers cold but steady. "What happened wasn't your fault. None of it. Trent..." Her voice faltered, and she swallowed hard, her eyes darkening with anger.

"Trent was a monster. And I should've been there. I should've stopped you."

Mia shook her head, fresh tears spilling over. "You couldn't have known. I was so stupid, Lara. So stupid."

"You weren't stupid," Lara said fiercely. "You were hurt, lost, and just trying to forget, for one night. That doesn't make what he did your fault."

A sob tore through Mia, her chest heaving as she clung to Lara. "I don't know how to do this anymore," she admitted, her voice breaking. "I don't know how to keep going."

Lara's own eyes burned with unshed tears, but she held Mia tightly, her thumb brushing lightly over her cheek. "You don't have to do it alone," she said softly. "You never have to do it alone. I've got you, Mia. I always have."

Mia's breath hitched, her tears slowing as she looked up at Lara, her expression raw and vulnerable. "Why?" she asked, her voice trembling. "Why do you even care? After everything, why haven't you given up on me?"

Lara hesitated, her throat tightening as she searched for the words. "Because I love you," she said finally, her voice barely above a whisper. "I've always loved you, Mia. Even when I didn't know how to say it. Even when I thought you'd never feel the same."

Mia stared at her, her chest tightening with an emotion so overwhelming she could barely breathe. "*You love me*?" she whispered, as if the words were too fragile to say aloud.

Lara nodded, her gaze steady despite the tears shimmering in her eyes. "*I love you*," she repeated, her voice stronger now. "I always have."

Mia let out a soft, broken laugh, her lips trembling as she reached up to touch Lara's face. "*I love you too*," she said, her voice laced with emotion. "*I'm sorry it took me so long to figure it out*. I was so scared, Lara. Of everything. Of what it meant. Of losing you."

Lara leaned in, pressing her forehead against Mia's, her breath warm against her cheek. "*You're not going to lose me*," she murmured. "*Not now. Not ever.*"

Their lips met in a kiss that was soft and hesitant at first, but it deepened quickly, carrying all the emotions they'd held back for so long. *Desperation. Relief. Love that had survived the storm.*

When they pulled apart, the wind seemed quieter, the world around them shrinking to just this moment. Mia rested her head against Lara's shoulder, her body trembling as she whispered, "*I don't think we're going to make it out of this*."

Lara's jaw tightened, but she didn't argue. Instead, she pulled Mia closer, her voice steady as she said, "*If this is the end, then we face it together*."

Mia closed her eyes, silent tears spilling as she clung to Lara like a lifeline. The snow continued to fall, covering them in a fragile layer of white, but for the first time in what felt like forever, she didn't feel alone.

They had nothing left to hold onto but each other. The snow kept falling, softening the edges of the world as if nature itself were trying to ease the harshness of their reality. Mia felt Lara's heartbeat through her jacket, steady, strong, a rhythm that reminded her she wasn't alone.

She lifted her head, her tear-streaked face pale but resolute as she met Lara's gaze. "We can't just sit here," she said, her voice trembling but firm. "If we stay, we'll freeze. We'll... we'll die."

Lara's eyes softened, her hands still cradling Mia's face. "I know," she murmured. "But if we move, there's no guarantee we'll survive either."

Mia swallowed hard. Her throat tight. "Maybe not. But if we keep going, at least we'll have tried. At least we won't just... give up."

Lara studied Mia for a long moment, her expression a mix of admiration and heartbreak. Despite everything, despite the fear, the pain, and the overwhelming odds, Mia still had fight left in her. And that fight, fragile as it was, sparked something in Lara she hadn't felt in days: hope.

"You're right," Lara said, her voice steadier now. "We keep moving. We don't stop. Not until we can't take another step."

Mia reached for her hand, their fingers intertwining in a silent exchange of resolve. The fear was still there, lurking beneath the surface, but it no longer felt insurmountable. Together, they could face it—whatever it turned out to be.

Slowly, they rose, their bodies stiff and aching from the cold. Lara tightened the straps on her pack, her movements deliberate as she glanced at Mia. "We stick to the trees," she said, nodding toward the dark line of forest hugging the mountainside. "The snow will slow us down, but it'll hide our tracks. If we can make it to the next ridge, we might find shelter."

Mia nodded, pulling her jacket tighter around her as she stepped out from beneath the rocks. The wind hit her like a slap, but she squared her shoulders, refusing to let it break her. She glanced back at the small hollow they'd shared, watching as the imprint of their bodies was already being swallowed by snow. A shiver ran through her, one that had nothing to do with the cold.

Lara stepped beside her, her hand brushing against Mia's. "*Ready*?"

Mia met her gaze, the fear in her eyes tempered by determination. "*Ready*."

The forest was silent except for the crunch of snow beneath their boots and the occasional crack of a branch underfoot. The trees loomed around them, their tall, skeletal forms casting long shadows in the fading light. The ground was uneven, the snow concealing rocks and roots that lurked beneath, waiting to trip them. But they kept moving, their pace steady but cautious.

As they walked, Mia's mind drifted to the letter she'd written to Noah. She pictured him holding it, his hands steady despite the starkness of her words. She hoped Patricia had sent it, that he'd read it and understood, *really understood*, how much she loved him. A lump rose in her throat, but she swallowed it down, focusing instead on the steady rhythm of her steps and the quiet warmth of Lara's presence beside her.

"What do you think happens to people like us?" Mia asked suddenly, her voice soft but clear in the stillness of the forest.

Lara glanced at her, brow furrowing slightly. "What do you mean?"

"People who've... lost everything," Mia said, her gaze fixed on the path ahead. "Who've done things they can't take back. Do we ever... get to come back from it?"

Lara was silent for a moment, her expression thoughtful. "I don't know," she admitted. "But I think... as long as we're still breathing, there's a chance. Maybe not to go back to who we were, but to become something else. Someone else."

Mia considered this, her steps slowing as she absorbed Lara's words. "Do you think we deserve that chance?"

Lara stopped, turning to face her. The wind tugged at her hair, snow clinging to her lashes as she looked at Mia with an intensity that stole her breath. "I don't know if we deserve it," Lara admitted, her voice raw. "But I know that you do. And if I have to keep fighting for both of us, I will."

Mia's chest tightened, emotion swelling inside her. Her tears threatened to spill again, but she blinked them away, nodding as she reached for Lara's hand. "Then we keep going," she said softly. "Together."

They pressed on, the wind howling around them as they climbed higher into the mountains. The snow was blinding now, a swirling tempest that swallowed the world in white, making it nearly impossible to see more than a few feet ahead. But the rhythm of their steps, the steady grip of Lara's hand in hers, kept Mia moving forward.

The sky deepened to an inky black, the temperature plummeting as night fell over the mountains. Their breaths came in short, visible puffs, their bodies trembling from cold and exhaustion. Yet, with each step, a quiet acceptance settled over them. A fragile peace in the face of the inevitable. They might not make it out alive, but whatever came next, they would face it together.

Lara glanced at Mia, her lips curving into the faintest hint of a smile despite the pain carved into her features. "You're stronger than you think, you know that?"

Mia let out a soft, breathless laugh, her fingers tightening around Lara's. "Only because I have you."

The wind howled, snow swirling in chaotic spirals around them, but they didn't stop. They didn't look back. And as the darkness swallowed the world whole, they clung to each other, their resolve the only light in an endless night.

29

The sharp whir of helicopter blades shattered the mountain's eerie stillness, slicing through the howling wind like a warning bell. Lara froze, her breath hitching as the sound grew louder, reverberating in the cold, thin air. She turned to Mia, her face pale beneath layers of grime and exhaustion, her eyes wide with alarm.

"Do you hear that?" Lara asked, though the question was pointless, the noise was impossible to miss.

Mia's heart slammed against her ribs as she nodded, her gaze snapping toward the slate-gray sky. The trees around them swayed violently in the ferocious wind, their skeletal branches groaning under the weight of ice and snow. The sound grew closer, deeper, vibrating through the frozen ground beneath their feet.

"They're looking for us," Mia whispered, her voice trembling as she instinctively stepped closer to Lara.

Lara grabbed Mia's arm, her grip firm despite the cold that had seeped into her fingers. "*We need to move,*" she said, her voice low but urgent. Scanning the terrain, her eyes narrowed as she spotted a dense copse of trees about fifty yards ahead. "There. Under the canopy. Go."

Mia hesitated for only a fraction of a second before nodding, her legs already burning as she followed Lara's lead. The snow was deep, their boots sinking with each step, and the icy wind bit at their faces but the fear of being found drove them forward.

The copse of trees offered the illusion of safety, their thick, frost-covered branches knitting together like a natural shield. The ground beneath was uneven, littered with roots and patches of ice, but the snow wasn't as deep here. Lara motioned for Mia to crouch behind a fallen log, dropping to her knees beside her, her chest heaving.

The helicopter's roar grew deafening, the sound bouncing off the mountain's rocky slopes and echoing through the narrow valley below. Mia pressed her back against the log, her breath shallow, fingers clutching the fabric of her jacket in trembling hands.

Lara's eyes flicked upward; her jaw tight as she tracked the helicopter's shadow through gaps in the trees. Its searchlight cut through the darkness, a piercing beam slicing across the forest, illuminating patches of snow in harsh white light.

"Stay low," Lara whispered, her voice barely audible over the noise. She reached out, her hand finding Mia's and squeezing tightly.

Mia's pulse thundered in her ears, her entire body trembling as the beam swept closer, its bright light creeping toward them, illuminating the snow just yards away. She couldn't breathe, couldn't think, her mind consumed by the terrifying possibility that they were about to be found.

"What do we do if they see us?" Mia asked, her whisper barely contained.

"They won't," Lara said firmly, though the tight grip on Mia's hand betrayed the fear she was trying to hide. "Just stay quiet."

The searchlight swept past them, shadows dancing wildly across the snow as the helicopter's blades churned the air above. The sound was oppressive, but the beam moved on, cutting through the trees before vanishing deeper into the forest.

Mia let out a shaky breath, her eyes fluttering shut as relief washed over her. "I think they're moving away," she whispered, her voice barely more than a breath.

Lara didn't respond right away. Her gaze stayed locked on the sky, her body tense, coiled like a spring. "Not yet," she murmured. "They're still close."

As if on cue, the sound shifted—the helicopter circling back toward them. The searchlight cut through the trees again, its beam sweeping the ground in wide arcs. Lara ducked lower, pulling Mia down with her, their bodies pressed tightly together behind the log.

Mia's heart pounded so loudly she was sure it would give them away. She clutched Lara's jacket, her nails digging into the fabric as she buried her face against Lara's shoulder. "Lara..."

"I know," Lara whispered, her voice steady despite the tension radiating from her. "I know."

The searchlight passed over them again, lingering on the branches above before moving on. This time, the roar of the helicopter blades began to fade, the sound growing softer as it veered away from the copse.

They didn't move. Didn't breathe. They waited until the noise was nothing more than a faint whirring in the distance. Even then, Lara kept them crouched behind the log, her body rigid, ears straining for any sign it might return.

When she was finally satisfied, she let out a slow, shaky breath, her muscles loosening slightly. "It's gone," she said, though the words carried little relief.

Mia nodded. Her head still buried against Lara's shoulder. "For now," she murmured.

Lara pulled back just enough to meet her eyes, her expression grave. "They know we're in the mountains," she said. "It's only a matter of time before they close in."

Mia's stomach twisted, fear bubbling to the surface. "What do we do?"

"We keep moving," Lara said, her voice firm. She glanced toward the deeper forest, jaw tightening. "We can't stay in one place for long. Not now."

Mia nodded, though the thought of leaving the fragile safety of the copse made her chest tighten. But she trusted Lara. She always had.

As they rose from their hiding place, the snowfall thickened, the wind howling through the trees like a warning. The distant whir of the helicopter still echoed in their minds—a reminder that the world hadn't forgotten them, that the chase wasn't over.

But as they pressed forward, their hands brushing as they walked, something stronger than fear flickered to life—resolve. They didn't know what lay ahead, but they knew they would face it together.

The tension in the makeshift command center was as thick as the bitter coffee Joel Barnes clutched in his hand. The converted conference room in the small-town police station buzzed with activity, a stark contrast to the quiet streets outside. Maps of the surrounding mountain ranges covered the walls, red pins marking the latest search efforts. Radios crackled with updates, and the low discussions of officers huddled around their computers underscored the chaos.

Joel stood near the corner, arms crossed tightly over his chest, watching as FBI agents pored over the latest reports. They had descended on the operation with an air of detached authority, their crisp suits and steely glares setting them apart from the local officers and search crews.

At the center of it all stood Agent Danforth, the lead investigator. His presence commanded the room, his clipped tone leaving little room for dissent.

"They've gone into the mountains," Danforth announced, his voice cutting through the chatter. He tapped the map pinned to the wall, his finger tracing the most likely routes Mia and Lara might have taken. "The helicopter crew reported limited visibility, but they saw tracks heading west. It's only a matter of time before they run out of places to hide."

Joel stepped forward. His jaw tight. "And when we find them?" he asked, his voice steady but sharp. "What's the plan?"

Danforth turned to him, his expression unreadable. "The plan is to apprehend them and bring them in."

Joel's eyes narrowed, his gut telling him there was more to it than that. "Apprehend," he said slowly, "or eliminate?"

Danforth's lips pressed into a thin line. "These women are dangerous fugitives. They've already demonstrated a willingness to use violence, and they're growing more desperate by the hour. If they pose a threat..."

"They're not a threat," Joel cut in, his voice rising. Heads turned, but he didn't care. "They're scared and running. That's not the same as being dangerous."

Danforth's gaze hardened. "They killed a man, assaulted law enforcement, and have evaded capture for weeks. That's more than enough to justify lethal force."

Joel's fists clenched at his sides. "And what about context?" he shot back. "Mia was sexually assaulted. Trent was a predator who, going by what we've been told, likely drugged her. She was trying to escape an abusive relationship. Or does none of that matter because it's easier to paint them as villains?"

Danforth's expression remained unchanged and his voice

cold, unyielding. "This isn't about context, Barnes. It's about eliminating a threat to public safety."

Heat rose in Joel's chest, anger and frustration boiling over as he stepped closer. "They're human beings," he said, his voice cracking. "Not animals to be hunted. This should be a rescue mission, not a manhunt."

Danforth didn't blink. "And that's where you're wrong," he said, his tone final. "This is a manhunt. And I suggest you remember where your loyalties lie."

The room fell silent. Joel stood there, fists clenched, chest heaving as he struggled to hold himself together. The other officers avoided his gaze, their discomfort apparent. Danforth barely acknowledged him, turning away to resume his discussion with another agent as if Joel's outburst had never happened.

A bitter taste filled Joel's mouth. Helplessness. Frustration. He swallowed hard, then turned on his heel and strode out, the door slamming shut behind him, louder than he intended.

The cold night air hit like a slap. Outside, the quiet town felt like another world, still, indifferent, so starkly different from the chaos inside.

He leaned against his car, tilting his head back to stare at the starless sky. The clouds hung low, reflecting the dim glow of the streetlights. Beyond them, the mountains loomed like silent sentinels.

Somewhere out there, Mia and Lara were fighting to survive. He couldn't shake the image of them huddled together in the snow, faces pale, hollow with exhaustion, lost in the relentless cold. He thought about Mia's bruises, the haunted look in her eyes whenever her name surfaced in interviews. He thought about Lara's unwavering support of her friend, standing by her in the most trying of circumstances.

They weren't criminals. They were survivors. And the system

—his system—was failing them. Joel's chest tightened. His breath hitched as he curled his hands into fists. He had become a cop to protect people, to stand for those who couldn't stand for themselves. But now, watching this operation twist into something monstrous, he felt powerless. He couldn't protect them. Not from this. Not from the system that had already decided their fate.

In the distance, the faint sound of helicopter blades echoed through the night, a grim reminder of the hunt unfolding in the mountains. Joel closed his eyes, his jaw clenching as a wave of sorrow settled deep in his bones. He had tried to help them, to humanize them, to give them a chance. But now, as the cold pressed in and the prospect of failure sank into him, all he could do was hope. Hope that somehow, against all odds, Mia and Lara would find a way to survive.

His voice barely more than a breath, he whispered into the empty street. "I'm sorry."

30

The helicopter thundered overhead, its blades slicing through the icy air and whipping the snow into a frenzied storm around Lara. The beam of its searchlight locked onto her, a blinding white circle that turned the clearing into a stage. She stood at its center, her breath rising in sharp, uneven puffs as the wind clawed at her jacket. The cold gnawed at her skin, but it was nothing compared to the crushing fear growing deep within.

Mia's muffled sobs drifted from the trees behind her, and Lara curled her fists at her sides, her nails biting into her palms. She couldn't think about Mia now. If she looked back, even for a second, her resolve would shatter.

The helicopter descended slightly, the roar of its blades a deafening pulse as it hovered above her. Through the blinding light, Lara could just make out the dark silhouette of the pilot and the figures leaning from the open sides, rifles trained on her. One of them lifted a megaphone, his voice slicing through the chaos.

"Stop where you are! Raise your hands and surrender now!"

Lara lifted her head, eyes narrowing against the glare. Snow stung her face, swirling in wild eddies around her boots, but she remained still. Her breaths came shallow and fast, her pulse hammering in her ears as she stared up at the faceless figures above.

"You are surrounded," the voice boomed, cold, commanding, impersonal. "Do not attempt to flee. Raise your hands and lie face down on the ground. This is your final warning."

Lara's lips pressed into a thin line, her jaw tightening as she slowly raised her hands, palms outward. To an outsider, it might have looked like surrender. But in her eyes, defiance burned. Her gaze flicked briefly toward the tree line, where the shadows of the forest swallowed Mia from sight. Stay hidden, Mia, she willed silently. Please.

The officers in the helicopter didn't waver. Rifles gleamed in the searchlight, steady and unyielding.

"Get on the ground!" the voice barked again, sharp and absolute, leaving no room for negotiation.

Lara didn't move. The wind lashed her hair across her face, snow seeping into her clothes, freezing against her skin. But she stood her ground. Her chest heaved with every breath, her heart pounding so violently she thought it might burst.

"Do it now!" The voice cut through the night, harsher this time, the tension in the air dense enough to choke on.

Slowly, deliberately, Lara lowered her hands. But she didn't drop to the ground. Instead, her fingers drifted toward her coat pocket, calm, unhurried. Her face remained unreadable, a mask of quiet defiance and unwavering resolve.

"Do not reach into your pockets!" The voice boomed, edged with panic. "Hands in the air, now!"

A scream shattered the night.

"Lara, no!" Mia's voice was raw, fractured, ripping from her throat as she watched from her hiding place, helpless to stop what was unfolding.

But Lara didn't stop. Her hand slipped into her coat, her gaze locking onto the shadowed figures above. She didn't beg. She didn't plead. She only stood there, resolute and unyielding, as the searchlight bore down on her like judgment.

The shot rang out like thunder, a single, shattering crack that split the night. It tore through the stillness of the mountains, its echo ricocheting through the valleys.

Above, the helicopter's blades roared on, the searchlight flickering for the briefest moment as the sound reverberated into the frozen wilderness.

And then nothing.

31

The gunshot shattered the air, slicing through the howling wind like a lightning strike. Mia froze behind the fallen log, the deafening echo reverberating through her chest. Her ears rang, the sound rippling through the snow-laden forest before fading into an eerie hush.

For a moment, she couldn't move, couldn't breathe, the magnitude of what had happened sinking into her bones like the cold itself.

"Lara," she whispered, the name catching in her throat, her voice swallowed by the endless white around her.

Her heart pounded as realization crashed over her. She stumbled to her feet, her legs weak and trembling. The world blurred, snow, shadows, the distant pulse of helicopter blades, all of it dissolving as she staggered forward, chasing the faint impressions of footprints in the fresh snow. Each step felt heavier, more impossible than the last, her chest tightening with every uneven breath.

"Lara!" she called, her voice breaking.

No answer.

The clearing opened before her, the stark whiteness

blinding under the harsh spotlight of the helicopter. And then, she saw her.

Lara lay motionless in the snow, her body curled slightly as if she had collapsed mid-step. The helicopter's beam illuminated her in sharp relief, highlighting the dark stain spreading across her chest. The crimson of her blood seeped into the pristine white snow, a vivid, terrible contrast that churned Mia's stomach and shattered her heart.

Mia fell to her knees, her hands sinking into the snow as she crawled toward Lara. Her breaths came in jagged sobs, each one tearing through her like shards of glass. When she reached her, Mia's shaking hands hovered over Lara's face, her chest, as though touching her would make it real, too real.

"No," Mia whispered, her voice breaking as she finally let her fingers brush against Lara's cold cheek. "No, no, no. Lara, please..."

Her hands trembled as she searched for a pulse, pressing against Lara's neck, her wrist, anywhere. But there was nothing. No warmth, no rhythm, no life. The quiet of Lara's still body was deafening, drowning out the roar of the helicopter and the muffled shouts of the officers above.

Mia let out a broken cry, the sound raw and primal as she collapsed beside Lara, pressing her head against her shoulder. The tears came in waves, hot against her frozen cheeks as they soaked into the fabric of Lara's jacket.

"You can't leave me," she sobbed, her voice shaking with the force of her grief. "You promised... you promised we'd face this together."

She pulled Lara's head into her lap, her fingers brushing through her dark, snow-dampened hair. Her eyes searched Lara's face, desperate for anything—anything—that would tell her this wasn't the end. But Lara's expression was peaceful, her lips parted slightly, her eyelashes dusted with snow. A quiet stillness that felt like a betrayal, a cruel reminder that Mia was too late.

The helicopter's blades roared above, but the sound barely registered. The searchlight flickered, casting long, eerie shadows across the clearing as the officers began their descent. Shouts and commands blurred together, meaningless noise in the face of what Mia had lost.

She pressed her forehead against Lara's, her tears freezing against her cheeks.

"I should've stopped you," she whispered, her voice cracking. "I should've told you how much I loved you sooner. How much I needed you. God, Lara, I was so scared... I didn't know how to tell you, but you..." Her voice broke into another sob, her hands clutching Lara's jacket. "You always knew. You always knew."

Her mind flashed to their last kiss, the way Lara had cupped her face, the warmth of her touch, the quiet determination in her voice as she promised Mia it would be okay. And now, here she was, cold and lifeless, her body lying in the snow as if she had given all she had left to protect Mia.

"I love you," Mia whispered, her voice barely audible as she pressed her lips to Lara's forehead. "I'll always love you."

The crunch of boots in the snow pulled her from her haze, but she didn't look up. The officers' shadows grew larger as they surrounded her, their dark uniforms stark against the relentless spotlight. Their helmets reflected the light, their faces hidden behind masks of authority. None of them spoke as they took in the scene.

"Step away from the body," a voice finally commanded, sharp and cold. "Put your hands where we can see them."

Mia didn't move. Her body trembled, not from the cold, but from the crushing weight of her grief. Her fingers tightened around Lara's jacket, clutching it as though letting go would shatter her completely.

"Ma'am, step away from the body," the voice repeated, louder this time, laced with urgency.

Mia turned her head slowly, her tear-streaked face lifting to meet the officer's gaze. Her eyes, swollen and red, burned with defiance and heartbreak.

"You've already taken her," she said, her voice trembling with emotion. "What more could you possibly want?"

The officer hesitated, her words settling heavily over the clearing. Somewhere behind him, a voice crackled through a radio, but Mia couldn't make out the words. She couldn't hear anything but the sound of her own ragged breathing and the gap where Lara's heartbeat should have been.

The snow began to fall again, soft and unrelenting, covering the clearing in a fragile, pristine layer. Mia lowered her head, curling protectively around Lara as the cold seeped through her clothes. She didn't care. The world could crumble around her, and it wouldn't matter.

She pressed her lips to Lara's temple one last time, her tears falling onto her pale skin.

"I won't leave you," she whispered, the words breaking as they left her. "I won't leave you."

The wind howled, the helicopter's blades roared, and the officers moved closer, their boots crunching loudly in the snow. But Mia stayed where she was, holding onto Lara as if she could will her back to life. And as the darkness of the forest pressed in around them, the only sound left in the world was her sobs.

The crunch of utility boots on snow echoed through the clearing as the ERT officers tightened their circle. Their dark, insulated uniforms, designed for combat, not grief, seemed out of place in the raw vulnerability of the moment. Their rifles, once held with rigid certainty, now hung uneasily in their grips as they exchanged glances, uncertainty flickering beneath their helmets.

Mia didn't notice. She couldn't see them, couldn't hear the sharp commands murmured into radios or the mechanical hum of the helicopter as it began to retreat. All she could see was Lara, lifeless in her arms, her body growing colder with every passing second.

"Ma'am," one of the officers tried again, his voice faltering. "You need to step away..."

"Enough."

The word was calm but firm, carrying an authority that cut through the tension like a blade.

Detective Joel Barnes stepped into the clearing, his coat dusted with snow, his breath clouding in the cold. His sharp eyes swept over the scene, narrowing as they landed on Lara's still body, then on Mia, who clung to her with a desperation that made his chest ache.

"What the hell happened here?" Joel demanded, his voice low but charged with authority.

An ERT officer stepped forward, his rifle slung across his chest. "She failed to comply. She reached into her coat..."

"And was she armed?" Joel interrupted; his tone sharp enough to make the officer hesitate.

"We couldn't take the chance," the officer replied defensively, shifting under Joel's scrutiny.

Joel's jaw tightened, his fists clenching at his sides. His eyes flicked to the fresh blood staining the snow, to Lara's open coat and empty hands.

"You couldn't take the chance?" he echoed, his voice laced with anger. "She was unarmed. You shot an unarmed woman."

"She was a fugitive," another officer muttered, but Joel silenced him with a glare.

"This was excessive," Joel said, his voice rising. "And I'm going to make damn sure this doesn't get swept under the rug."

The officers exchanged uneasy glances, but Joel had already

turned away, his focus shifting back to Mia. She hadn't moved, hadn't acknowledged the conversation happening around her. Her head was bowed, her tears soaking into Lara's hair as she whispered something Joel couldn't hear.

His heart twisted. He crouched beside her, moving slowly and carefully, as though approaching a wounded animal.

"Mia," he said softly, his voice gentler than he expected.

She didn't respond at first, her hands still clutching Lara's jacket, her body trembling from cold and grief. Joel reached out, his fingers brushing her shoulder.

"Mia," he said again, more firmly this time.

She looked up, her tear-streaked face a portrait of devastation. Her lips trembled as her red, swollen eyes met his, and Joel felt her pain like a physical blow.

"Come on," he said gently. "You're freezing. Let's get you somewhere warm."

Mia shook her head, her grip tightening on Lara.

"I'm not leaving her," she whispered, her voice barely audible.

Joel's throat tightened. He crouched lower, his hand still resting lightly on her shoulder.

"You don't have to leave her, Mia," he said softly. "But you can't stay here. Lara wouldn't want you to get sick or hurt. She'd want you to take care of yourself."

Tears streamed down Mia's face as she looked back at Lara, her lips trembling.

"I should've stopped her," she choked out. "She didn't have to… she didn't have to do this."

Joel swallowed hard, his own grief swamping his chest.

"She was trying to protect you," he said gently. "And I'm so sorry I couldn't stop this from happening. But we have to go now."

Reaching into his coat, Joel pulled out a thick woolen

blanket and draped it over Mia's shoulders. The motion was deliberate, as though shielding her from more than just the cold. She shivered beneath its warmth, her hands trembling as they fell to her lap.

"I'll help you," Joel said, his voice steady. "But you need to let me."

For a long moment, Mia didn't move. Then, with a broken sob, she released her grip on Lara's jacket and let Joel guide her to her feet. She swayed, her legs weak, but Joel steadied her, wrapping his arm firmly around her shoulders.

The clearing seemed impossibly quiet now, the only sound the soft crunch of their steps as Joel led Mia away. The officers didn't move to stop them, their earlier confidence replaced by an uncomfortable pause.

Joel glanced back once, his gaze lingering on Lara's still form lying in the snow. Regret twisted in his chest, sharp and unbearable. He had failed her. He had failed both of them.

"I'm so sorry," he murmured under his breath, the words meant for no one but himself.

As they disappeared into the trees, the helicopter began to rise again, its blades slicing through the cold air. But the sound was distant now, swallowed by the quiet grief that settled over the forest like the snow itself.

Joel tightened his hold on Mia, his mind racing with everything he couldn't undo. And as they walked, he silently vowed that if he couldn't save Lara, he would do everything in his power to protect the woman she had died for.

32

The little town buzzed with quiet urgency, the kind of subdued energy that came when something extraordinary collided with the ordinary. People whispered in the diner, their eyes flitting to the grainy news broadcast playing on the television above the counter. The word fugitive floated through conversations, laced with the curiosity of those who had never imagined such chaos reaching their remote corner of the world.

Patricia lingered on the edge of it all, wrapped in her old green coat, her hat pulled low over her brow. She sat in the farthest booth of the diner, her back to the wall, her coffee growing cold in front of her. The voices around her blurred together, bits and pieces of news filtering into her thoughts.

"One of them's dead," a man at the counter murmured, shaking his head. "Shot out in the woods. What a damn shame."

"And the other?" the waitress asked as she poured his coffee.

"Arrested, I think," the man replied. "They're sayin' they were dangerous, but I don't know... sounds more like desperation to me."

Patricia's fingers tightened around the mug, the warmth seeping into her chilled hands. She stared into the dark liquid, her heart bruised by an ache she hadn't expected. She had known their names but not their story, not really. But she had seen enough in their eyes, fear, love, determination, to know they weren't who the media wanted them to be.

With a slow, deliberate motion, Patricia slid her hand into the pocket of her coat, her fingers brushing against the envelope she had carried for days. The edges were soft from handling, the creases deep where she had folded and unfolded it. Noah, it read in shaky handwriting, a name that carried a mother's love, a bond she could comprehend.

The cold air hit her like a slap as she stepped out of the diner, the wind whipping at her hat and tugging at her coat. The streets were empty, save for a few cars parked along the curb, their tires dusted with snow. The sky hung low and gray, a reflection of the heaviness in her chest.

Patricia walked with purpose, her boots crunching against the icy sidewalk as she approached the red post box on the corner. It stood like a sentinel, its bright paint chipped and dulled by years of harsh winters. She hesitated only a moment before pulling the letter from her pocket.

Her fingers brushed over the name again, her lips pressing into a thin line as she stared at it. She had no idea which of the women had fallen, no idea who had survived. The thought gnawed at her; a hollow ache deepened by the uncertainty.

Patricia slid the letter into the slot, her breath clouding in the air as her fingers lingered on the edge of the envelope. "I hope this gets to you, kid," she murmured, her voice barely audible over the wind. "I hope it gives you something to hold onto."

She stepped back, watching as the letter disappeared into the box. For a moment, she stood there, snow swirling around her and thought of the two women and their raw desperation, their quiet moments of love and connection and how society had chewed them up and spit them out.

As Patricia walked back through the streets, she couldn't shake the bitterness settling in her chest. This wasn't the first time she'd seen the world fail people like them. It wouldn't be the last. The townspeople might call it justice, but to her, it was something else, something colder, more calculated—a system that valued appearances over humanity.

She thought of her shack in the wilderness, how the forest wrapped around her like a cocoon, shielding her from the noise and cruelty of a world she no longer wanted any part of. Society was broken, fractured in ways that couldn't be mended. She had been right to walk away from it. The headlines, the whispers, the judgment, it was all so hollow, so meaningless when stripped down to what truly mattered.

Patricia reached her truck, climbing into the cab and slamming the door against the cold. She rested her hands on the steering wheel, her gaze fixed on the snowy street ahead.

She turned the key in the ignition, the engine rumbling to life beneath her. As she drove away, the town faded in her rearview mirror, the red post box shrinking into the distance until it was nothing more than a speck against the gray horizon.

The ache in her chest remained, but she didn't look back.

The police station was a stark contrast to the snow-covered wilderness Mia had just left behind. The harsh fluorescent lights buzzed faintly, reflecting off sterile white walls and a cold, tiled floor that amplified every footstep. The rush of activity echoed down the hallways, murmured voices, the shuffle of papers, the occasional static crackle of a radio but to Mia, it all felt distant, like sound muffled through a thick fog.

She sat in the corner of the interrogation room, the metal chair unforgiving beneath her, its edges digging into her back.

Her wrists were cuffed in front of her, resting limply on the table, her fingers trembling slightly from the cold that still clung to her body. The cuffs were too tight, the metal biting into her skin, but she didn't flinch. She didn't even look at them. Her eyes remained fixed on the scratched surface of the table, as if she could disappear into the jagged lines etched into the steel.

Her reflection stared back at her in the polished surface, distorted and fragmented. Her face was pale and drawn, her lips cracked and tinged with the faintest trace of blue from hours spent in the snow. Her hair hung in limp strands, damp from melted snowflakes, clinging to her cheeks and neck. Dark circles hollowed her eyes, red and swollen from crying—though no tears fell now. She was empty. Hollow. A shell of the woman who had once clung to hope.

Every officer who passed by the glass window of the room gave her the same look, a mixture of curiosity, pity, and quiet judgment. Mia felt their eyes on her, their unspoken questions and silent assumptions. She heard their murmurs in the hallway, the words indistinct but sharp enough to cut through her haze.

"Is that her?"

"The fugitive?"

"God, she looks awful."

"Poor thing."

Poor thing. As if those two words could encompass the ruin of her life, the devastation carved into her chest like an open wound. She kept her gaze down, her fingers twitching slightly as she fought to shut out the whispers, the glances, the sharp stab of humiliation.

The door creaked open, and the sound made her flinch, her shoulders tensing involuntarily. Joel Barnes stepped inside, and the room seemed to shrink with his broad presence. He was no longer wearing his coat, but the chill of the mountain air still clung to him. His dark hair was slightly disheveled, a faint redness marking his cheeks from the cold. His jaw was tight, a shadow of stubble lining it, and his gray eyes were clouded with something that looked like regret.

He closed the door quietly behind him, his boots scuffing against the floor as he approached the table. In his hand, he held his hat, the brim creased from how tightly his fingers gripped it. He looked at Mia with a mixture of empathy and exhaustion, like a man who had seen too much and carried every second of it all.

"Mia," he said gently, his voice soft in the sterile room.

She didn't look up. Her gaze remained fixed on the table, her body stiff and unmoving, as if acknowledging him would take more effort than she could summon.

Joel sighed, pulling out the chair across from her and sitting down with a quiet scrape. He set his hat on the table, his fingers brushing over the creased brim as he studied her. The minutes stretched between them.

"I wanted to check on you," he said after a moment, his tone careful. "See how you're holding up."

Her lips twitched faintly, the ghost of a bitter smile that never reached her eyes. "How do you think?" she murmured, her voice hoarse, barely audible.

Joel leaned forward slightly, his elbows resting on the table. He searched her face for a flicker of something, anger, fight, even resentment, but all he saw was devastation. "I know this is... unbearable," he said quietly. "And I know you've been through more than anyone should ever have to face. I'm sorry, Mia. I'm so damn sorry."

Her head snapped up at that, bloodshot eyes blazing with a spark of anger, one that was quickly drowned by despair. "Then why is she dead?" she demanded, her voice cracking. "Why didn't you stop them? Why didn't you do something?"

Joel's chest tightened, but he didn't flinch under her glare. "I tried," he said softly. "I tried to de-escalate, to make them see there was another way. But I wasn't the one holding the rifle, Mia. I couldn't stop what happened."

She stared at him, her breaths coming in sharp, uneven bursts as the words sank in. Her anger flickered briefly, but it couldn't withstand the crushing grief. Her shoulders sagged, and her head fell into her hands as fresh tears streaked down her cheeks.

"She was all I had left," she whispered, her voice trembling. "And now she's gone."

Joel swallowed hard, guilt tightening like a vice. He wanted to tell her it wasn't her fault, that there was nothing she could have done to change what had happened, but the words felt hollow. Instead, he leaned forward, his voice steady as he said, "Mia, I need to tell you what happens next."

She didn't respond, but her hands clenched into fists against the table. He hesitated, jaw tightening before he continued. "You'll be extradited back to the U.S.," he said carefully. "Once you're there, it's up to the courts to decide your fate. There's nothing I can do to stop it."

Her laugh was sharp and hollow, cutting through the room like shattered glass. "Fate," she repeated bitterly. "Like I ever had a choice."

Joel winced but pressed on. "I don't know what's going to happen to you," he admitted. "But I do know Lara wouldn't want you to give up. She..."

"Don't," Mia snapped, her voice breaking. She lifted her head, her eyes burning with fresh tears. "Don't tell me what Lara would've wanted. You didn't know her."

Joel leaned back, his hands tightening around the brim of his hat. He let the words hang in the air.

"You're right," he said finally, his voice quieter. "I didn't know her. But it was clear how much she loved you. And she gave everything to make sure you had a chance."

Mia's lip quivered, her breath hitching as she looked away. "What kind of chance is this?" she whispered. "Even if I don't go to prison, my life is over. Noah will never forgive me. I'll never see him again. I'll never have anything. Not without her."

Joel's chest ached as he watched her crumble, her voice trembling with a sorrow so profound it seemed to fill the room.

He stood slowly, reaching for the door, but hesitated before leaving. Turning back, he said, "I wish I could've done more."

She didn't respond, her head bowed, tears falling silently onto the table. And as Joel stepped out of the room, closing the door behind him, the legacy of his failure settled over him like a storm cloud.

Inside, Mia sat alone. The sterile walls, the clinical lights, the distant activity of the station—all of it blurred into the background as grief swallowed her whole. And though she was still breathing, it felt as if the parts of her that mattered had been left behind in the snow, with Lara.

33

Noah sat on the edge of his bed. His suitcase open but mostly empty on the floor. Late afternoon light filtered through the thin curtains, casting soft, golden hues over the faded posters on the walls and the scattered remnants of his life before everything fell apart. A hoodie lay crumpled at his feet, next to a pair of sneakers he wasn't sure he wanted to take.

He stared at the suitcase as if it were an unwelcome reminder of how much his world had changed. In less than forty-eight hours, he'd be on his way to live with his aunt, a woman he barely knew beyond obligatory holiday cards and a few awkward conversations at family gatherings.

It felt strange, packing his life into a suitcase when he couldn't even make sense of what his life was anymore. His mom was gone, lost to a legal system he barely understood, and Dane had been arrested just two days ago. That memory brought a bitter sense of satisfaction.

Noah had been in the kitchen when the police came for Dane. The image of him handcuffed and furious, still played vividly in his mind. For all of Dane's shouting and struggling, the officers had stayed calm, their voices firm as they led him out the door.

"Domestic abuse," they'd said when Noah asked. They didn't give him the details, but he didn't need them. He'd lived it. He knew.

Later, one of the officers handed him a card, explaining that his mom had given them everything they needed to arrest Dane. Noah hadn't known whether to feel proud or angry. She'd stood up to his dad, finally, but at what cost? She wasn't here. She was locked away somewhere, her name plastered across the news alongside words like fugitive and homicide.

He sighed, running a hand through his fair, unruly hair. His mom's absence hung in the air. Everywhere he looked, there were traces of her, her favorite coffee mug still on the hook over the counter, the blanket she used to wrap herself in draped over the couch.

But she wasn't here. And she wouldn't be.

Noah bent down, grabbing the hoodie and stuffing it into the suitcase. He moved mechanically, his thoughts a whirlwind he couldn't control. He reached for a stack of books on his desk but froze when he noticed a small envelope tucked beneath them. How had he not seen it? But then looking at the chaos of his room, he knew why.

His name was written across the front in his mom's handwriting. His mom must have left it there before she went on her trip. Noah's heart skipped a beat as he picked up the envelope, his fingers brushing over the familiar scrawl. His breath hitched, and his hands trembled slightly as he turned it over, breaking the seal with careful precision.

Inside was a single sheet of paper, folded neatly. He unfolded it, his eyes scanning the words as his chest tightened.

His vision blurred as he read, his throat constricting with emotion. He held the letter carefully, as though it might crumble if he gripped it too hard, his fingers tracing the lines of her handwriting.

Noah,

I know you're probably rolling your eyes right now because I'm leaving you a note and not a text, but I'm old school and didn't want to go without saying something.

I'm going away for a few days. Just a short trip with a friend, someone who reminds me that life doesn't always have to be so hard. I promise I'll be back before you even have the chance to miss me (but I hope you miss me at least a little).

There's food in the fridge, and I made that pasta bake you like, so don't let it go to waste. Try to get some sleep, and for the love of God, don't spend the entire weekend in front of the PlayStation. You know I'll check your screen time when I get back.

I love you, Noah. I know things have been... complicated lately, but I need you to know that none of it changes how proud I am of you. You are the best thing in my life. You always have been.

I'll see you soon. I promise.

Love,

Mom

Tears streamed silently down his cheeks as he sat on the bed, the letter pressed against his chest. The anger and confusion that had been building inside him for weeks cracked open, leaving him raw and exposed.

"She wrote this for me," he whispered, his voice trembling. "She didn't just leave me. She was going to come back."

Noah placed his mom's letter gently on his desk, the words still imprinted in his mind like the faintest echo of her voice. The heaviness in his chest hadn't lifted, but for the first time in weeks, it felt like there was space to breathe. Her words had given him something he hadn't realized he was longing for —hope.

As he sat there, the quiet of the house settling around him, the faint creak of the mail slot echoed from the front door. Curious, he wiped his damp cheeks with the sleeve of his hoodie and made his way downstairs. As he reached the bottom step he noticed a pile of mail on the floor, which he grabbed before wandering towards the kitchen.

A single envelope lay on top, its edges slightly crumpled, as if it had traveled far to reach him. Noah frowned, the handwriting was familiar, scrawled in the same uneven loops as the letter his mom had left him. He hesitated, his heart pounded, the envelope in his hands feeling far heavier than the paper inside. Carefully, he slid a finger under the seal and pulled the letter free.

The words leapt off the page, unmistakably his mother's.

Dear Noah,,

I don't know where to begin except to say that I'm sorry. I've failed you in so many ways, and I'll carry that guilt for the rest of my life. I should've been stronger. I should've protected you from him. But I wasn't, and for that, I am so deeply sorry.

I know I've made mistakes, big ones. But please don't believe what they are saying about me. I didn't kill anyone, I swear. I know you probably hate me right now. But I want you to know that everything I've done, I've done because I believed it was the best way to keep us safe. You are my world, Noah, and I never stopped trying to do right by you, even when I got it wrong.

I've found the strength now to leave. I've finally found the courage to break free and be the person I've always wanted to be, the person you've deserved all along. It's terrifying, but it's also freeing in a way I can't put into words. I wish I could take you with me right now, but I need to make sure this freedom is real, that I can build a life for us without fear or anger or regret.

One day, I hope you can forgive me. I hope you'll grow up to be the strong, kind, and gentle man I know you're capable of being. I hope you'll find someone who loves you for who you are, who sees the good in you the way I always have. I hope you'll follow your dreams, no matter how impossible they might seem, and make a life that makes you proud.

I will come back for you, Noah. When the time is right, I promise I will. And when I do, I want us to start fresh. To build something new, something better. Until then, please know that I love you more than words can say. You will always be my son, my heart, my reason for fighting.

Always yours,

Mom xxx

Noah stared at the letter, his hands trembling. She had written this before everything spiraled out of control, before the mountains, the helicopter, the snow. Before Lara died.

She had believed she would find freedom. That she would come back. That there was still time. His gaze shifted to the date scrawled in the corner of the page, and his chest tightened. It was days before she and Lara had gone into the mountains. Days before everything fell apart.

A lump rose in his throat, and he swallowed hard, his eyes burning. She had written these words with hope, with determination, with love. And though the world had taken so much from her, it hadn't taken that. Noah carefully folded the letter, slipping it back into the envelope before tucking it into his hoodie pocket. As he stood there, the honesty of his mother's words pressed against his heart, his decision solidified. He would visit her. He would go to the jail, look her in the eyes, and tell her what she needed to hear.

That he forgave her.

For the first time in weeks, a fragile but resolute sense of purpose ignited within him. He had lost so much, but he hadn't lost her.

EPILOGUE

The clang of the cell door echoed behind Mia as she stepped inside, the sound reverberating off the gray concrete walls. She let out a slow breath, her shoulders sagging under the weight of the day.

Her fingers drifted to the spot on her chest where Noah's head had rested just hours earlier during their goodbye. She could still smell the faint hint of his shampoo, the same kind she used to buy for him and the thought tugged at her heart.

The cell was small, the kind of space that forced you to confront your own existence every time you entered it. But Mia had made it hers. A stack of borrowed library books sat neatly on the shelf above her narrow bed. A photo of Noah, its edges worn soft from handling, was taped to the wall near her pillow.

It wasn't much, but it was enough to remind her why she was still fighting.

The door rattled faintly as Mia's cellmate, Bea, glanced up from where she sat cross-legged on the bed, a well-worn novel in her hands. Bea had a wiry build, her arms covered in tattoos that told stories Mia had only begun to understand. Her face was sharp, her features weathered by years of hardship, but her dark eyes were warm, softening the rough edges of her exterior.

"How'd it go?" Bea asked, her voice low but not unkind. She set the book aside and leaned forward, resting her elbows on her knees.

Mia lowered herself onto the edge of the bed, her hands clasped tightly in her lap. "It was good," she murmured, her voice laced with both sadness and hope. "He's grown so much. His hair's longer now, and he's starting to look like..." Her words faltered, but Bea didn't press.

"Like you?" Bea offered, a small smile tugging at her lips.

Mia shook her head, a faint laugh escaping. "Maybe a little. But mostly, he looks like himself. He's so confident now. Strong. He told me about school, about how he's thinking of joining the debate team." Her voice wavered, and she took a steadying breath. "He's doing okay. Better than okay, really."

Bea shifted, her hands resting loosely on her thighs as she watched Mia carefully. "That's good," she said. "Sounds like you did something right, even from in here."

Mia turned to her, a bittersweet smile tugging at her lips. "I still wish I could be out there with him. Three years doesn't seem long compared to everything that's happened, but when you're watching your kid grow up without you..." She shook her head, her voice breaking. "It feels like a lifetime."

Bea leaned back against the wall, her expression softening. "You'll make it through," she said simply. "And when you do, you'll still have him. You've already done the hardest part, getting him to see you're still his mom, no matter what."

Mia nodded, the lump in her throat easing slightly. Bea had a way of cutting through the noise in her head, grounding her when everything felt too much. It was one of the many reasons Mia had come to rely on her, to care for her in a way she hadn't thought possible after losing Lara.

She reached up, pulling her hair free from its ponytail, letting the strands fall around her shoulders. The room felt smaller at night, the dim light from the hallway casting long shadows on the walls. Her gaze drifted to the photo of Noah, her chest aching with a mix of longing and pride.

"He said something before he left," Mia murmured, her voice barely above a whisper.

Bea tilted her head, waiting.

"He said he forgave me."

The words hung in the air between them, settling over Mia like a warm blanket. She let out a shaky breath, her eyes slipping shut as she replayed the moment in her mind, the way Noah had held her, his arms wrapped tight as if afraid to let go. The quiet strength in his voice when he'd said, "I forgive you, Mom."

Bea shifted, patting the narrow space beside her. "C'mere," she murmured.

Mia hesitated only a moment before sliding onto the bed. The two women fit together in the cramped space like puzzle pieces, Bea's arm draping over her, a steady presence in the quiet. Her hand rested lightly on Mia's hip as their bodies curved into each other.

"You're going to be okay," Bea whispered, her voice soft, certain. "You've got people who love you—on the outside and in here. You're not alone."

Mia rested her head on Bea's shoulder, her fingers tracing the edge of one of Bea's tattoos, a delicate rose blooming from a crack in a stone wall. The symbolism wasn't lost on her. She let her eyes drift shut, breathing in the quiet comfort of Bea's warmth, the steady rise and fall of her chest.

"I didn't think I'd ever feel like this again," Mia whispered. "Like I could care about someone. Trust someone."

Bea pressed a light kiss to the top of her head. "You don't have to rush it," she murmured. "We've got time."

A soft laugh escaped Mia, blending with the faint noise of prison-life going on around them. “Time,” she echoed, the word tasting different now, lighter, full of something that felt dangerously close to hope. “Yeah. We do.”

As the world outside their small cell spun on without them, Mia let herself sink into the moment. She had a way to go yet. But for the first time in a long time, she could see the possibility of a future. Because somewhere at the end of a long and winding highway, freedom and Noah were waiting patiently on the horizon.

The End